HOLD BACK THE TIDE

MELINDA SALISBURY

HOLD BACK THE TIDE

SCHOLASTIC PRESS / NEW YORK

All rights reserved. Published by Scholastic Press, an imprint of
Scholastic Inc., *Publishers since 1920*. SCHOLASTIC, SCHOLASTIC PRESS,
and associated logos are trademarks and/or registered trademarks of
Scholastic Inc.

The publisher does not have any control over and does not assume any
responsibility for author or third-party websites or their content.

Library of Congress Cataloging-in-Publication Data available

ISBN 978-1-338-68130-7

1 2021

Printed in the U.S.A.   23
First edition, January 2021

Book design by Christopher Stengel

FOR MY SECOND-FAVORITE SCOTSMAN. I DOUBT DAVID TENNANT READS MY BOOKS, SO NEIL BIRD, THIS ONE'S FOR YOU. SLÀINTE MHATH!

HOLD BACK THE TIDE

"Hell is empty and all the devils are here."

WILLIAM SHAKESPEARE, *The Tempest*

"Let all men know how empty and worthless is the power of kings . . ."

HENRY OF HUNTINGDON, ON KING
CANUTE, *Historia Anglorum*

"The form of the monster on whom I had bestowed existence was forever before my eyes . . ."

MARY WOLLSTONECRAFT SHELLEY,
Frankenstein; or, The Modern Prometheus

ONE

Here are the rules of living with a murderer.

One: Do not draw attention to yourself.

It's pretty self-explanatory—if they don't notice you, they won't get any ideas about killing you. Be a ghost in your own home, if that's what it takes. After all, you can't kill a ghost.

Of course, when you live with a murderer, sit opposite them at every meal, share a washroom and a kitchen, and sleep a mere twelve feet and two flimsy walls away from them, this is impossible. Even the subtlest of specters is bound to be noticed. Which leads to the next rule.

Two: If you can't be invisible, be useful.

Cook huge, hearty meals that make them too full and sleepy to feel like slaughtering you. I'm talking meaty stews, thick casseroles. Heaps of potatoes—no one ever ate three pounds of mash and then went on a killing spree. Serving a bit of bread and hard cheese is not going to keep you alive.

You should also keep your home spotlessly clean. Get those floors swept, pillows fluffed; shine that cutlery so bright you can see your face in it. Never let them run out of fresh laundry, always sew on loose buttons before they're lost, and darn socks the moment they show any signs of wear. Be sure to collect the eggs and milk the goat each morning before sunrise, no matter the weather—better to be cold and damp than dead, my girl. In short, make it so your death would be very inconvenient. Murderers hate to be inconvenienced.

It's still not enough, though. Not nearly enough.

On to rule three: If you can't beat them, join them.

Not in murder, obviously; the last thing you want is to get into some kind of rivalry. Find some *other* way to become an apprentice, and turn yourself into the thing they didn't know they needed. Become their right hand so that cutting you would only make them bleed.

Build the stamina it takes to walk around the loch day after day, rain, snow, or shine; do it with ease and speed. Learn to set and cast the nets around the loch edges to catch the fish that live there. Where to slit those fish to and harvest what's in their bellies, and how to sift through your findings, panning for information like the luckless pan for gold. Then train yourself not to be sick at the sight of fish guts strewn across a table you spent half an hour polishing to gleaming just the day before.

Clean the table again.

Study hard. Learn how to test the loch to make sure it's clean. How to draw the tables that predict what the water level should be so you know at a glance how much can be used and how much should be spared. Master these calculations, be sure you can do them in your head, and keep those numbers on your tongue, ready if they're ever needed. Record the signs that mean rain is coming or that drought is likely. Prepare.

More than that. Familiarize yourself with spears, knives, and guns. Learn how to sharpen a blade on a whetstone so it sings when you slash it through the air, how to clean a barrel, oil a trigger. Practice until you can assemble a long gun in under thirty seconds. Know where the bullets and gunpowder are kept and make sure there's always plenty.

Four: Don't make them angry.

In my experience, a murderer is much more likely to kill you if you make them angry.

Right now, my father is furious with me.

TWO

"Alva."

It takes a lot of practice to keep your back turned when a murderer is standing behind you. But then, I've had a lot of practice.

"Alva."

I know he's angry from the way he says my name. It's how he snaps the word: the sharpness of the *v*, the second *a* strangled to death almost before it passes his lips. The tiny hairs on my arms rise reflexively. Then there's the dread swooping in my stomach, like an owl for a mouse. When he says my name like that, it's a snarl in the dark, telling me to run, to hide. To be careful.

So what do I do?

I let out a long sigh. "Just a moment, Da."

I write the last three words of the sentence I'm transcribing with a flourish and calmly put my pen down. Then, and only then, do I turn away from my desk to face him.

Because there's a fifth rule, and this one is the most important of all:

Don't let them know what you know.

To survive, you have to be smarter than they are. If I listened to my instincts, if I fled whenever he came into a room, startled every time he picked up a knife or a hammer or a gun, he'd know something was wrong. He'd start asking questions, start getting anxious, and then I'd really have to worry. The last thing in the world you want is to make a murderer skittish. The trick is to hold your nerve and behave as though everything is fine. So instead of cowering, I act like any other sixteen-year-old would if their father came into their room uninvited.

"What is it?" I try to sound bored, even a little annoyed. I'm pleased with myself, though the sense of achievement trickles away when I look at him. He is most definitely *not* pleased with me.

I attempt a smile. He doesn't return it.

Oh hell.

My father fills the doorway, ducking his head so it doesn't bump the frame, and I swallow the realization that he's blocking the only way out. He's a real giant of a man; when

I was wee, I'd sit on his clasped palms while he bent double and swung me back and forth between his legs, and my feet never even came close to touching the ground. I didn't inherit his height, though I did get the Douglas bird's nest of dark curls and their coal-chip eyes. Right now, my father's eyes are fathomless, cold and deep as the water outside, and I fight not to flinch as I meet them.

"Did you check the nets?" he asks.

"Yes."

"All of them?"

I nod, even as my gaze moves to the bundle of rags gripped in his right hand.

No. Not rags. Net.

Oh holy hell.

Here's the thing: I did not check all the nets. For once, I decided to leave the farthest one up by the north mountain so I could get back and finish my transcribing work. In my defense, I've checked those nets twice a week for the past three years. There's never anything in them—not even the smallest of fish for me to examine—and they've never needed more than the most basic repairs. Until today.

"Alva?"

There's no point in lying. Again. Not that that stops me from trying. "I forgot. They were fine last week," I say, standing, my pulse rising at the same time.

In reply, he unrolls the net, and I wince as I see the size of the rents that have been torn in it. After seven years, I'm good at repairing them, but there's not enough twine in Ormscaula to get this one back into working order. I could fit inside one of the rips.

My father glares at me through the net, and for a moment, it looks like he's caught in it. Then I realize that from where he stands, I would be the catch. My mouth dries.

I look away from him, forcing myself to step closer and peer at the damage. I'm surprised to see that the holes are neat, no fraying, like they've been cut, not chewed. Whatever did it must have teeth or claws like knives.

"What could have done this?" I ask, for a second forgetting to be wary of him, reaching to touch the clean edges as if they might answer me. The biggest predators in the loch are otters, but there's no way they're responsible, nor any of the fish that live there. "A wolf? A bear?"

Da shakes his head immediately. "There're no bears in these parts anymore. And we'd have heard wolves if they were around."

That's true. You always know when wolves are close. "A lugh, then? Maybe a deer was trapped inside the net, and it went after it?"

I have found deer in the nets before. Deer are pretty stupid. And lughs—mountain cats—do hunt by the loch, although usually during winter.

My father stares at the net, as if expecting it to tell him how it got in this state.

"Is it likely to be a lugh, do you think?" I ask.

"A lugh would have to be starving to come down the mountain in spring," he says finally. "Starving or rabid. I'd better set some of the cages." Then his tone turns pointed. "Either way, the net will need replacing today."

My heart sinks. It's bad enough that I skipped checking it, worse that he found it in this state. Any other day, I'd already be halfway to the sheds to fetch a new one, muttering prayers and apologies as I went. But today, I need to go down into the village to meet Murren Ross and get my *things* from him. Finding, inspecting, and hauling a replacement net almost ten miles around the north mountain shore will take the rest of the morning and most of the afternoon, and then I'll have to rig it up, too. I'll lose the whole day. I can't afford to lose a whole day.

The timing couldn't be worse.

A nasty thought occurs to me. The north nets have been fine for years, and yet today, the sole time I didn't check, one is damaged. Not just damaged, but ravaged by cuts that look like they were made with a blade. And he just so happens to have found it . . .

The skin along my shoulders tightens and prickles. Could *he* have done this? Does he know what I'm planning? Because if he knows, then that means—

"Alva? The net. Today, if it's convenient."

The irritation in his voice yanks me from my thoughts.

"Sorry." I shake my suspicions away. Now *I'm* being stupid. If he knew what I was planning, he wouldn't bother to sabotage his own nets to keep me here. He'd probably just kill me.

I cover the transcription with a calfskin cloth to keep it clean and hastily roll up the old scroll I've been copying, disturbing a few tiny flakes of gold leaf that drift onto the desk. I have a jar of scraps I've harvested over the years, collecting the leftover fragments the monks forget, or can't be bothered, to remove properly. The bottle they're in is probably worth more than the contents, but I like the thought of my little pot of gold.

"I'll go now, then," I say, still hoping for a reprieve.

A normal father would hesitate to send his only child ten miles around the loch shore to fix up a new net with a potentially rabid lugh lurking nearby. He'd take pity on his daughter and allow her to go down into the village to collect the paper she told him she needs to finish her work. But not mine.

"Take a gun, and mind yourself," he says, turning away. "And be back before nightfall."

Aye, Da. I love you, too.

The sheds, where we keep the spare nets, our boats, and a whole mess of other things, are a mile west of the cottage, huddled together like gossips on the south shore of the loch. I'm warm by the time I reach them, hands damp inside my woolen gloves, my *earasaid* heavy on my shoulders.

When I was a wean, the sheds were my playground; I'd ride there on my father's back and spend the day with him. I'd sit in one of the boats and play at being a pirate, or get inside one of the cages and howl like a wolf until he threatened to toss me into the water. Sometimes, I'd thrash in the nets, pretending to be a mermaid, trapped, able to grant wishes in exchange for the cake I knew my mam had packed for us.

Then there were the times I'd sit quietly beside him, practicing knots on old scraps of net while he sorted through the newer ones, pausing occasionally to ruffle my hair.

I don't remember the sheds being creepy back then, but today, even in the bright spring sunlight, they're undeniably sinister: tall and thin, the wood black and warped so that they lean together, crowding me. Goose bumps rise the moment I move out of the sun and into the shade they cast, owing less to the cold than my own unease.

The ominous feeling worsens when a fat magpie lands on top of one of the boathouses, watching me as I pass, cruel beak parted like it's silently laughing at me. They're supposed to have a bit of the devil caught under their tongues.

Lore says that if you give them human blood to drink, it feeds the devil in them, and they'll speak like a person.

It had better bloody not.

I take my *earasaid* off and wave it at the bird, but all it does is eyeball me, dipping its head like it's taking my measure. I have the sudden, irrational feeling it's about to speak, drink of blood or not.

"Away with you," I say before it can. "I don't have time for devils today."

I'm both embarrassed and relieved when it simply cocks its head at me, then begins to preen, combing through feathers that glint inky blue and emerald green in the sun. Obviously dismissed, I leave it behind and head for the storage sheds at the back.

Inside, I light a lamp and watch the shadows play against the wood, pausing to give the rats time to get out of my sight. I listen to the sound of tiny feet scurrying deep in the recesses of the shed and the creak of the wood as it contracts in the rising heat of the day; winter has finally loosened her grip on the mountain. The place smells musty, dank from the droppings and the nets strung from the ceiling to dry before they're mended and rolled up for reuse.

It's the rolled nets I'll need, and the lamp isn't bright enough to check them properly. I spend a couple of sweaty, sweary hours dragging them outside, unrolling them, examining them, then rolling them back up, disappointed. At last,

I find one long enough to replace the ruined one, only to see that something has been nibbling on it, leaving a mess of frayed edges and loose threads that will need reinforcing before it can be used. I groan aloud at the thought of coming back here to repair it.

With a start, I realize I might not have to. This could be the last time I ever come to the sheds. If all goes to plan, I'll be gone in a few days. And I won't ever return. I'll never sit here again, sorting through nets. This place will be nothing but a memory.

Stunned, I sit back on my heels, crushing the net in my fist until my palm hurts, bringing me back to the present.

I roll the net up no less carefully than before and try another, and another, until finally I find one that's right.

By the time I've hauled it ten miles around the shore in one of the wooden carts, I'm roasting alive; my hair is stuck to my forehead, I'm panting with every breath, and thirst has seen me empty and refill my water canteen four times from the loch. Though I've kept my gloves on to protect my hands, my *earasaid* is flung over the nets, and I'm seriously considering shucking my vest off, too, and fixing the net in just my blouse and skirts, propriety be damned.

My arms and legs are killing me, and I think dark thoughts about mountains, earthquakes, secret underground lochs, and how they've all ruined my life. Why couldn't I have lived three hundred years ago, when the loch was a third the size it is now? Why did a stupid earthquake have to shift this particular mountain and release an underground reservoir no one even knew about? If it hadn't, I'd be done and on my merry way to the village by now. But instead, I'm still here, still dragging the bloody net, sweaty, tired, and cross.

Stupid, *stupid* earthquake.

The traveling priest who comes to Ormscaula twice a year to remind us of our sins says the one true god caused the earthquake to teach us Highland heathens a lesson and that we should remember it, so I cast a wary eye to the sky for a stray lightning bolt. But instead of thunder, it's my stomach that rumbles.

I'm *starving*. I didn't bring anything to eat with me, and my stomach's growling like a wild thing, which makes me think of the lugh, and I remember to look around, minding myself like I was told.

That's when I spot something that makes me very grateful I didn't strip down to my underskirts.

And it's worse than a lugh. Worse than the devil talking through a magpie.

Watching me approach, leaning against a tree with his satchel of sins over his shoulder and his ice-blue eyes fixed on me, is Murren Ross.

THREE

"For mercy's sake, what are you doing here?" I drop the handles of the cart and shove my hair out of my face before putting my hands on my hips. "Are you insane?"

"You stood me up. I thought we were meeting." He pushes himself away from the tree and walks toward me. Despite his limp, he clears the distance between us quickly. Then he's right in front of me, and I'm looking up into his amused face.

"If I could make it," I said.

Ren raises one eyebrow. "So I wasted my morning waiting for you in a clandestine location? There was me thinking it was a definite commitment."

"I wouldn't exactly call Mack's Tavern a clandestine

location. And, for the record, I would throw myself in that loch before I entered into a definite commitment of *any* kind with you, Murren Ross."

He clutches his heart. "Ouch."

I roll my eyes. "Seriously, why are you here? I told you not to come up the mountain. I said I'd come to you."

The look he gives me is appraising. "Aye. And then you didn't show up. It might not have been set in stone, but you've always come before when you've said you would. So I was concerned." He gives me a sour smile. "You could try being a little grateful. I just climbed up half a mile of mountain and trekked ten miles around a loch to make sure you weren't dead."

I don't mean to glance at his twisted leg, but I do, and he sees it. We both blush.

"Well, thank you," I mutter without meeting his eyes. "I'm fine. One of the nets needed replacing, that's all." I hesitate. "You should probably go. You know my father doesn't like villagers coming up here, nosing in his business."

Ren laughs.

"I'm not nosing in your da's business. I'm nosing in yours. Besides, how do you think I found you? He told me where you'd be."

For a moment, I'm speechless, fingers of alarm tightening around my throat. "You went to the cottage? *My* cottage? You spoke to him?" I manage to choke out. "Ren, do you ever listen to anything I say?"

"Yes. Every word. But sometimes after I've listened, I choose to ignore you. I call it 'free will.'"

"Seriously—"

Ren holds out his hands to calm me. "He didn't seem to mind. He offered me tea."

My jaw drops.

"I said I was in a hurry, but maybe next time." Ren grins, exposing pointed canines that give him a wolfish look. I turn away, trying to reel in my temper.

Wolfish is the perfect way to describe Ren: All sharp cheekbones and watchful eyes. Rangy, canny, a bit unkempt. And, above all, not one to turn your back on, because he'll be behind you before you know it. As if to prove me right, his arm slips around my shoulder; he's gotten closer while I've not been paying attention.

"Don't be mad," he coaxes, pulling me against him, his too-long hair tickling the top of my ear. "He really didn't seem angry."

I push him away and fold my own arms over my chest. "How would you know?"

"I know what angry men look like. You've seen the type that court my mam."

There's a twist in his voice, but his expression is still amused, mouth curving upward, the skin at the corners of his eyes crinkled in a way that makes him look older than seventeen.

"Can I help?" He nods to the cart behind me. "Make up for disturbing your peace?"

"Shouldn't you be at work?" I ask.

"Night shift. I'm all yours until dark." He grins suggestively.

"Stop it."

Ren shrugs lazily. "I'm serious. Let me help."

I hesitate, then nod. It'll go faster with both of us, and the damage is done—my da already knows he's here. I might as well benefit from it. "All right. You see the posts there, along the side of the shore?" I point to them. "There are loops at the top and bottom of the net. They need to be threaded onto the posts, both ends. We'll keep the net on land while we do that. You stay here, and I'll go to the far end. We'll meet in the middle."

Ren slips off his satchel and places it carefully beneath the tree while I fold my *earasaid* and drape it over the cart handles. He helps me carry the net and unroll it, and we begin hooking it to the poles. We work in silence, setting a good rhythm of lifting, threading, and then threading again, working in tandem until a short while later, we're heaving the center of the net onto the last pole.

He's kept up with me the whole time, matching my pace, and—annoyingly—he barely seems the worse for wear. The underarms and back of my blouse are soaked with sweat, and I know without looking that my face is bright red, but he looks as though he's just woken from a refreshing nap;

there's barely a hint of pink in his cheeks. I suppose working in the mill keeps you fit.

He straightens and pushes his hair out of his eyes.

"You need a haircut," I tell him.

"Are you offering?"

I pull a small switchblade from my pocket. "Aye, come here."

He laughs, sweeping his hair back, and nods toward the net. "Now into the water?" he asks.

"Coward," I mutter, catching his grin as we push the bottom of the net into the loch. It sinks down, bubbles rising. And then they stop, half of the net still above the surface.

We take a moment to get our breath back, looking out over the glassy loch.

"It's low," Ren says, nodding at the waterline. "Look, you could almost walk out to the mountain there."

He points over to the right, where the shallows of the marsh expose parts of the loch bed, leaving a boggy trail out toward the mountainside. Along it is a dark line that marks where the water used to reach. The surface now is far below it, and Ren frowns.

"Have you told your da—" he says.

"Of course I have," I cut him off. I told my father what was happening before the waterline had even dropped to the first notch on the poles that measure the depth. "Besides, he isn't blind." I nod toward the nearest pole, three nicks visible in its side, showing just how much the loch has fallen. "He can see for himself."

As I stare at those marks, my stomach clenches. Because I know my da can see what's happening but he's not doing anything about it. And he should be. It's his job. It's the only reason we haven't been run out of the village yet.

My father is the *Naomhfhuil*—the caretaker of the loch. A Douglas has been the *Naomhfhuil* of Ormscaula since the village was just four wattle-and-daub huts with delusions of grandeur, centuries before the earthquake and the merging of the lochs. It's more than a job. It's his calling—his *sacred duty*—to care for the loch: to read it, and tend it, and guard it. To let the villagers know when it's in trouble. Except right now it is, and he hasn't. And from what I can tell, he doesn't plan to.

Which is a big problem, because these days Ormscaula revolves around one thing—Stewart's Paper Mill. And Stewart's Paper Mill is powered by the river that comes from our loch.

"Is your father not worried?" Ren asks, as if reading my thoughts. "Surely this doesn't bode well for the mill? You know what Giles is like."

I scowl, because I know *exactly* what he's like. Cross Giles Stewart, and you might suddenly find that your or your family's hours are cut at the mill, or that folk won't buy milk or eggs from your farm or drink in your tavern. Where he goes, others follow, if only to keep him onside. It's cold in Ormscaula if Giles Stewart isn't your pal; I speak from experience. But there's nothing I or anyone else can do about it.

Ormscaula is too small to need a mayor—we only see the mailman and the priest once or twice a year—but that hasn't stopped Giles from styling himself lord and master of the place. And who's going to challenge him when it's his mill and his money that pays everyone?

Except my da and me. And there's no love lost between Da and Giles as it is; they're old enemies. So if Giles finds out my father has been keeping something this big from him, he'll come for us. Heavens know he's been waiting long enough for a chance.

"He's planning to expand once summer comes. If the loch gets any lower . . ." Ren looks at me with questioning eyes.

"Since when do you care about Giles Stewart?" I say lightly. Ren is no gossip. But if he mentions the loch level to someone, even in passing, and it gets back to Giles, he'll be straight up here to see for himself. And I can't have that. Not now. "I didn't think you liked working there, anyway. Surely you'd be happy if it had to close for a bit?"

Ren's expression darkens.

"Aye. You know me," he says, a sharp note in his voice. "Any excuse not to put in a good day's grind. Work-shy and feckless, like all my kind."

"What? I didn't mean . . . Ren . . ."

He walks back to the tree, lowering himself carefully down beside his satchel and opening it, his mouth pinched tight, and I stare after him, confused.

The thing is, I *do* know him. And I know what it's like when everyone has an opinion about you. I'm the daughter of Lachlan Douglas, a man everyone despises because Giles Stewart told them they ought to. So I'm disliked and distrusted by association. And Ren is Murren Ross, a slatternly Sassenach for a dam, and no idea who his sire is.

We're bad apples, he and I. Fallen clean at the roots of the trees that grew us.

I hadn't thought that bothered him before now.

"I was joking," I say softly. "I know you're not . . . I know you."

He pulls out a canteen of water and takes a long swig, then holds it out to me without meeting my eyes.

Recognizing it as a gesture of forgiveness, I flop down beside him and take it, grateful for the cool, clear water. When he pulls out a packet of sandwiches and hands one to me wordlessly, I almost hug him.

Even in my ravenous state, I take the time to taste them properly. Thin slices of marsh lamb and red currant jelly stuffed between doorstep-thick slices of crusty bread that are slathered with so much salted butter I can see my teeth marks in it. I chew happily, and the pair of us pass his canteen back and forth between mouthfuls until it's empty and the sandwiches are just crumbs.

"That was great," I say after we're finished. "Thanks for sharing."

Ren smiles. "No bother. I made them especially."

Sure he did. More like he swiped them from someone not paying enough attention.

I glance at the satchel as he reaches back into it and pulls out a wedge of fruitcake, breaking it in two and offering me the larger chunk. "Did you bring my *things*?" I ask as I take it.

He looks out over the loch, chewing his own cake thoughtfully. "I couldn't," he says after he's swallowed, giving me a sideways look. "Guess that means you'll have to come to the village tomorrow."

For a moment, I think he's joking again, because why else would he have walked up the mountain with his leg if not to bring me what I asked for? But when he doesn't smirk or wink, when he just keeps staring out over the calm surface of the water, I realize he's serious.

"Right." I try to hide my confusion and disappointment. I think rapidly about what I need to do in the next few days before the mail cart comes. "That's fine. Maybe not tomorrow, though. It depends." On my father and his mood. "Can you keep them until I come and find you?"

He smiles. "So long as no one else wants them. I'm joking!"

he adds when he sees the look on my face. "They're yours. I got them for you. So I suppose you should tell me what they're for."

I shrug. "I would have thought that was obvious."

"Of course. But what are they *for*?"

I'm tired of this conversation. It's far from the first time we've had it. "Ren, I'm not going to tell you. Not today, not tomorrow. Not ever. So stop asking."

The look he gives me is fierce, but I don't back down. I'm very good at keeping secrets. Ren blinks first and turns toward the loch.

"Mist's coming in," he says, and when I follow his gaze, I see he's right.

Eddies of mist are gathering in the rushes at the edge of the water, lending them a blurry quality. A fish surfaces, sending ripples out. The temperature seems to drop at the same time, and I rub my arms, suddenly chilled.

"You could tell me, you know." Ren keeps his eyes on the water, his tone careless. I'm not fooled by it, especially when he continues, "You can trust me."

"It's not about trust. It's just none of your business," I say gently, pushing myself to my feet. "Come on, you've work to get to, and we don't want to be on the mountain after dark. My da and I think a rabid lugh destroyed the net. We shouldn't hang around." I offer him a hand, but he ignores it, rising awkwardly, all his weight on his left leg.

Before we go, I check the water level one more time. I'm

stunned when I realize it has dropped again, a full inch, in the hours we've been there. Though I can't see it from here, I turn east in the direction of the village, where I can picture the mill down by the river, the waterwheel turning relentlessly, sucking up the loch water, the vats steaming away as logs are pulped, turning the loch to cloud.

I'll talk to my father again, I decide. Something has to be done.

"Look." Ren points through the mist to a part of the loch we can't normally reach, bordered by the mountain. "See that hole? I bet it leads to the otters' dens."

"Holts," I murmur, correcting him. "Otter dens are called holts."

I peer in the direction of his finger, narrowing my eyes to focus. Just visible above the waterline is a dark hollow in the side of the mountain.

"That's surely too big to be the opening of a holt," I say.

"It'll be the waves eroding it now that it's at surface level. The otters won't like it. Maybe they sabotaged your net. In protest."

I snort a laugh, then fall silent and still. Otters are shy creatures. In a lifetime living by the loch, I've never actually seen one, though I've found their tracks a few times. I've certainly never seen the loch so low the underwater entrance to a den is visible, if that's what it is.

"Or . . ." Ren's voice turns dramatic, sinister. "Maybe it

was a loch monster that ruined it. Some horrible ancient beastie emerging from the depths to wreak its revenge on Ormscaula."

"Maybe," I say, allowing myself a smile. There's only one monster up here, and it doesn't live in the loch. But I don't say anything, and neither does Ren.

The mist thickens, and the sun gets a little lower in the sky.

"Come on," I say again. I put my *earasaid* back on and begin to walk, dragging the cart behind me.

The journey back is mostly silent, both of us lost in our thoughts, though every now and then one of us points out a falcon or a fish as the mist chases us all the way to the path down the mountain.

"Will you be all right going back alone?" I ask when we reach the fork that will take him on to Ormscaula and carry me back to my cottage in the opposite direction.

Ren gives me a look. "If I said no, would you offer to walk me home? Or invite me back to yours?" I am silent, and he smiles. "I'll be fine. Will you?"

In response, I move my outer skirt aside, exposing the gun tucked into a holster. It's one of a pair of flintlock pistols my father has in addition to his two long guns, which I'm not allowed to use. The pistol is half-cocked already; I didn't want to mess around with gunpowder and a bullet if a lugh did attack. Thankfully, I'm a good shot. And I have the switchblade in my pocket, just in case.

Ren doesn't seem surprised by the gun. But then, why would he be, given what I've asked him to get for me?

"So that's what you wanted the bullets for?" he asks, his eyes narrowing. "They're going to be too small for that."

I guess we're not calling them *things* anymore. I smooth my blouse down. "That's not your concern."

He looks as though he might say something else, but then he throws his arms wide and turns, sauntering down the mountain path toward Ormscaula. I watch him until he's out of sight around the bend; the last thing I see is his hair, dyed red by the setting sun. Then I make for the sheds, dragging the cart with one hand, the other on the gun, before heading home.

FOUR

I open the door to the cottage and almost die of shock.

From the kitchen comes the sound of pans clanking. Someone else is in there, doing the work I've been doing since I was nine. And the smell—I know that smell. There are days and nights that I've *craved* it, would have done almost anything for it. For fluffy potatoes cooked in their own skins, swimming in cheese and herb cream, studded with crisp smoked bacon. Stunned, I lean against the doorframe, mouth watering, mind whirring.

He's cooking. My father is cooking.

That can't be good.

I don't go into the kitchen right away. Instead, I go to his study to replace the gun in the lockbox, then to the washroom to clean myself up, taking the time to puzzle over why he's suddenly cooking but coming up with nothing to explain it. Back in my room, I put on a fresh blouse and skirt, secreting the switchblade in a pocket before attempting to tame my wild curls into something resembling a braid. The string snaps as I try to knot it at the end of the plait, too old to cope with my mop any longer. I search for another bit but quickly give up, tying a yellow scarf I find at the back of one of my drawers over my head instead.

When I finally go through to the kitchen, my father stands facing the stove. A knife glints in his hand, and I pause in the doorway, heart stuttering.

I swallow. *Relax*, I tell myself. He's not gone to all the effort of cooking only to kill you before dinner. If he's going to do it, he'll do it after.

Small comfort. Gallows humor.

"Smells good," I say as I enter the kitchen. If he's pretending this is normal, then so will I. "The new net is in place. I'll check it in a couple of days. No sign of a lugh there."

My father keeps his back to me but grunts in acknowledgment, and I light candles and gather plates and cutlery. He opens the oven door and pulls out a sizzling tray that fills the room with the scents of thyme and loss.

As he turns with it gripped in gloved hands, he glances at me and halts, startling so suddenly I'm afraid he'll drop the food. But he recovers and carries it to the table as I pour a dark beer for him, setting the glass down at his place and fetching water for myself.

"Is everything all right?" I dare. He's still looking at me, his expression unreadable.

"Your hair . . ." I wait for the rest of the sentence, but instead he follows it up with "Sit down. It's ready."

I look at the tray and see that he's cooked enough for three people, like he used to. Me, him. And Mam.

It hurts. For the first time in forever, I feel an old, familiar pain under my ribs, like someone has elbowed me sharply from the inside. Soul side. I close my eyes and breathe through my mouth, waiting for it to pass.

When I look up, I see my father has begun eating as though nothing is wrong. And maybe it isn't. I'm being stupid; I doubt he even realizes what he's done.

Pushing down the sorrow in my chest, I sit and lift one of the potatoes from the tray. It drips cream onto the plate, cheese and bacon oozing from its core. This was his specialty when I was little. I used to ask for it at least twice a week, though it was closer to twice a year that he'd make it. He bakes the potatoes in the stove, packed deep in a tray of ashes. When they're almost done, he brings them out and cleans the ash off, then makes a hole in each, scooping the innards out. He mixes the potato with cheese and bacon, then crams it all back inside the skin, covering the hole. To serve, he slashes the tops and drizzles cream spiked with garlic, chives, thyme, and tarragon over them. They taste salty and smoky and fatty and creamy. They taste like home, but I'm too nervous to take a bite, too frightened of what might come bubbling up to the surface if I do. I take a sip of water instead.

"Is he courting you? Murren Ross?"

I almost spit the water across the table. Ren, courting me? As though he's a gentle laird and I'm a pretty maiden whose hand he seeks in marriage. I half wish Ren were here to hear it. He'd die.

I manage to keep a straight face as I reply, "No. No one's courting me. Ren just gets the paper I need for transcribing cheap from the mill. He came to deliver it because I didn't go down to the village. The mail cart is due at the end of the week, you see, so I have to finish my work in the next couple of days."

My father gives a displeased *hmmm*, then falls silent, as he always does when I talk about my job.

Which is exactly why I brought it up.

It started as another way for me to make myself indispensable to my father, to bring in some money. Being the *Naomhfhuil* pays only a nominal amount. And that was fine way back when the *Naomhfhuil* also earned a tithe in meat, cows' milk, and grain, but those days are long gone, along with my mother's dowry and my family's reputation.

I, on the other hand, earn a decent wage. I'm a lot cheaper

than the town scribes, thanks to Ren's willingness to get paper for me, and my penmanship is exceptional, even if I do say so myself. I'm in demand.

So much so that I've got a job waiting for me in Thurso.

See, I've been clever—most runaways would head south, to Inverness. But if anyone's going to look for me, they'll go there. So I'm heading east. I'll be working for the clerk at St. Peter's as an underclerk. He doesn't even mind that I'm a girl. This job has been four years in the making, four years of planning and squirreling money away and making inquiries, but now I'm just days from telling Ormscaula to kiss my arse as I ride away from it for good.

Farewell, judgmental villagers. Goodbye, bad reputation. So long, risk of murder.

I can't wait.

The taste of freedom is enough to wake my appetite, and I dig into my dinner with relish, swallowing memories down with the crispy bacon and fluffy potato.

"So, will he be back?"

I pause mid-chew and look at my father as understanding dawns. This is why he cooked. That's why he made enough for three. It wasn't out of habit. It was in case Ren came home with me. This is a performance, not a supper. *Everything's fine up here, laddie. Just a normal da, caring for his daughter. Won't you have a potato?*

He thinks that if Ren is interested in me, then he's also

someone who will notice if I'm all right, someone keeping an eye out for me. Someone who will tell the village if I pull a vanishing act. After all, losing one family member might be excused as careless; losing two is undeniably suspicious.

"He's Liz Ross's son, isn't he?" my father continues when I don't answer. "And he works at the mill, you say?"

"Of course. Who doesn't?"

"Even with his leg?"

"He doesn't need his leg for cutting paper."

He grunts again.

We finish the meal in silence, splitting the last potato as though the reason he cooked so much was so we could have more, not that he planned for company.

I'm relieved when we return to the old routine afterward; I clear the table as my father melts the base of a candle before sticking it to a saucer. He does this every night, even though we have candlesticks, a fine pair of silver ones that came with my mam when he married her.

As he passes me, making for his study, I'm rocked by a vision of my mother. For a moment, she's there beside me, telling him in a stern voice that doesn't match the curve of her lips or her sparkling eyes that we're not saving the candlesticks for best, that he doesn't have to worry about using them up.

Too many memories fighting their way to the surface lately. If I were the superstitious kind, I'd worry.

I shrug the past off and put the kettle on the stove for tea, listening to the sound of his chair creaking as he settles into it, the thud of the logbook when he opens it, the heavy wooden cover knocking against the desk.

My father writes in the *Naomhfhuil* log every night without fail. Even two winters ago, when a fever rendered both of us bedridden and delirious, he still got up and made his checks, meticulously recording what he'd seen before passing out at his desk. He could no more take a day off than he could grow wings and fly over the mountain. That's what it is to be the *Naomhfhuil*.

Naomhfhuil roughly means "holy saint" in the old tongue, a throwback to a few centuries ago when everyone believed a whole bunch of gods lived in the loch, demanding sacrifice and worship, and the *Naomhfhuil* was the person chosen to act as the liaison between them and us. It was the most important role in the village, once upon a time.

Until the one true god did his earthquake trick, splitting the mountain and killing the old pagan loch gods, rendering the *Naomhfhuil* mostly pointless and the loch big enough to drive me around the bend when I have to walk its perimeter.

I light more candles and dot them about the kitchen, lending it a false sense of cheer. By candlelight, it looks inviting: the red-and-white-checked cloth on the table; the dresser with its fine china that I dust every week, even though we haven't used it in forever; the rack of copper pans, bushels of herbs drying in between them. Nothing has changed in years.

I catch my reflection in the window as I wash our dishes, blurred by the condensation beading there and distorted by the thick bull's-eye glass. It rounds out my cheeks, and for a moment, my mother looks back at me.

Spooked, I swipe at the pane, sending rivulets of water trickling down, erasing the image. I pull the scarf from my head and pocket it, running my fingers through my hair to return to it its natural volume. When I check my reflection again, I only see myself.

Resting my hips on the edge of the sink, I lean forward, pushing the window open to allow the steam out. As I do, the mist creeps in, bringing a chill with it. I stand still for a while, listening to the faint sound of the loch lapping the shore and the larger, denser silence around it. I wonder what it will be like to live in a big town, surrounded by the roar of coaches and people and whatever else towns sound like.

Leaning forward once more, I pull the window shut and drop the latch, then close the shutters. I make the tea, holding two mugs in one hand and taking a candle with me, blowing out the others.

"You replaced the net, you said?" my father asks when I enter his study. He murmurs thanks as I set down his tea.

"I did. Oh, and the water level has dropped again. Another five inches since yesterday. It's so low in the marshes that the bed's starting to dry." I pause. "I think it fell even while we were there. An inch, I'm sure of it; I could see by the measuring stakes."

He half turns, stern profile caught by the lamp on his desk. "Did you mention it to the Ross boy?"

"I didn't have to. He noticed it himself."

My father turns fully to face me. "And is he likely to say anything about it to Giles Stewart?" He sneers as he says the mill owner's name, spitting it out like poison.

"No, of course not. But Giles will know anyway, once you write and tell him," I say. When he stays silent, I ask outright, "Da, you have written a report, haven't you? Because Giles is planning to expand the mill. He needs to know that he can't; the loch can't handle what he's taking from it now."

His mouth is set as he replies, "I've not written. Not yet."

"But—"

"I said not yet," he thunders. "Do you think I don't know my job? I don't want them all traipsing up here unless it's absolutely necessary. More fool is Giles if he doesn't realize that mill can't run day and night like it does without it meaning trouble."

He dismisses me by turning back to his desk, and I beat a hasty retreat to my room, berating myself as I go. That was all five rules broken in one go. I'm an idiot. I'm so close to getting out of here; how could I be so stupid as to risk my life now?

I shut my bedroom door and put my tea and candle on

the little stool beside the bed before lying down. My da's right about one thing—Giles Stewart's greed is the reason the water level is dropping so fast. He's the one who's been increasing the mill's output all winter, and he's the one looking to expand and build another pulping tower. There's no denying it's because of Giles that water is being used faster than it can be replaced. Surely he can understand that? He must know the loch isn't infinite.

I stop myself; I shouldn't care about this. I'll be long gone by the time it matters. It's not my business, and it's not my problem. My problems lie miles away, in Thurso. *That* should be taking up every spare bit of space in my mind. Building my new life.

Pulling a pillow under my head, I try to imagine it. New town, new me. A place of my own. Work. Friends.

Maybe even—

The sound of a woman screaming outside tears my fantasy apart.

I almost knock my tea over in my haste to stand, the switchblade in my hand before I'm on my feet. It'll be the lugh, I realize. Not a woman. They sound almost the same.

As I reach my bedroom door, my father strides past, a long gun in his hands, the barrel open as he shoves shells into it, snapping it closed with a flick of his wrist.

He turns to me as he pulls the safety back. "Stay here."

Then he's gone, out into the night.

I rush to the window, but the reflection of the room blinds me to the outside. I pinch the candle out, but even so I can't see more than a few feet ahead, thanks to the mist. There's no sign of my father or any cat. I hold my breath, keep myself still, waiting.

The scream comes again, from the back, by the henhouse.

Still clutching my knife, I dart from my room, staying close to the walls as I move through the hall to the kitchen. I pull the shutters back and listen.

It's silent, but the skin on the back of my neck prickles. Like I'm being watched.

Something crashes into the front door, and I cry out. Then I run toward it, arm raised, knife gripped tightly . . .

It flies open, and I manage to stop myself just before I stab my father.

His face is blank, eyes unseeing, apparently unaware how close he came to being the sheath for my knife. I lower it, my heart thundering like a thousand horses racing, but still he says nothing, staring at me—through me. He doesn't seem to notice the blade in my hand at all.

My blood runs cold.

"Papa?" I haven't said *Papa* since I was a child. My voice is high like a child's, too.

At last he looks at me.

"Put that away," he says, glaring at the knife. I close it and shove it back into my pocket.

"Did you get it?" I ask, realizing I already know the answer, because I didn't hear the gun go off. "Do you want to go back out and look?" I offer. "I could come—"

"No!" he snaps, his eyes blazing. "You're to stay in the house, do you hear me? And you keep away from the windows. Do you understand me, Alva?"

I stare at him, fright rooting me to the spot, deadening my tongue.

"Do you hear me?" he says again, grabbing my shoulders and shaking me until my teeth rattle. "You do not leave these walls without my permission."

I manage to nod, and he releases me.

Without another word, he storms away, back into his study, closing the door.

I stay where I am, my bowels turned to liquid, too scared to move. I don't know if I'm going to faint, or be sick, or cry, or worse. So I do nothing until I'm sure I can move without losing control. Then I go back to my bedroom, closing the door, pausing in the middle of the room, counting my heartbeats. So much for being ready for it. I wasn't ready at all. I didn't even try to defend myself.

I pull the shutters over my window, and when I'm sure my father isn't coming back, I drop to my knees and push aside the raggedy rug my mother made for me. Digging the knife into the wooden floorboards, I prize one of them up.

Hidden beneath my bedroom floor is a sturdy canvas bag;

a brand-new *earasaid*—plain, not plaid; a pair of thick-soled boots; two impossibly pretty lace-trimmed dresses I could never wear in Ormscaula; a set of carved calligraphy pens— brown, black, red, and blue ink; a sheaf of gold leaf; almost two hundred crowns in gold, silver, and bronze pieces.

And the gun my father used to kill my mother seven years ago.

FIVE

I wake early the next morning to find that my father has already left the cottage. At first I'm relieved, until I discover he's taken all the milk with him, the rest of yesterday's bread, half a block of cheese, and some of the dried sausages from the store.

I break my fast with watery porridge and tea as black as my mood. I could milk the goat—I can hear her bleating outside—but knowing my luck, he'd return while I was in the yard, and there'd be hell to pay for disobeying him. Better to wait for him to get back.

It's when I head to his room to straighten it and find his bed neatly made, the blankets still tucked with my sharp corners, that I realize he hasn't slept in it. And when I check his study, I find one of the long guns gone, the box of shells half empty. He must have left the cottage last night, after I fell asleep, to hunt the lugh. He's been out all night.

Back in my room, my own gun hums beneath the floorboards, and once again I prize the board up and free it, holding the now-familiar weight in my hand.

I don't know why I took it. I don't know why I still keep it. It's pretty, if a gun can be such a thing. The flintlock pistols I'm allowed to use belonged to my father's grandmother. The wood is scratched, the metal dulled; even though they've been well cared for, they're old, and it shows. But the gun that killed my mother is a real beauty.

The handle is pale wood, inlaid with iridescent abalone shell, and rounded, designed to be cradled in a palm. The barrel is long—elegant, really. It takes different bullets than the flintlocks: shiny, silver-pointed things that look nothing like the lead balls the flintlocks use. Most importantly, you can load more than one at a time. Six will fit snugly in the chamber, which revolves to line them up. And there's no need to mess around with gunpowder; the whole mechanism is clockwork smooth. I know because I've tried it, though not while it's loaded. It must be devastating when it is. *Bang. Bang. Bang. Bang.* Faster than a heartbeat.

It used to be too big for my hands, but now it fits just fine.

Sometimes I think about throwing it in the loch and letting water and time make it into nothing. Other times, I fantasize about putting it on the table between my father and me while we're eating, just gently setting it down, finally there, out in the open. Or handing it to the sheriff when he next comes through. Telling him what I should have said seven years ago.

In darker times, I imagine using it for retribution and finding the natural home for those last two bullets.

If I'm honest with myself, I expect I'll take it with me and hide it under some different floorboards for seven more years. But at least I'll have bullets for it. I've wanted them for so long; just four, enough to fill the chamber. I can't shake the feeling the gun *wants* to be full. Complete.

Of course, to do that, I have to get down to Ormscaula and find Ren, which is a lot trickier now that I'm forbidden to leave the house.

You could be down the mountain and back within three hours, a sly voice says in my head.

I hide the gun away once more, then look out my window, scanning the loch. No sign of my father. But that doesn't mean he couldn't come back at any minute.

He took all that food, the voice continues. *That's a lot of food. I bet he plans to be out at least until supper tonight.*

In the kitchen, the clock chimes eight times. We eat supper around six, usually.

Down and back in three hours . . . It may be your last chance . . .

Oh hell.

Before I can think better of it, I find myself outside with a basket in my hand, creeping along the edge of the loch in a plain brown *earasaid*, eyes peeled for any sign of him. When I make it to the mountain path unseen, some of the fear eases up; the chances of bumping into him on it are pretty remote, unless he has finally gone to see Giles. But something in my gut tells me that's not where he is, and I look north one last time before beginning the journey down.

Almost an hour later, as I round the last bend on the mountain path, trailing my fingers through the heather, the low hum of Giles's mill reaches me, disturbing my peace. Then I see Ormscaula: pretty cottages with thatched roofs and white walls, glowing in the sunlight, tiny dots of chickens scratching in neat squares of fenced-off dirt behind them. It's like something from a storybook; I have to fight the urge to sing as I approach it, rosy-cheeked from the wind, my hair tucked neatly under my *earasaid*. A simple country maiden, wending her way to the picturesque village she calls home . . .

The walk back up the mountain will be pure hell on my thighs.

Still, that's ahead of me, along with the rest of my troubles, and it's hard not to feel cheerful under the warm sun. The basket rests in the crook of my left arm, and in my right hand I have a trusty flintlock, half-cocked once more. I like the weight of it, the same as I like the weight of the knife that bounces gently against my leg with each step. What kind of girl—what kind of person—takes comfort in that?

This girl. This person. What can you do?

Just outside the village proper, I pass the mill: a long, windowless building with a single tower churning white steam into the air as the giant waterwheel sucks up water from the river. The noise this close to it is deafening, all roaring and creaking and thumping, and I scrunch my nose up against it, as if that'll help. It'll be a hundred times worse when Giles expands the mill. And the water it'll need . . .

Not my business, I remind myself. *Not my business, not my problem. Not anymore.*

I uncock the gun and tuck it into the basket as I arrive in Ormscaula, where my mood immediately sours. Up close, it's still like something from a storybook, but the moment I cross the bridge and enter the village, the story changes from one where I might be the plucky young heroine to one where I'm the monster. Or, if not the actual monster, then the monster's daughter. That's what Giles would have the villagers believe, at any rate.

And he's right. My father is exactly what Giles says he is. He is a murderer.

I know, because I was there.

It's why I can't be angry with them for the way they treat me.

I pass Auld Iain Stewart, some third or fourth cousin of Giles, sitting out in his garden. He spots me and sucks in a deep breath, then kisses his knuckles and presses them to his forehead, warding against me like I'm a mountain geist. Women pull their children away from garden gates as I walk by, like being motherless is catching. Men passing me on their way to the mill stare at me through narrowed eyes, as if trying to figure out who I'm more like: my maybe-murderer recluse of a father, or my maybe-child-and-husband-abandoning mam. I don't know which they think would be better.

From what Ren says, no one really believed Giles when he came haring down the mountain, shouting about murder. They nodded and said, *Aye, how terrible*, but most folk reckon my mother left of her own free will, making for Balinkeld and beyond when she realized she'd shackled herself to a man who would always put the loch first. They saw enough in the days and weeks leading up to her disappearance to believe she finally snapped and ran away.

It's what gave me the idea to leave, actually. I like how they believe my mam is out there, living a life she's chosen. I couldn't save her from my da, but I can do this for us.

When I finally reach the village square, I'm surprised to see people tossing old furniture and scraps from the mill to build a bonfire at the center. Then I remember it's almost time for the *feis samhaid*—the festival to bring on summer.

As I stare at the burgeoning pile, I can almost taste charred sausages, salted butter, and hot bread. I think of the last of the harvest apples from the autumn before, dried over winter, then sliced, speared on sticks, and dipped in hot caramel that dripped onto your hands so you had to lick them clean. Birch sap in tiny cups, tasting like silk. My father lifting me onto his shoulders so I could see over the crowd to where the violinists were sawing away, the dancers spinning about the Staff, the lovers kissing.

I remember one particular year, him setting me down while he bought hot whiskey for himself and my mother and a cone of pine candy for me to suck while they supped. How my mother pushed her cup away and laughed.

"I can't drink that now, can I?" she'd said, and he'd stared, baffled for a moment, before slapping his forehead.

"I forgot," he said, grinning.

"Lucky you," my mam had replied, and they'd both laughed.

I didn't understand what was funny at the time. When they'd hugged, I remember feeling left out and alone . . .

Another memory pushes through of the same *feis*, one of a scrawny boy with dirty-blond hair falling in his eyes, sitting alone on the well, a sturdy brace strapped to his leg, glaring around him as though he could repel people with the power of his mind. But not me. I walked over, away from my embracing parents, and sat next to him. I offered him a candy. I remember the crack it made when he bit into it, the crunching sound of teeth on hard sugar. He asked for another, and I gave it to him. He ate the whole cone while I sucked the one sweet until it was gone.

Ren.

That was the last *feis samhaid* I went to. Just before . . .

"Alva?"

I realize Gavan Stewart, Giles's son, is right in front of me, tentatively waving his hand before my face. Behind him, his friends—who used to be my friends, too—are watching. Their faces are amused, confused, and maybe a little disdainful, all at once. I straighten in response.

"Hallo there," Gavan says, brown eyes lit with pleasure. "It's nice to see you. It's been a while. How are you?"

"I'm fine." I nod toward the bonfire. "How's it going?"

"Good. It's going to be a great night. The best one yet, I reckon. Will you . . . Are you planning to come this year?"

Not many would ask me that without a snide note in their voice, but Gavan means it sincerely. He's genuinely interested. He's his father's double—same reddish-gold hair, same ruddy complexion, same stocky build—but in temperament, Gavan's as sweet as can be. And he doesn't need to be, not with Giles as his father and everyone desperate to curry favor because of it. The mill will be his one day—which means Ormscaula will be his, or as good as. Most boys would turn nasty with that sort of power.

But Gavan . . . He was always kind.

"No," I say, finally answering him and putting the others out of their misery. Gavan might be decent, but Hattie Logan, Cora Reid, and James Ballantyne aren't. It's been a long time since we were friends. Seven years, in fact.

"You should think about it," Gavan continues. "We never see you anymore."

"Da keeps me busy," I reply. "Lots to do on the loch."

"Well, if you change your mind, I'll save you a dance." He smiles at me, and it's so bright and lovely that I smile back without meaning to.

And then I see Ren, who gives me the briefest wave before ducking down the alley toward the tavern, reminding me I'm not here to annoy the villagers.

"I have to go," I say.

"Until tomorrow?" Gavan says, his tone hopeful.

"I'll see you," I say, only realizing as I walk away that it could be taken as a promise.

I go to the general store first, lurking in aisles stacked with jars of pickled cabbage and onions and cans of milk and oil, pretending to choose between sacks of flour until the only other customer leaves.

"Has the mail cart been sighted?" I ask Maggie Wilson as I approach the counter, not bothering to greet her first. There's no need to pretend we're pals.

I once heard her telling Mrs. Logan, in a too-loud whisper she meant for me to hear, that I'd cut myself one day if I carried on being so sharp. Old hypocrite. She's not exactly soft herself.

Maggie Wilson knows everything about Ormscaula— Giles Stewart uses his money and his mill to grease the wheels, but Maggie is a born leader. She's been the sole proprietor of the store since her husband died a few months into their marriage. Local legend says she took three days to grieve: one to cry, one to bury him, and one to rearrange the layout of the store to suit her better. After that, she opened the doors once more, and they haven't been closed a day since. That was some forty years ago, and she's still going, iron haired and hearted.

I'd rather be sharp than dull. Knives are better sharp. You'd think she of all people would agree.

She peers at me over half-moon spectacles. "Aye. He'll be here midday tomorrow, by my reckoning. In time for the *feis* this year, it seems." Then her eyes narrow. "I just hope everyone behaves themselves while we've got company."

And right on cue, my cheeks start to burn.

I had a crush on Duncan Stroud, the mailman, a couple of years ago. I was hardly the only one; the first time he came, age twenty and new to the job, the square was packed to the walls with every woman in Ormscaula, eager for a look. I went half-daft watching the muscles in his arms move when he bore the weight of each sack to the ground. I'd never seen anything like it.

"I'll be back before you know it," he'd said as he was leaving, tipping me a wink, and I was done for. That was all it took.

I spent six months waiting for him to come back. I'd already hatched my plan to leave the village, but after Duncan, my fantasies of escape took a different turn, ones that involved him throwing me over his shoulder and saying he had to have me as his bride, he couldn't live without me, and he was taking me with him.

In my defense, I was fourteen. I didn't know any better. So I suppose what happened next served me right.

When he returned, I was waiting. Sitting at the side of the road outside Ormscaula in my best skirts and blouse, trying not to squint when the sun got in my eyes. He recognized me and pulled his cart over, offering me a ride. I promptly got in, gave him the completed transcripts I'd done, and as he leaned forward to put them away, I tried to kiss him.

I caught his cheek. He didn't laugh, to be fair, just moved me away and told me in a heartbreakingly gentle voice that I was very bonny, but too young for him. And in response, I ran. Jumped out of the cart and bolted back up the mountain to lick my wounds.

He left the new manuscripts for transcribing with Maggie, who glared accusingly when I slunk into the store to ask if she knew what he'd done with them. I'm sure he never told her what happened, but since then, she's always had a censorious look in her eye when I've asked her about him.

"I suppose you'll be back to meet him, then?" Maggie says, right on time with her sniff of disapproval. "For your work," she adds, and I fight not to blush again.

If only she knew that Duncan is my unwitting escape out of here. That in a few days' time, I'll be hidden under sacks of mail and goods, grateful I never have to see her mug again.

"Got to keep the wolf from the door, Mrs. Wilson." I smile widely at her.

"I should think it's the wolf already inside you'd want to worry about."

My chest tightens. "And what does that mean?"

"Nothing at all," she says in a tone that means the opposite. "Well, I won't keep you."

She means *get out*, so I do, before I say something I'll regret.

SIX

I find Ren in Mack's Tavern.

It's got what a generous person would call "a lot of char-acter": ominous dark stains on the wooden floor, tabletops scarred with pocks and scratches, a mangy one-eyed cat sit-ting sentinel on the bar that would bite you as soon as look at you.

It's got what *I* call a death-trap air about it, but beggars can't be choosers.

The tavern sells two types of stout, one type of whiskey, and that's your lot. For the nobler folk, like Giles Stewart, there's the inn, where you can buy a nice dinner from Rosie Talbot and wash it down with wine. But for the likes of Ren and me, and a lot of the folk who work nights at the mill, there's the tavern. Today, though, it's nearly empty; everyone is at work or asleep before the night shift.

Ren sits in a corner, nursing a clay tankard. He's wearing a black coat with the collar turned up, his hair spilling over it. He doesn't look up until I sit opposite him, and then his sharp blue eyes meet mine.

He ate the whole bag of pine candy. All but the piece in my mouth.

How had I forgotten that?

"Hi," I say, covering my confusion by reaching for his tankard and drinking from it.

It's not ale; it's apple juice. Refreshing after my walk, but surprising. I push the tankard back toward him.

"Have you got the money?" he says quietly.

I reach into my basket and pull out the money for my bullets: a discreet bag of coins, each one wrapped in a scrap of cloth to keep them from chinking together and revealing themselves. I check that Mack isn't in sight before I slide it across the table to Ren. The cat eyeballs us, supercilious.

It looks like Ren simply waves a hand over it, and then it's gone and his hands are clasping the tankard once more. He still doesn't say anything, just lifts his cup and drinks.

"And my half of the deal?" I ask when the bullets don't appear on the table with the same sleight-of-hand trickery.

His eyes slide to the side, where Mack has appeared,

joining the cat in watching us with mild derision as he dirties a tankard with a grubby-looking cloth. "Not here."

I lower my voice. "Then where?"

"Come on," he says, standing and sliding out from the table, his bad leg making the movement awkward.

I stand to follow, only for Mack to step out from behind the bar, thick arms folded ominously.

"It's a groat for the drink."

Trust Ren not to have paid.

I pull my purse from the basket and hand Mack a dull silver coin, then follow Ren outside.

He's already halfway across the square, coat flaring behind him like wings, courting the same unfriendly looks from Gavan's circle as I did, though he does a better job of ignoring them. At the edge of the square, he stops, waiting for me to catch up.

"Everyone is looking at us," I mutter, glancing back to where James Ballantyne and Cora Reid are giving us both filthy glares.

"And that bothers you?" he asks, a curious expression on his face. "Ashamed to be seen with me? Don't want them to think you're friends with *that Ross boy*?"

He does a surprisingly good impression of Maggie Wilson. It takes me a few seconds to recover, and all the while, he watches me.

"I just mean I don't want people gossiping that I'm following you around Ormscaula like a lost lamb," I say.

He grins but doesn't reply, stalking off again.

I follow him, silently seething, through the village, past the butcher and the baker, past the village hall and the tiny chapel and Iain the Smith's smithy. We walk on, leaving behind the neat houses with their white fences and brightly painted doors, past scrubby wee houses that are run-down, the paintwork chipped, the yards overgrown and littered with bottles, houses where the windows are dirty, smeared with grease and fingerprints.

There's a moment when I think maybe he's taking me to his home, and I feel a thrill of excitement. Domestic Ren isn't something I can imagine; he seems too fey to live in something as mundane as a cottage. But we pass the last of the dwellings with their sparse thatch and patched walls and move into a pasture, heading toward the forest.

"Are we going to the woods?" I ask. "Ren? I have to get back." I've been away for nearly two hours. I don't have time to mess around.

"We're almost there," he says, his limp more pronounced now that the ground is uneven.

"Where?" I ask, but he doesn't answer.

It's much cooler under the canopy of the trees, the scent of resin and pine thick and clean. Again I think of the candy and his tiny, boyish face, the greed and fear on it, and I wonder if he remembers or if he's forgotten, like I had.

Brown pine needles crunch under my feet, and I drag my boots through them, kicking them, until Ren stops in a small clearing and sits on a fallen log, extending his legs in front of him. The right one turns inward slightly, but that's the only tell that he was born with a twisted leg. Carefully, I sit, too, perching on a raised root, resting the basket in the space between us.

"Was this really necessary?" I ask, shifting to face him.

"I've not brought you here before, have I?" he says, and I shake my head. "It's my favorite place. I come here to think."

I look around, trying to see what's special about it, but my attention moves back to him when he reaches into his coat and pulls out a package. The bullets. My pulse quickens.

"What are they for?" he asks, weighing the parcel in his hands.

"A gun." I give him my best grin.

He fixes me with a glacial look. "What are they *for*?"

"I just told you."

He tilts his head. "Fine. So they're for a gun. What about the new *earasaid*, and the dresses?"

"I decided I need to get out more."

He doesn't return it. "You're leaving, aren't you? That's what it's all been about. All the stuff you've asked for. You're running away."

I don't even blink. "No."

"Where are you going?" he continues, as if I haven't spoken. "Inverness, it has to be."

"Ren . . ."

"I want to come with you."

I choke on thin air.

"Is that so strange?" He looks at me. "I have as much reason to want to leave. More. I'm not from here, remember?"

I shake my head. "Can I just have my bullets, please?"

He puts the package back in his pocket. "You want them, let me come with you."

"Will you get it out of your head that I'm going somewhere, Murren Ross? This is ridiculous." I stand and walk toward him, holding out my hand.

"Full-naming me, gosh—it must be serious. So am I: no me, no bullets. You can have your money back." He reaches into his pocket and pulls out the bag I gave him, dangling it in the air, where it twirls one way, then the other.

Maybe I don't need those bullets. I can take another gun; it doesn't have to be that one. I'll throw the gun into the loch, let it go. It's about time. What would I even need a gun for in Thurso?

But the thought of not having it makes me feel panicky; immediately, sweat prickles along my shoulders, my heart beats a little harder. No, I can't leave it behind. I can't get rid of it. I need it. I need the bullets for it. I don't know why, but I do.

"I thought we were friends," I try.

"We are. That's why you should tell me when we're going. That's what friends do."

I growl in frustration. "Ren, give me the bullets, or I swear—"

"Swear what?" He looks me up and down, smirking, as he tucks the money pouch away once more. "Alva, come on. You don't need to put on your tough-girl boots. *I know you.*"

I hear the echo of my words from the other day, on the loch. But there's no soft apology in his tone. Instead, he's sure I'll back down, now that he has something I want—*need*. He's so confident he knows me, but he doesn't know anything. Doesn't know what I know, or what I've done.

Before I realize I'm doing it, I reach into the basket and pull out the gun.

His eyes widen with surprise for a second, and a bolt of triumph bursts through me. He doesn't know me that well.

Then his mouth splits into a grin, and I falter as the heat of my fury gives way to icy shock at my own behavior. What the hell am I playing at?

But Ren doesn't seem frightened by the gun. Or even bothered.

He reaches out, taking the barrel of the gun in his hand. He pulls it—pulls me—forward until the tip is kissing his forehead, all the while watching me calmly.

"I'm not going to shoot you," I say quietly.

"Says the girl with a gun to my head." He smiles. "They're in my top inside pocket, if you were wondering."

I try to pull the gun away, but he holds it fast, keeping it pressed into his skin.

"Do you have a death wish?" I ask. "This isn't funny. Stop it."

"Take them."

I hesitate, looking into his eyes, trying to read the intention there. Slowly, I reach into the inside pocket of his coat, find the box resting against his heart. I pull it out, my knuckles feeling the rhythm behind his ribs, beating hard and fast. Despite his arrogant smile, he's frightened.

Or excited.

He smiles at me: a pure, open smile.

"You're insane."

"Am I?"

As I lift the package free, he raises his other hand, resting it over mine. One still keeping the gun to his head, the other pressing my hand to his chest. His heart is wild beneath it, the twin of mine. Glacier-blue eyes watch me, clear as the sky above. A girl could drown in eyes like that, and not in the fun way.

Then he blinks and releases both the gun and me.

"Alva?" he says, his voice low, a purr to it that makes my mouth dry.

I raise an eyebrow, not trusting myself to speak.

"I knew you weren't going to shoot me," he says in his

normal voice, folding his arms behind his head and leaning back. "You didn't cock the gun."

I turn on the spot and run, leaving him there, a faint red ring on his forehead like a faded lipstick mark. This last image of him is burned into my brain: sitting on a stump, cheeks flushed, breath coming fast. Flushed as mine, fast as mine.

I have what I came for. So why does it feel like I've lost?

SEVEN

I race back up the mountain, shame dogging my heels. I can't believe I drew my gun. How reckless. How idiotic. A despicable thing to do.

There's no excuse, *no reason*, for pulling a weapon on an unarmed person, no matter what they've done. I should know that better than anyone. Like father, like daughter. What's wrong with me? What if it had gone off? What if I'd hurt him? What if it had been worse? *Ren* . . .

I rage at myself the whole way home, the fury only ebbing away as I get closer to the cottage, when it's replaced by the fear that if Da is back, then he knows I disobeyed him and left. Maybe it's no more than I deserve.

I find the cottage still and silent, heavy with the feeling of emptiness. And it frightens me. I should be relieved, but I'm not. I'm worried.

"He's fine," I say aloud to the kitchen, as if that will make it true. "Of course he's fine. Why wouldn't he be fine?" Concern for my father is a new feeling. "You just worry about your-self," I mutter as I put the kettle on to boil.

While it does, I hide the bullets beneath the floorboards in my room, replace the flintlock in the cabinet in my father's study, and brush the mud from my skirt. There. What he doesn't know won't hurt him.

Everything is fine.

I mix dough for bread and leave it to rise. Then, starving after my hike, I throw together a potato soup, leaving it on the hob to simmer while I fuss over the already-tidy cottage, dusting surfaces that are spotless, straightening quilts and polishing cutlery. When the soup is finally ready, I lace it with dill, taking the bowl through to my father's study.

Settling in his chair, legs curled under me, soup balanced on my knee, I flick through the huge logbook that represents his life as the *Naomhfhuil*, going back, back, until I reach the year I was nine. The year he—

I stop dead as I find a piece of paper folded between the pages of the log.

Lachlan is written on the front. My father's name in my mother's handwriting.

Suddenly, I can smell lavender and hear her singing off-key

as she hangs the washing out. I remember running through a maze of white sheets on the first good day of spring, her chasing after me. I remember her making shadow-puppet monsters with her hands, and screaming with delight when they tickled me through the washing.

She'd been pregnant in the weeks before my father shot her, but something went wrong. She lost the baby, and a lot of blood, too. She almost died. Harry Glenn, who was the nearest thing Ormscaula had to a doctor of any kind, told my father to stay home with her, that she would need him. But he didn't. As always with him, the loch came first.

She wasn't the same afterward.

She slept later and later; some days she never got out of bed. She stopped eating, stopped talking, stopped getting dressed. Her hair grew lank, her eyes bloodshot. It was summer, and she started to smell unwashed and sour, so bad I didn't want to go near her. When she did get up, she'd leave me at home and wander the lochside for hours, returning after dark and going straight back to bed.

My father begged her to pull herself together, and I wanted that, too. I wanted my mam back; I didn't understand why I wasn't enough to make her happy, like before. She barely seemed to know I was there. My father would come home from his rounds to find me eating jam from the jar because it was all I could reach on the shelf and I was starving. He told her over and over that he was sorry for what had happened, but that he needed her to get better. For her own sake. For my sake. And she didn't. Wouldn't. Couldn't, I see now.

It was her screams that woke me up the night he killed her. Her voice that dragged me from my bed. After weeks of silence, there was suddenly sound: guttural, furious shrieking, rage shredding her throat, making each cry raw and ragged. Something in my father must have snapped, because I opened my bedroom door in time to hear a scuffle in the parlor, and then a gun going off. Four times, one after the other, with no pauses. *Bang. Bang. Bang. Bang.* Faster than my heartbeat.

The revolving barrel made it quick. You wouldn't be able to shoot someone four times like that with a flintlock; you'd have to keep pausing to reload each bullet, to stuff more gunpowder down the barrel. You'd have to really mean it, to shoot someone four times with that. Maybe it's easier with a revolver.

One more outraged cry, and then the window shattering. I ran back to bed and hid under the covers. I told myself it was a dream. I was in bed, so it had to be a dream.

When I heard my father's tread outside my window, I shut my eyes until I couldn't hear it anymore. He was gone. That was when I went to the parlor.

I longed to see my mam crouched on the floor, picking up bits of glass with careful fingers, plucking them from her pretty carpet, a spark finally back in her eyes, reignited by the shock of the gunfire and the thunderstorm air-clearing of the row. I wanted her to tell me to go back to bed and not to worry. I hoped to lie awake and hear my father return, and the sounds of them making up. But there was none of that. No sign of her. Only a little gun left on the floor. I picked it up and went back to bed, where I put it under my pillow.

When he came back, he looked for it, of course. I screwed my eyes shut tight and listened while he lifted up the sofa, while he reached under the sideboard. I lay still as the dead when he came to my room, the gun hard beneath my pillow as the door opened and the beam of light hit the wall. I thought he knew I had it. I thought he was coming to take it back and finish me off, too. Those last two bullets, waiting for me. But all he did was bend and kiss my head gently, as though he hadn't just gunned my mother down two rooms away and dumped her body in the loch outside my window.

When he finally closed the door, I thought my heart would fly from my chest.

The next morning, the door to my mother's parlor was closed, forbidden now, and he told me she'd left in the night. When I asked if she'd be back, he said he didn't know.

A week later, when Giles Stewart came around, oh-so-concerned after hearing she'd lost the baby, and found her missing, I repeated what my father had said—that she'd left us.

Even when he sent for the sheriff, I never wavered. I looked right into the sheriff's solemn gray eyes, and I told him she left of her own free will. I didn't mention the gun or the shots.

I didn't say that my mother's body probably lay at the bottom of the loch.

I remember later that night, a great storm began, a sky-breaker, rain lashing down, churning the loch. My father spent most of the night by the window, watching it. Waiting to see if what he'd done would come to the surface.

Now I lift this slip of paper out of the log, this note from my mam written so long ago, and slowly I open it.

I've gone down into the village to see Maggie, it reads. *Alva is with me. We'll be back for tea.* Then a single kiss, an *x* slashed across the bottom of the page, instead of a name— because of course he'd know who it was from.

And he kept it. A note like those she must have left a hundred times before. A nothing note. Folded away in his precious *Naomhfhuil* logs.

My soup has gone cold, but I don't have the stomach for it anymore. Usually I try not to remember that night, but once you decide not to think of a thing, you can't get away from it.

I uncurl my legs, needle pricks stabbing my soles when I put them on the floor. Once the pain has passed, I hobble to the kitchen and dump the soup back in the pot before crossing to the window. Outside, the loch is so calm it's as though a looking glass has been lain on the ground, reflecting the clear sky above. There's no sign of life out there at all.

Filling a pan with water, I set about making tea, putting my bread in the oven while the water boils. I wish I had something else to do—more transcribing work, sewing, anything. The kitchen feels too big and my bedroom too full of secrets, so I take my mug to the front stoop, sitting on the thick slab and blowing at the steam. I tell myself I'm not watching for my father.

I check on the chickens and am surprised to find them huddled in their coop instead of out scratching for worms. When I rummage in the straw, there are no eggs, and when I head to the goat shed, I find the goat dry, too. I wouldn't have been able to have milk in my porridge this morning even if I had come out then. It's that wildcat, scaring away my breakfast. I hope my father catches it soon.

Locking the goat in, I return to the stoop, my attention on the horizon, until the sky turns pink, mauve, then mulberry. When the polar star emerges above me, I go back inside. The cottage smells of fresh bread, like a real home.

It's just before midnight when I decide enough is enough. He's been gone for a whole day and night now, and I've spent the last three hours watching the clock on the mantelpiece, ears straining toward every sound, heart jumping with every imagined lift of the door latch. I'm never going to sleep feeling like this—I have to do something. I fetch my *earasaid* and my boots and go to my father's study for a weapon, deciding in a fit of rebellion to take the other long gun.

I'll walk to the sheds and back. Just to see if there's any sign of him.

The night is clear and light enough to see, a hundred thousand stars glittering in an indigo sky, the moon a fat, bold sphere that makes me think of Ren, of all things, though I've no idea why.

A splash to my right has me whirling on the spot, raising the gun as my eyes lock on to something moving in the loch. Then I laugh, delighted.

An otter. After all these years, there's one right there, swimming parallel to the shore.

I watch it dive, its sleek brown body slipping under the water without making a sound. Then it resurfaces, flipping onto its back and scrubbing its face with its paws. My heart lifts. If ever there was an omen that things are going to be all right, it's this.

My step is much lighter as I walk on, eyes tracking the otter until it vanishes into the depths of the loch and doesn't return.

The joy lasts until I reach the sheds. I didn't bring a lamp because the long gun needs two hands—it's a more powerful gun—but I regret it now. A flintlock pistol would have meant I could have had both weapon and light.

"Da?" I call softly, moving from shed to shed, pushing the doors open and allowing what little light there is to spill inside. I hesitate to go in, suddenly scared a door will close behind me and I'll be trapped, but force myself to do it anyway, leading with the gun.

"Are you here?" I whisper, both wanting and dreading a reply.

Rats squeal at the intrusion, bold enough in the dark to dart in front of me, but otherwise the sheds are still, the nets hanging dolefully from their hooks, the cart where I left it. If he's been here, there's no sign of him now. When I check the boathouses, both boats are there, their hulls bone dry when I pat them.

Defeated, I turn for home, looking to the loch, hoping to see the otter again, watching the whole way back.

The cottage is in sight, the kitchen glowing a welcome at me, when something breaks the surface of the loch again.

But it's not an otter.

It's fish-belly pale and long.

The world falls away as I realize what it is.

A body.

Her body.

Then it moves.

It barely makes a ripple as it swims toward me, slowly cutting through the water with a sinuous grace. And as it dives, I see its tail, mottled and gray.

It's a pike, nothing more.

I laugh with relief, embarrassed by my imagination. I soon sober when I realize it's a bad sign that pike are coming to the surface. Though I suppose it's not so much the pike coming to the surface as much as the surface is closing in on the pike. Even in the dark, I can see the water level has dropped again. That decides me. I'll write to Giles myself, I think. He has to know—

Something grabs me from behind.

EIGHT

I drop the gun and scream. Within seconds, I'm flung into my own hallway. Miraculously, I manage to stay on my feet, stopping myself before I crash into the wall. I turn to find my father standing in the doorway, both long guns over his arm.

He slams the door closed and throws the bolt, leaning against it, breathing heavily.

"Da?"

"What did I tell you?" he says in a low voice.

"I was just—"

"What did I tell you?" he turns and roars, spittle spraying from his lips.

His eyes bulge so wide that I see the white around his dark irises, his face purple with fury.

I back away until I'm against the wall with nowhere else to go. My knife is in my pocket; my fingertips brush the hilt. Then my father lets out a long, rattling sigh and walks away, into the kitchen.

My head falls back against the wall, my heart making a frantic bid to exit my body directly through my chest, my hand trembling against my hip.

Slowly, I exhale, breathing through my mouth, until everything is steady. When I follow him through to the kitchen, he's sitting at the table, shoveling cold soup into his mouth straight from the cooking pot. He doesn't look at me, just eats, spooning soup up with a punishing rhythm.

I pull the loaf I made earlier from the bread box and slice it, depositing thick slabs before him.

He glowers at me over the rim of the pot but accepts the bread.

When he pushes the pot toward me, I take a piece of bread and dip it in the soup. We eat until it's gone.

The air settles between us, the tension and rage dissipating with the sharing of a meal. Even a cold one.

"Did you see the pike?" I ask.

He stares at me, then nods. I wait for him to tell me he's finally going to tell Giles, so I won't have to.

"What were you doing out there?" he asks. "I told you to stay in the cottage."

"Looking for you. You've been gone a whole day."

His eyebrows rise in surprise. "I didn't mean to worry you."

I shrug and begin to clear the table.

"Alva?"

I turn, soup pot in hand.

He doesn't say anything for a long moment. Then: "You look so much like your mother."

Abruptly, he stands, heading to his study, closing the door behind him.

The moment I hear it click shut, my knees buckle and I hit the floor, the soup pot landing beside me with a gentle thud.

Sleep comes in snatches, punctuated by terrible dreams. In them, I hear screaming, see carpets of blood creep toward my feet, my mother's face mouthing words I can't make out from beneath glassy waters. I wake between these nightmares and can hear my heart in my ears as sweat cools on my skin. Each time is worse than the last, as though my brain is trying to outdo itself.

The worst, though, is the time I wake and realize I'm not alone. A thin shaft of light shines on the wall by my head, and soft breathing comes from the doorway behind me.

My father is there, watching me sleep. Just like he did that night.

Almost as soon as I realize it, the beam narrows and vanishes, the latch closing so quietly I wouldn't have heard it if I wasn't awake. A moment later, I hear his bedroom door close, a distinctive sound because it always sticks.

I don't even attempt to go back to sleep. Instead, I get up, throwing a shawl over my shoulders. I tiptoe to the bedroom door and lift the latch silently, sneaking to the kitchen to light a candle before returning to my room and wedging my shawl between the bottom of the door and the floor to keep the telltale glow from giving me away. Then I sit at my desk and pull a sheaf of paper toward me. I open a jar of ink, dip my favorite pen in it, and begin to write.

I compose two letters. Both are to Giles Stewart.

The first tells him the level of the loch is falling rapidly. It details everything I can remember from the *Naomhfhuil* log over the past few weeks, up until tonight, when the bottom-feeding fish began to come to the surface. I tell him in no uncertain terms that his mill is using too much water. He'll care if his income and status is threatened, maybe. I can't do more than try.

The second tells him that I lied about the night my mother vanished. That he was right all along; my father did kill her. I tell him everything I remember—the shots, the gun, my mother's missing body. I don't bother with apologies or excuses or explanations. They won't matter to him, or to the sheriff he'll have to pass the information on to. They'll just want facts, so that's what I give them.

I seal both letters inside envelopes and hide them under

my pillow. Then I lie back down and watch the candle burn all the way till dawn.

I'm still awake when my father leaves the cottage, not long after the sky has finally begun to lighten. Thanks to my sleepless night, my head is full of wool, and I know from experience that the only thing that will get me through the day is raiding my father's stash of coffee. I brew a huge mugful, opening the window to let the aroma out. Then I lace it with obscene amounts of honey and carry it back to my room.

Closing the inner shutters over my window, I open the switchblade and dig it into the seam between the floorboards, levering the loose one up. Duncan should be almost at the village by now; he'll stay overnight in the inn, hosted by Giles, and leave the next day with an extra, unexpected package—though he won't know it. He'll make his way down the mountain toward Balinkeld, where I'll hop out and find a convenient barn or outbuilding to stay in overnight before getting the stagecoach onward to Thurso. Easy as you like.

Tomorrow morning, I'll be gone.

I unroll the canvas bag I made from scraps of old sail from the boats. It's ugly but sturdy, and that's all I need it to be. In go my two pretty dresses—I want to look like I belong in town, and I know from listening to the gossips in Maggie Wilson's store that women down there wear a lot more lace than we do. I add my nicest everyday clothes, stockings, and underwear, all of it a mix of what I salvaged of my mother's old clothes and what I could bear to buy from Maggie.

Next is my new, thick winter *earasaid*, lined with what Ren assures me is the finest lamb's wool. It's soft, so soft, and when I lay my head on it, I swoon with sleepiness. I hastily fold it and shove it in the bag, taking a hefty gulp of coffee after. No more of that, thank you.

I leave the boots where they are—I plan to wear them for the journey—but I pack my pens and ink with care, wrapping them and my jar of gold leaf scraps in an old blouse. I also split the money up—only a fool would keep it all together. I fill small bags: one for each boot, to tuck down beside my ankles, another to put in my underclothes, and a fourth to attach to my belt.

Then I add the gun.

I lay it on top of the *earasaid*, reverently as a mother lays down a newborn. Finally, I reach for the bullets. Curious, I open the box. Six tiny rounds sit in two neat rows. I asked for four, only wanted enough to fill the gun, but here's a full set. Including the two bullets still in the gun, that's eight deaths at my disposal. I take one bullet out and hold it up. It's as long as the first joint of my little finger and just a little slimmer. The casing is silver, and so is the rounded surface of the actual bullet embedded at the tip. It looks so elegant. I shudder and put the bullet back in its place, then slip the box into a special pocket I sewed especially into the bag.

There. I have everything I need.

Thanks to Ren.

I squash down thoughts of him, trying to bury my guilt beneath my fluttering heart. I close the bag, realizing it won't fit back under the floorboards now that it's full. I shove it under my bed instead, wishing I could do the same with my conscience. Ren's the only person in Ormscaula to be a real friend to me in the last seven years, and I held a gun to his head.

I need to apologize to him before I go. Today.

Screwing up my face, I drain the last of my coffee and push myself to my feet, throwing open my bedroom door.

Only to come face-to-face with my father.

My stomach drops. I don't know how long he's been out there, listening through the door. I wasn't paying attention, and now there will be a reckoning.

It's only when he swears sharply, clearly as startled as I am, and I see the net clutched in his hands that I understand why he's there. A strange sense of déjà vu comes over me.

"Get dressed," he commands. "I need you at the sheds. The net at the north shore wants replacing. Again."

It's not until the afternoon that I finally make it to the mountain path, my mood sour as early cherries as I head toward the village. My hands are sore from needle pricks and rope burns, and my nerves are shredded worse than the net. The only saving grace was that when I started to load the repaired net into the cart to take it north, my father told me in dark tones that he'd do it himself this time.

"I fitted it properly," I insisted, outraged at the implication.

"Did I say you didn't?" he said gruffly.

"No. What time will you be back for supper?" I asked.

"I don't know. Likely not until late, if at all. Leave my supper in the warmer. Don't come looking for me if I don't come back," he warned. "And keep your hands off my coffee."

We walked back to the cottage together, where I waited until he was out of sight. He'd said not to go looking for him, but he hadn't said I was to stay in the house . . .

I repeat those words like a magic spell as I make my way down to Ormscaula. I just need to find Ren and say I'm sorry. And goodbye, although he won't know it.

By the time I reach the bridge, I've almost walked off my temper. I pause at the peak and look down into the river. It's flowing as fast as ever; little wonder no one has noticed anything is wrong with the loch. I watch a pair of moorhens flirting and smile at them. Then my smile falls as I remember the *feis samhaid* is tonight. The whole village will be out and about.

Instead of taking the main path and risking running into just about everyone, I duck behind a row of cottages and walk around the outskirts, listening to the bustling crowds homing in on the center of Ormscaula. Already I can smell roasting meat and onions, and it makes me hungry; fool that I am, I didn't grab anything from my cottage before I came down. My stomach rumbles aggressively, emphasizing that I'm an idiot.

Deciding to take a chance, I make a turn and head toward the bakery, hoping to buy a roll to tide me over. But of course it's closed, a sign hanging from the silver horseshoe above the door saying the Campbells will be serving food at the *feis*. I sigh in annoyance.

"Alva?"

I whirl round to see Gavan Stewart standing there, a bunch of keys in his hand.

"You came," he says, smiling.

"Oh," I say, confused. "No, I just wanted a roll."

Gavan holds up a set of keys. "You're in luck."

His grin widens as he steps past me and slips a key into the lock, opening the door.

"The Stewart Pastry Kitchen and Cookshop is open for business," he says. "Come on in."

NINE

I follow him inside, and he disappears into the back of the store, behind the curtain. I walk over to the counter and hoist myself up, sitting on it and kicking my legs.

"Here."

I turn and catch the small cloth bundle Gavan tosses at me. It fills my hands with warmth, and I unwrap it to find a fresh crusty roll topped with cheese. I used to love these when I was little. I tear a bit off, dropping it into my skirts when a string of still-molten cheese burns my fingers.

"It's hot," Gavan says, and I narrow my eyes at him.

"Thanks for the warning." I blow on my sore fingers and retrieve the fallen piece, eating it carefully.

Gavan disappears again, returning with a huge basket, the

contents covered with a cloth, before he goes back and gets a second. He leaves them both near the door, then reaches into one for a roll, juggling it in his hands as he comes to sit beside me.

"Why do you have the bakery keys?" I ask, chewing.

"Mhairi Campbell needed someone to come and take the rolls out of the oven, and Wee Campbell has vanished. I volunteered."

Of course he did.

"Well, I'm glad," I say before popping a fluffy chunk of bread in my mouth.

"I'm glad you're here," Gavan says sincerely.

I have no idea what to do with that, so I shove the last of the bread in my mouth. I need to find Ren and get back. I'm about to hop down, thank Gavan, and be on my merry way when he turns to me, his expression sly.

"You see, I can't take both baskets at the same time. I was hoping you'd help, now that I've sated your hunger with a nice cheese roll."

The sneaky little . . . I fell right into his trap.

"Come on." He widens his brown eyes at me. "There's more food in it for you. Mhairi Campbell is going to pay me in roast pork. I'll get some for you. You can't say no to that, fresh off the fire."

It's like trying to say no to a baby cow. He just keeps looking at me, all soft-faced and hopeful, long eyelashes batting.

Say no. Alva Douglas, say no. Say no.

"Fine." I jump down and march to the door.

We each take a basket. Gavan locks the bakery diligently behind us, then leads the way, winding down toward the square. I'm already sweating, my stomach cramping with nerves. It's been seven years since I've seen some of these people. I can't imagine I'll be a welcome sight.

"You all right?" Gavan calls back over his shoulder.

I swallow instead of answering.

It feels like every face in the square turns to us as we enter. In the middle is the huge pyre I saw them building yesterday, not yet lit; they'll wait for sundown to do that. To the left is the Staff, loose ribbons fluttering in the breeze, waiting for the dancers to come and take the strands and swaddle the Staff to sleeping. Lining the outskirts of the square are stalls selling spiced cider, whiskey, ale, and birch wine, juice for the kiddies. I scan each one for Ren, knowing it's not likely he'll be here, but hoping that, like me, he'll have braved it today. The sooner I see him and apologize, the sooner I can go back to the cottage. There's no sign of him, though. No hint of blond among the browns, blacks, and reds. No devilish laugh causing old crones to cross their chests.

At the far end of the square, Iain the Smith—not to be confused with awful Auld Iain—has been co-opted by the butcher into turning a huge pig on a spit while the butcher himself is carving another into thick slices and tossing them onto a tray. Mhairi Campbell, the baker's wife, is beside him at the end of their production line, cramming meat into a dwindling supply of rolls.

"Looks like we're just in time," Gavan calls cheerfully.

I stay close behind Gavan, keeping my head down as I follow in his wake, trying to stay out of sight, both for his sake and mine. I stay so close that when he stops, I walk into his back.

He turns, amused, and takes the basket from me, handing it to Mhairi.

"Thanks, lad, you're a lifesaver," she says, wiping her forehead with an apron. "Here you go."

She stuffs a roll and hands it to him. Then her gaze falls on me. She stills, fork held aloft.

"Alva helped," Gavan says, seemingly oblivious to the tension that's suddenly rolling off Mhairi in waves. "I promised her a roll, too." He gives her the kind of wide, bright smile that would charm the birds from the trees.

But Mhairi just stares at me. I lift my chin. I won't cower. I can feel the gazes of everyone nearby on us, waiting to see what she'll do.

Without breaking her stare, she stuffs a second roll and holds it out to me.

"Thanks, Mhairi, that's kind of you," I say.

"That's Mrs. Campbell to you," she snaps, and turns away, aggressively filling more rolls, pretending I'm no longer there.

"Come on," Gavan says, tilting his head, beckoning me to follow.

It seems that Mhairi's decision to turn her back and ignore me has decided everyone else, because now it's as if I'm not here. As we cross the square, skirting around the pyre, people call out to Gavan, greeting him, slapping him on the back and chatting with him, but their gazes slide from me like butter off a hot knife.

Being ignored is somehow worse than their dagger eyes, and I chew my roll with vigor, taking my frustrations out on it, throwing myself onto the wall outside the tiny village jail, kicking my heels against it angrily.

"Don't mind them," Gavan says. "They don't mean any harm."

He's lucky my mouth is full of food.

"They just don't know you," he continues. "Come on, Alva, you know what it's like here, everyone in everyone's business." He looks at me, those big eyes miserable, and I soften. This isn't his fault.

"It's fine, Gavan. I get it." I look across the square. "Why don't I fetch us some cider?"

"I'll go," he says eagerly, and I sigh. It was supposed to be an excuse to leave and find Ren. Still, a wee cider to wash my food down won't hurt. I might even find some courage in it.

Gavan hops off the wall, heading into the sunlit square. I realize we've been sitting in a patch of shadow, and the aptness of it almost makes me laugh. I spy Duncan Stroud across the square. He gives me a wave, and I nod back at him before noticing who he's standing with.

Giles Stewart. He is laughing, patrician face tilted to the sky, teeth gleaming, the picture of the jovial leader. Employer. Husband. Father. Pillar of the community.

He was in love with my mother.

It's one of the reasons—probably the biggest one—that no one really believes him when he says my father killed her. Everyone knows Giles Stewart was sweet on her and sour that she didn't feel the same.

I had no idea until he came to our cottage one afternoon. He hadn't been there before, and it felt exciting that he'd come all the way up to see us—few ever did. My mam sent me to my room and kept him on the doorstep, but I opened my window to listen. It was near my birthday, you see, and I'd gotten it into my head that he might have come about my birthday party. I hoped he would offer his big house for it as a surprise, because I'd been hinting . . .

I used to go to Gavan's house for tea on Friday nights after school, just the two of us, and Giles—Mr. Stewart, as he was to me then—would hover, asking me questions about my da and mam and our lives while Mrs. Stewart stood in the background, mousy and silent. He used to say I was welcome anytime, that I was like a sister to Gavan. I didn't notice at the time that my mam never went there. That it was always Mrs.

Stewart who'd walk me to the bridge, where my da would collect me.

Giles wasn't there about my birthday party. He was distraught my mother was pregnant again. I heard him say two Douglas children were too many. She was pushing her luck, and his love wasn't limitless.

My mam tried to interrupt him, but he kept going. He could forgive her for marrying Lachlan Douglas and for having me. But he couldn't forgive another baby.

"Giles, I never promised you anything." My mam tried to sound gentle; I recognized it as the voice she used on sick or frightened animals. "We never had an understanding. I don't know where this is coming from."

"Not a spoken one," Giles had insisted. "What we had was deeper than an understanding or a silly promise. Look at this place," he'd said, gesturing up at our cottage. "It's a hovel. You can't be happy here—not you, not with what you came from. I can give you a town house, make you a lady." She tried to speak again, and he held up his hands. "I know you're worried about your reputation, but you don't have to be. No one would dare say a word to us, not with the mill now up and running. I can give you everything you want."

A silence, and then my mother said, "Don't you see? I have everything I want."

"How? How can you be satisfied with this?"

"Giles," my mother said, and her voice was firm now. "You

have to know I'd never leave Lachlan. Never. Nothing on earth would make me leave this place or my family."

Giles would remember that. He would remember that when she went missing.

I stopped going to Gavan's for tea after that, saying I was needed at home. I didn't like how hungry Giles looked to me, like a caged bear waiting for its moment.

Now, in the shadow of a sunlit square, I watch Giles Stewart laughing. And as if he can sense my attention, he turns and looks straight at me.

"Sorry it took so long. There was a queue." Gavan takes his place by my side again.

Across the square, his father sees us and frowns.

"Actually, Gavan, I need to be getting on," I say. "I'm sorry."

"At least drink your cider."

"Why don't you—"

"Miss Douglas."

I fall silent. I have no idea how Giles crossed the square so fast, but here he is, standing too close. Duncan is at his side, a tankard in his hand.

"Giles," I say as politely as I can. "Duncan." He gets a smile from me.

Giles's face is thunder dark. "I'm afraid I need to take my son from you, Miss Douglas," he says, not sounding sorry at all.

"Let me finish my drink," Gavan says easily.

"Now," Giles says, taking both mugs from Gavan and setting them down on the wall. After a moment, Gavan stands, and Giles puts an arm around him, steering him away. I watch him try to turn to say goodbye, only for his father's grip to tighten on his shoulder, preventing him.

Duncan watches Giles's retreating back.

"Is it just me, or was that a wee bit awkward?" he says.

"Giles is not a fan of mine," I tell him.

"More fool him," Duncan says, and my cheeks flush. "I'm afraid your monks didn't send any work for you this time," he continues.

Of course they sent none; I'll be joining them in a few days' time. But he can't know that.

"They don't want me anymore," I say, and shrug. "Sent me a note last time thanking me for my services, but telling me I was no longer needed."

Duncan tuts, shaking his head. "Ah, Alva, I'm sorry. After you worked so hard for them all these years. Shame on them to cut you loose with no warning."

"Aye. But what can you do?" I shake my head. "I'll send the last lot back with you and get paid for that, at least. What time are you leaving tomorrow?" I say it as casually as I can.

"After lunch, I expect." He looks down at the tankard in his hand. "I won't be wanting an early start."

I smile. "Of course not. Say around one?"

He smiles. "One sounds about right."

"Although"—I look at my own drink and raise my brows—"if I haven't brought it by then, don't hang about," I add. I don't want him waiting for me while I'm huddled in the back of his cart, desperate to get on.

"Too right." He grins. "No more than they deserve, to be left in the lurch after ditching you."

Giles beckons Duncan to join him.

"I'm being summoned by my host. But I hope I'll see you tomorrow."

"Enjoy the *feis*," I call after him, and he raises a hand in acknowledgment.

"You're a curiosity," a voice says the moment Duncan is out of earshot. "That's the only reason he's interested in you. Same with Gavan. Novelty."

Hattie Logan is at my elbow, upturned nose in the air.

"Nice to see you, too, Hattie," I say. "Thanks for that. I'll be sure to keep it in mind."

"The strange girl from up on the mountain. That's your allure."

"At least she has some." Ren has appeared unnoticed on my other side. Now he looks out across the square with the air of a man surveying his lands and finding them wanting. "Unlike certain others here, who are about as enticing as sheep dip and twice as loathed."

"As if I care what some Sassenach thinks of me," Hattie says, spitting the insult at him.

"Whisht, you mardy coo," Ren says, thickening his accent to mimic Auld Iain's Highland brogue.

I laugh as Hattie's neck flushes beet red and she stalks off.

Ren picks up one of the mugs of cider Gavan left and holds it out to me.

"Here. Waste not, want not," he says. "Happy *feis samhaid*."

"Same to you. Thanks for standing up for me just then." I take a deep breath. "Ren . . . I'm sorry—"

"Don't." He stops me. "Neither of us was at our finest yesterday, and if you say sorry, then I'll feel obliged to say it back, and I really don't want to. So let's just agree we had a mad moment and there's no harm done."

But I still don't feel absolved. "Ren, it was more than a wee mad moment. I—"

"Do I need to tell you to whisht, too? I said forget it. Know when you've won. Or lost. Or both."

I shake my head and drink my cider, both hands around the mug, until it's gone.

By now, the light is starting to fade, and people are drawing closer to the pyre, waiting for it to be lit, but we stay back, outside it. Though for once I don't feel outside. I suppose that's the difference between standing alone and standing with someone else.

"Do you want another drink?" he asks, holding his hand out for my cup.

"You've not finished yours yet." I nod to the other tankard, still sitting on the wall.

"I don't like cider," he says. "I'll get something else."

"All right," I reply. "You owe me, anyway. I paid Mack for your apple juice."

He smiles wickedly, canines denting his lower lip as he bites it. "So you did. Can I tempt you with a birch wine?"

"Go on, then."

He starts toward the square, then turns back. "Close your eyes and hold out your hands." I raise my brows. "Just do it," he says.

I do as he says, cupping my hands before me and shutting my eyes.

He places something solid in them and whispers, "Count to ten," in my ear. I feel him move away.

I start to count, feeling foolish. Once his footsteps have faded, I stop and heft whatever he's handed me cautiously in my palms. I hear rustling—paper—and feel small, solid objects within. I open my eyes and peer into the brown bag in my hands, and it's full of pine candy.

Oh.

TEN

By the time he returns, my face is a normal color again, the sweets tucked into my pocket.

"Thank you," I say. "For these." I pat my pocket, not meeting his eye.

"I owed you, if I remember right." He hands me a wooden cup of sweet birch wine. "My lady."

"Thanks. Again."

Across the square, we watch as Giles Stewart lights the pyre. The dancing will begin now. Gavan stands with Cora, James, and Hattie, close to the Staff, waiting to snatch up the first ribbons and take their spots. Hattie and Cora have their arms linked, though Hattie is pulling her red hair around her finger, gazing at Gavan with naked adoration. He doesn't seem to notice; he's laughing at whatever James is saying, who in turn keeps glancing at Cora, as if to be sure she's noticed how funny he is.

And from the looks of things, she hasn't; her attention is occupied by subtle glances over at Ren. Well, I never. Cora Reid, from one of our finest and oldest families, has a yen for Ormscaula's black sheep. Her mother would have her hide if she knew. Maybe that's part of the attraction.

"Do you mind?" Ren asks.

"Mind what?" I watch Cora scowl as Ren leans closer to me.

"Not being part of that crowd anymore?"

"I was never part of that crowd," I scoff.

It's not true, though—not quite. We were friends once. I was always closest to Gavan, but I'd had tea at Cora's and Hattie's a couple of times, me the awkward third point of their triangle. In a place the size of Ormscaula, you don't have much choice; it's pals or pariahs. And then there's the uncomfortable truth that you'll probably end up marrying one of your classmates. We have to keep records of every marriage to make sure we're not too interbred. That's why Duncan caused so much excitement; he wasn't related to any of us.

"You were," Ren says. "So . . . do you?"

"Yes. And no," I say. The musicians are starting to tune up; I hear the warm hum of the fiddle, the boom of the drum. Ruairidh Cross will be somewhere with his pipes. "What about you?" I ask. "Do you mind when they call you 'Sassenach'?"

"Yes. And no." He repeats my words back at me. "It's true, isn't it?"

"Only half. Your father's from here."

"Is he? You'll have to introduce me sometime," Ren says. "Because as far as I know, my mam and me are the only Rosses in Ormscaula. Unless you see someone out there that's the spit of me."

We both look out across the square at the villagers gathered around the fire, which has finally taken hold of the pyre and is burning merrily. Ren's mam came here just before he was born, claiming his da was a villager, but he's right— there are no Rosses here. Never have been. Only Liz Ross knows the truth of Ren's father, and she swears blind he's a Ross from Ormscaula and that's why she came.

"I think," Ren continues, his voice soft, "the truth of it is that my mam met some man who said he was called Ross and from someplace called Ormscaula. And after he was done with her, he vanished. Then she found out about me and came here looking for him. Though I can't account for why she stayed, because it's certainly not the friendly neighbors." He smiles ruefully. "It would be the last place I'd run to." He gives me a pointed look. "It's more somewhere you'd run from."

I keep my eyes fixed on the cup in my hand.

He throws back his drink, leaving the cup on the wall. "Come on."

"What?"

Ren grabs my hand. "We're going to swaddle the Staff. We two outsiders."

"Oh no, we're not," I hiss, but he's already pulling me toward the square. "Murren, I don't want to dance!"

"Of course you do." He turns and grins. "Just imagine the looks on their faces when they have to make room for us. Don't tell me this hasn't been your dream since childhood."

I'm spilling wine everywhere, dragging my feet as he pulls me toward where everyone is pairing off. But he's right; a teeny, tiny part of me does want to dance. Growing up, I couldn't wait to take my place among the older boys and girls of Ormscaula, ribbon in my hand and music in my heart. I've never done it before. I won't ever get to again.

"They won't let us," I protest.

"Like they can stop us."

In the fading light, he looks wild, his blue eyes alight with glee. Like he's from another world, some sprite or puck sent to tempt me into behaving stupidly.

"Ren . . ."

He stops. "Do you think I can't?" He gestures down at his leg.

He would have grown up watching the older kids swaddle the Staff, too. I bet he's never danced it before, either.

And he's right. It'll put an itch in the knickers of every single one of them to see us taking part in their precious festivities instead of hiding in the shadows. I'm not ashamed to admit that the thought of it makes me giddy.

"To hell with it," I say, tossing the cup to the ground and picking up my skirts, pulling him behind me this time. "Let's show them how it's done."

He whoops, which is enough to make some people on the outskirts of the crowd turn, their jaws dropping as they see the two of us pelting toward them.

"Coming through, mind yourselves, there," I announce, slipping between people. Soon enough, we're standing behind a furious Cora and James, frozen in the act of reaching for a ribbon. "We're in, too," I say, locking eyes with Rhona Logan, Hattie's mother, as she glares at us from her lofty position as mistress of the dance.

"There's no room," she says immediately.

"I see two ribbons right there," I say, before I can think better of it.

"I'm holding them for . . ." She peers over my shoulder, casting about for anyone she can rope in. "For . . . Ah, there they are. Aileen!" Mrs. Logan bellows at her eldest daughter. "Come on through, you two! You'll miss your place."

Sure enough, there's jostling behind us, and Aileen and Connor Anderson, who danced last year as newlyweds, are pushed forward. I look down at Aileen's heavily pregnant stomach, ballooning under her apron, and then at the confusion on her face.

"Of course," I say, stepping back, and gesturing for them to step forward. "After you."

Connor makes to take a ribbon, only for Aileen to whack him in the arm.

"Connor, I cannae swaddle the Staff any more than I can see my toes," she hisses. "You try heaving this weight about."

"So, can we?" I ask. "If Aileen and Connor can't?"

"There are others waiting for turns," Mrs. Logan says. She is gripping the ribbons tightly, scanning the crowd behind us for anyone to prove her right, when Gavan speaks.

"Murren can have my spot, if he likes. And I'm sure Hattie will give hers to Alva, won't you, Hattie? We don't mind."

Hattie looks as though she's never minded anything more, but she nods and holds her ribbon out without looking at me.

There is a pause. "No," Mrs. Logan snaps. Loath to lose a chance to throw her daughter at the son of the richest man in the village, she shoves the ribbons in her hand at me. "It's fine. Seeing as they're so keen, I suppose they can have them."

I snatch them before she can change her mind, and pass one to Ren. "Thanks," I say, slipping past her and following my ribbon to its spot, aware the whole village is watching. Suddenly, I'm not sure we're doing the right thing.

Ren follows me and we stand back-to-back.

"Have we made a terrible mistake?" he asks in a low voice.

"I expect so," I reply grimly. "Can you remember how this goes?"

"Nope."

"Me neither." It's been seven years since I last practiced. "Just make sure you take out Hattie Logan first."

He laughs as the music starts up, and the drum counts us in. To my surprise, my body knows what to do—my muscles remember even if my mind doesn't—and I put my left foot out, tilting at the ankle before swapping to my right.

I flash a quick smile at Ren as we begin to orbit the pole, kicking our legs in time to the drumbeats, weaving in and out of the others. Gavan gives me a radiant smile as he passes me, and James Ballantyne ignores me completely, but I don't care, suddenly filled with the joy of the dance. I skip past Ren and hear him laugh.

Each circuit brings us closer and closer to the Staff as we swaddle it, the ribbons crossing and shortening, so we have to take care not to knock into one another. In a flash of foresight, I know what's going to happen just before it does, but it's too late to do anything to stop it.

Hattie Logan moves to the side, as she should, so I can go around her, but she puts her foot out at the last second.

And I trip.

I grip the ribbon so hard in a bid to stay on my feet that my arm is almost wrenched from its socket. Ren slams into my back, and I fly forward, almost smacking into Tam Reid, one of Cora's brothers, as he makes to cross beside me.

The music falters, but I keep dancing, determined not to give them any more reason to stare or mutter. I throw myself into it, eyes on the middle distance, teeth gritted, until the pipes finish with a flourish and the dance is over. As the village begins to clap and whistle, we all take our bows. Gavan is looking at me with pity, and Ren steps closer, maybe to keep me from flying at Hattie and murdering her.

But just then, there's a commotion from the back of the square.

"Help! I need help!" a voice cries, and the people part to let Fergus Brown from the Ballantynes' stables stagger into the center.

He bends double, wheezing but trying to speak through it.

"What is it, man?" Giles steps forward.

"Someone's let all the horses out of the stables. They're gone."

Ren nudges me. "Let's get out of here," he says in a low voice as Jim Ballantyne pushes through the crowd.

"What do you mean, *gone*?" Jim asks.

"I heard them carrying on from the hostler's cottage, sounding afeard, so I went to look. But when I got there, the stalls were all open, and they were gone." Fergus stands upright and looks his employer in the eye. "The fences are all bust. Whoever took them just smashed clean through them, didn't even bother with the gates. I followed the tracks as far as the forest."

"Who would do this?" Jim Ballantyne spits. "Who would dare?"

"Come *on*," Ren says, reaching for my hand. "Alva, if there's trouble, it's best we're not in sight." He's right, and I let him draw me away from the square as everyone crowds around Fergus.

He drags me all the way to the bridge. We stop then, drawing breath. He stands and looks at the village for a while, then turns to face me.

"Listen, Alva . . . I was serious the other day. I want to come with you when you go. I'll be useful; I'll get a job. And I'll watch your back. I know you can take care of yourself," he adds hurriedly when my eyebrows shoot north in outrage, "but people will try to take advantage of a lass on her own— you know that."

"And who will you be to me, Ren? My guardian? My brother? My husband?" I ask. He's been planning this, trying to sweeten me up—literally, I realize, remembering the bag of pine candy.

"I wouldn't expect—"

"I'd cut your balls off if you even thought about it," I snap, wrenching my hand from his.

I step right up to him, in his face, lowering my voice. Ren

tenses, watching me, the moonlight washing him into black and white.

"Hear me, Murren Ross. I like you well enough, but I'll not be your wife, pretend or otherwise. If you want to leave Ormscaula, leave. But you'll not come with me. Do you understand?"

He gives a single nod.

"Good night, Ren." I cross the bridge at a march, leaving him staring after me.

I hadn't meant to stay down in the village until after dark, and I soon regret it as I climb the mountain toward home. The moonlight is bright enough when the skies are clear, but wreaths of cloud keep scuttling across it, plunging me into darkness and forcing me to stop walking until the light returns and I can see the track once more.

Twice I think I hear something behind me, and I turn, half expecting to see Ren following, ready with a new argument. But the track is always bare, the fire in the village square visible as a glowing dot in the distance.

That's when fear starts to creep in. Lughs, mountain geists . . . all the things that could hurt a girl alone on the mountain, and I didn't bring a gun with me. I see a rock that looks to have decent weight and pick it up, grateful to have some kind of weapon.

But still, it's a long, creepy walk home, and for the first

time in my life, I'm relieved when I finally step onto the cottage path and see there's golden light inside, winking like a friendly eye.

Of course, that means my father's home tonight and therefore knows I'm not. My stomach begins to churn as I imagine his fury.

Screwing up my courage and preparing to face him one last time, I start toward the cottage.

The reflection of the moon makes a pretty path on the water of the loch, and I stop just outside the cottage, taking it in for the last time, breathing in the smell of the water, and the rushes, and the mud. It looks like a scene from a fairy tale, everything cast in pewter and black, the reeds silvered by the moonlight, the shadows between them velvety dark, the water beyond the mirror of the sky above glittering as though a thousand stars sit just beneath the surface.

I will miss it, I think, taking it into my heart and holding it there. *Even if I don't want to, I will.* I take my time, committing it to memory.

One last look, and then I turn for home. And freeze.

There is a tall bone-white creature standing between me and the front door.

ELEVEN

It has its back to me, facing the door. It stands seven, maybe eight feet tall, its skin corpse pale. It has no hair at all, its head and long limbs bare, and it wears no clothes or covering; I can see its ribs and every vertebra of its spine, the buttocks flat, the skin tight over the wrists and ankles, as though it's starving.

When it turns slowly, I freeze, my rock gripped in my hand so tight it hurts.

Shock ripples through me as I take it in. The eyes are large but filmed over, the nose nothing more than two holes, like a snake's. The lips are the same bone white as the rest of its skin, stretching wide across its face. I can't tell whether it's male or female; its crotch is completely smooth, its chest flat and unmarked.

Whatever it is, it's not human.

My entire body turns to ice as it looks toward me, its head weaving oddly from side to side, but its eyes stay unfocused, no jolt of connection with mine. Then it raises its chin. It's smelling the air, I realize. It can't see me. It's trying to locate me by my scent.

I don't move a muscle, not a single one, locking my knees.

It tilts its head. One long, pointed nail—no, *talon*—at the end of a slender finger with too many joints taps against its thigh as it sniffs the air again.

I feel the breeze against my face. I'm upwind of the creature, my scent blowing away behind me, out toward the loch.

But it still knows I'm here. It's waiting for me to give myself away.

Behind it, the cottage goes dark; my father must have snuffed the candles out in the kitchen. He'll be heading to his study on the other side of the cottage.

If he looked out of the kitchen window, he'd see me. He'd see it.

Look out, Papa. Please. Please look out, I think, a tear escaping my eye.

The creature turns back toward the house, head canting as it listens. Then, fast as I can blink, it turns and runs toward the sheds.

Still I don't move. Can't move. For all I know, there is a horde of them behind me. For all I know, it's a trap, and the only thing keeping me alive is the fact that I haven't moved.

Somewhere to my left, down near the sheds, I hear a scream. It sounds like a woman being murdered.

It's the same scream I heard a few nights ago outside my bedroom window.

It wasn't a lugh.

The shutters on my window open slightly, drawing my attention. Then my father throws them wide, staring out at me, still rooted to the spot, silvery tracks on my cheeks.

He vanishes, and a second later the front door opens. I move then, flying toward it, throwing myself into the house. I collapse to the floor, my legs no longer working.

I can't take my eyes off the outside, expecting the pale thing to come after me any second.

My father shuts the door and throws the bolt, and I see a flintlock in his hand, cocked and ready. He walks past me into the kitchen, and I hear the sound of a chair being dragged over the slate floor, then a cork being pulled from a bottle, liquid hitting the bottom of a glass.

He's back, scooping me up like I'm a wean, carrying me into the kitchen. My skirts are cold and damp against my legs, and I realize I've wet myself. Shame burns through me, but he doesn't seem to notice, dropping me into a chair near the stove.

He opens the stove door, releasing a blast of heat that scorches my face, and shoves the glass into my hand.

"Drink," he says, and I do, relishing the burn of the whiskey as it sears a trail down my throat and into my stomach. If it hurts, it means I'm alive.

I glance at him. He's moved to the sink, leaning over, peering out of the window. I can't help looking, too, terrified I'll see it again, blind eyes somehow fixed on me anyway. But the only thing in the window is his reflection.

He closes the shutters and walks toward me, topping up the glass up again.

"Slowly this time," he says, and I take a sip, and then another, until I notice the glass in my hand isn't shaking anymore.

He watches me. And then he says, "So you saw one."

I nod.

And then his words sink in.

Saw one. As in, there are more. And he knew about them.

I understand now. His fury when he caught me outside the other night. His forbidding me from leaving the cottage. It makes sense. He knew they were out there. And he didn't tell me.

"What are they?" I ask.

He is quiet for a long moment.

"You remember why the *Naomhfhuil* role was created originally? That the *Naomhfhuil*'s job was to deal with the gods of the loch?" he says finally, filling a glass for himself and sitting at the table, his eyes in shadow. "What you saw tonight is what our people once believed were those gods."

For a moment, I think I've misheard him. "As in, the gods that were supposed to have been killed in the earthquake?" He gives a brief nod. "*That* was a god?"

"No," he says immediately. "They're not gods. They were never gods. It was a word people used to explain things they didn't understand, creatures they couldn't comprehend." He pauses, looking at me over the rim of his glass. "Do *you* understand?"

"Aye," I say, the whiskey turning me bold. "They're not gods. Though I can't imagine why anyone would think giant white bald things with no private bits were gods."

Da's mouth twitches, and for a second I think he's going to smile. Then his face becomes stern once more.

"You don't need to worry about them. They won't bother you again. I'll make sure of that. Best to forget what you saw."

Is he joking? How am I supposed to forget them? I shake my head, questions spilling from me.

"Are they dangerous? How many of them are there?"

"Alva—"

"Where do they live? Why haven't I seen them before? Did they go away? Do they migrate?"

"Please, lass," he snaps. "Enough. I've told you." He

wipes his hand across his face. "You don't need to concern yourself. Get some rest." His tone makes it clear it's not a suggestion.

I close my mouth, biting my protest back. I still need to play by the rules. "All right. Good night, then," I say, standing slowly.

My father nods, looking away from me to the open door of the stove. The firelight reflects in his eyes, flames dancing there like he's the devil. It sends a shiver through me.

As I reach the kitchen door, he stops me. "Wait," he says. "Are you planning on going into the village tomorrow? To take your work to the mailman?"

"Yes." I wait for him to forbid me, to order me to stay in the cottage again, but he merely gives a single nod.

"Will you answer me one thing?" I ask. "You say they're not gods, so what are they?"

His expression is bleak. "Something else. Now, off to bed. I'll deal with it. Trust me."

It's the one thing I can never do.

I leave the room on wobbly legs that owe just as much to the whiskey as leftover fear. I lock myself in the washroom and strip, rescuing the pine candy from my pocket. I leave the dirty skirts on the floor while I wash myself.

When I close my eyes, I see the creature turning toward me again. My teeth start to chatter, though I don't feel cold.

I wrap my *earasaid* around me and head into my room.

My father is at my window, turning the key in the lock on the shutters.

"For peace of mind," he says gruffly, stepping around me without meeting my gaze, shutting the door behind him. He's left his candles on the stool by my bed, three of them welded to the plate with wax.

Crouching down, I peer under my bed. My bag is still there, tucked back in the shadows, and I shove the bag of candy inside before pushing it to the wall again. The morning won't come soon enough. If I didn't already have enough reasons to flee, the existence of these gods, or whatever they are, would have made up my mind.

I change into my nightshirt and climb into bed, deciding it won't hurt to leave the candles burning tonight. Then I tug the blankets up over my head. The walls feel too thin, not strong enough to keep that thing out. I curl up smaller, pulling my pillow down and dislodging the letters I wrote to Giles. I sit up, holding one in each hand. It feels like a lifetime ago that I wrote them.

I'll need to write another, I realize. I have to warn the villagers there are monsters up here, in case my father doesn't. They've a right to know what they're facing.

Then I sigh. *I* don't know what they're facing. "Not old gods" is all I have. Something else.

Like that helps.

I'll do it in the morning, before I go. Hopefully, things will be clearer then. That decided, I push the first two letters back under the pillow and hunker down under the covers.

Fear is a funny thing. Moments ago, I was worried the walls wouldn't keep that thing out. But now, whiskey warming my veins, my heart beating at a normal pace again, covered in the blankets I've had since I was little, I feel . . . if not safe—because I haven't felt safe for a long time—then steady. Even the sound of my father in the kitchen is comforting for the first time in years, because it means I'm not alone. I'm glad he was here tonight and that he looked outside. If he hadn't . . . I turn from that thought. He did. And he came for me. I'm grateful.

I still shiver when I think of the creature's face and hands, and I expect it would be a whole other matter if I blew the candles out and lay in the dark, but my fear feels manageable now. It helps that it's quiet outside, except for the familiar sound of the loch hushing and shushing. I let myself sink into the floating feeling the whiskey has given me. I leave the flames burning, and I don't think of the *thing*, even as my eyelids grow heavy.

I sleep.

The room is dark when I wake, except for a thin golden line of daylight between the shutters.

And it all comes back to me.

I sit up, gasping for breath like I'm breaking through water, my hand clutching my nightshirt.

Bone-pale skin, hairless, blind. Wide mouth. Those terrible, terrible fingers.

Within a blink, I'm out of bed, throwing open my bedroom door.

"Da? Da?" I call.

He's not here.

To be sure, I check every room: the washroom, his study, his bedroom, the kitchen. In every room, the shutters are closed, and when I try to open them, I find they're all locked. I look for the key, expecting to see it sitting in one of the locks, but it isn't.

By the time I try the front door, I already know what to expect, though it doesn't stop me from punching it with the base of my fist and swearing.

He's locked me in.

Whether to keep me safe or to keep me from running screaming all the way down to the village, he's made me a prisoner.

I lean my forehead against the door. How am I going to leave Ormscaula today if I can't even leave the cottage?

TWELVE

By candlelight, I ransack the place, going through every drawer in the kitchen, tipping over every cup and jar and rummaging in the contents, spilling years' worth of useless knickknacks onto the table. I find broken clothes pegs, single buttons, rusted nails, a dull penknife, but no key. He'll have the one for the front door with him, but the spare key for the shutters might still be here; I just have to find it. In my hunt I leave a trail of wreckage behind me, letting everything lie where it falls as I move on.

Into my father's room I go, placing the candle on the stool by his bed as I lift the mattress and peer beneath it. I check inside his drawers, turn his shoes out. I pull every item of clothing from his chest, patting down the pockets, tossing them aside when I find nothing. I even try prizing up some of the floorboards in case he has one like mine, perfect for hiding things under. But still no key, and my heart beats like an executioner's drum.

I don't care if he comes back; I don't care if he catches me. I have to get out of here today. This is my chance—maybe my only chance. My job, everything I've worked for, saved for . . .

I need that key.

By the time I get to his study, I'm in a rage, a human hurricane tearing through the house, not giving a damn what's in my way or whether I destroy it. I only stop when I see that both long guns and both pistols are gone from his gun cabinet. I check the bullet and powder store and see it's depleted, too.

My father, the god slayer.

I search the room, pulling books out and checking behind them, standing on the window seat to feel across the tops of the bookshelves, going through the drawers in his desk. My heart leaps when I find a leather pouch, feeling the outline of a key inside, until I pull it out and realize that it's too small for the shutters and the wrong shape; the end is a twelve-pointed star, narrow at the tip like an arrow, the bow a wide hole I can easily grip. I don't know what it's for, but it's not what I need.

At the bottom of the same pouch, I find a cameo of my mam, and I pause. I've not seen it before. I take it over to the candle and examine it. She's young, only a little older than I am now. It's uncanny how alike we look: the same wide cheeks and pointed jaw, the same insolent quirk to the mouth. Aside from my dark hair and eyes, I could be her twin. I pocket the cameo and the strange key and think about what to do next.

There is a place I haven't checked. But he wouldn't dare . . . Would he?

I walk back to the hall, candle in hand, and face the closed door to the parlor.

It's been shut since that night. As far as I know, my father hasn't set foot in there since. Neither have I. It was always my mam's special room, even before it became her cenotaph.

But it's the only room I haven't looked in. The only one he'd never expect me to enter.

Gritting my teeth and pushing my shoulders back, I open the door.

I know at once that he hasn't been in here. The shutters on the windows have been locked for a long, long time; the room smells stuffy and stale. Dust begins to dance as fresh air rushes in, glittering in the light from the candle. I take a deep breath and step inside.

I'd forgotten how pretty it was. Mam decorated it to her taste: the walls with their fine floral paper, the long, low twin sofas upholstered in yellow silk patterned with pink roses. The delicate tables with their long, spindly legs, and the ornamental boxes inlaid with mother-of-pearl and tortoise-shell. Fine things she brought up here from her childhood home after her parents died and her brother moved away. Before Giles began building his empire, my mother's family was the richest in Ormscaula.

Crossing over a thickly piled rug, I open one of the boxes and find pine candies inside, old now. When I lift one, it smells of nothing. The scent is gone forever.

All the fight goes out of me, and I put the candy back, closing the box.

Defeated, I close the door to my mother's parlor and return to the study. I might as well tidy up. My eyes sting, and I rub them viciously.

"I will not cry. *I will not*," I mutter through clenched teeth as I cross toward the bookcase.

The next thing I know, my ankle twists as a pen rolls beneath my foot, my arms windmilling for balance I can't find. I scrabble to save myself, grabbing uselessly at the cushion on the window seat.

It comes away in my hand with a violent tearing sound, and I hit the floor hard, yelping as the impact jars my spine and my teeth snap together with a loud *clack*, rattling my skull. With my free hand, I slap the floor, biting my lip to keep from screaming. Jesus Christ, it *hurts*.

When my ears finally stop ringing, I slowly haul myself to my feet, rubbing the bottom of my back, and examine the window seat. There are strips of fabric stuck to the bare wooden top where the cushion had been fixed on to it; I've ripped it clean off. My heart sinks as I realize I can't reattach it.

It's as I lower it back into place, vainly hoping my father won't notice, that I see a small hole in the top of the seat, the exact size and shape of the odd key I've just found. My jaw drops as I understand what I'm seeing.

It's not a seat, but a box, built into the recess under the window. With the cushion on, you'd never be able to tell.

I forget my pain and pull the key from my pocket. As I turn it, the lock releases, and the key becomes a handle. I lift the lid.

And I stare.

There are seven books hidden inside, bound in kidskin and nestled in the softest wool I've ever touched. I lift one out; it's the same size as the *Naomhfhuil* logs on the shelves, but so old that when I open it, the paper starts to disintegrate. I hastily replace it before it's completely destroyed. The next two are just as fragile, and I leave them alone.

But the fourth seems sturdier, so I sit on the floor, crossing my legs and resting it gently on my lap. The cover is so soft, like chamois or fine suede. Real fancy stuff. I open it and give the page a careful prod, relieved that it stays intact. So I begin, cautiously, to flick through it.

I can't read it. The oldest books I've seen are written in Old Scots, and I needed help reading those—but they were nothing compared to the book I hold now. It's all symbols, not even words; either it's some kind of code or a language more ancient than Old Scots. I scan a few paragraphs, but nothing makes sense.

And then I turn a page, and I see it.

All the fear I felt last night comes back threefold as my fingers clutch at my nightshirt collar with remembered panic.

The artist was skilled—I'll give them that. The ink has faded to rust, like old blood, but the images are still sharp, the details still true. It's the thing I saw last night, here in this book, drawn over and over.

As I gaze at the pictures, unable to look away, I can see exactly why the one I saw seemed so wrong to me, out there on the path. So inhuman. Its limbs are too long, making the creature look spindly, almost frail. It doesn't look as though it should be able to support its own weight, not an ounce of meat or fat on it. *Cadaverous* is the word, I think. Or starved. Just sinew and hollows.

I keep looking. The next few drawings are of faces, etched with astonishing detail. In the pictures, the creature's eyes look bright and alert, not like the filmed-over eyes of the one I saw, and I wonder if maybe it's an anomaly, or if it's much older than those in the book. The ears are high on the head, a little pointed at the ends. The lips are the same, long and thin, the nose two depressions in the center of its face. Its skin has been shaded—it looks like it would be coarse to the touch.

Not that I ever plan to find out.

I flip to the next page and shove the book off my lap, swearing freely.

Every hair on my body is on end, my breath caught somewhere between my mouth and lungs. I don't want to look at the book again, but I force myself, my hand trembling as I pull it back onto my knees and find the page once more.

If the creature had opened its mouth last night, my heart would have burst. The picture has been drawn as though the creature was frozen, lunging at the viewer, and it's petrifying.

Its maw is a gash that stretches across its entire face, two rows of teeth inside it. The back row contains masses of short, needle-thin teeth, all wickedly sharp, crowded together and crossing over each other in places as if they've grown in haste.

The front row contains just four teeth. Two pairs of canines in the same places mine are, except mine are maybe a quarter the length of these. The creature's are so long, I don't know how they fit inside its mouth when it's closed.

How could anyone have ever thought these were gods? Demons, maybe, escaped from the pits of hell, but not gods. I can't imagine how the artist got so close to it, and I don't want to.

I'm lost in the image, staring at it, when something batters at the front door, and I jump.

Scrambling to my feet, leaving the book on the floor, I cast around for a weapon, cursing my father for taking the guns and leaving me trapped in here like bait.

I think of the knives in the kitchen and run into the hallway, my pulse thundering in time with the thumping at the door.

"Alva?" a voice calls from the other side. It is sharp with fear, but I know it. "Alva? Are you there?"

"Ren? Ren? I'm here! I'm in here!" I press myself against the door as if I could push through it.

"Alva!" he says again. "Are you all right?"

I laugh weakly. "Well enough. My da locked me in. The shutters and the door. I can't get out."

A moment's pause. "Do you want me to get you out?"

"No, I'm happy being held prisoner," I snap before I can stop myself.

I can hear laughter in his voice when he replies. "I'll just ignore this axe in the woodpile, then, shall I?"

Hope rises, but I think fast. "Not the door," I say. "The washroom window." It's small, easy to board up afterward. "Around the back."

"Meet you there."

I follow Ren through the house to the washroom, then remember I'm still in my nightshirt, now stuck to my back where my skin is clammy, and my soiled skirts are still on the floor where I left them last night.

"Wait!" I cry. I bundle them up and carry them to the tiny mudroom off the hallway, dumping them in the laundry basket and washing my hands. Then I dash back to my room and dress, throwing on the only set of clothes I haven't packed, my hair an untamed black mess.

"All right," I shout when I've returned to the washroom. "I'm ready. Aim for the lock."

A second later, I hear the sound of the outer shutters being destroyed, followed by the thick glass of the window cracking.

"Keep back," Ren calls, and I listen as he knocks the glass out of the frame.

Then the blade of the axe splits a hole in the shutter, at least six inches to the left of the lock.

"Oops," Ren says. "I missed."

"You don't say," I reply, grinning wildly.

I wait in the doorway, wincing every time he hits the wood, never in the same place twice. When he's made so many holes the shutters look like nets, he pushes the axe through and twists it, using the sides of it to pull the splintered timber out. Then his face appears, his cheeks red from exertion, his hair sticking up. He beams, pleased with himself.

"Good day, fair damsel. I believe you ordered a rescue."

"Stop messing about and get in here," I say. I don't know

if the creatures hunt during the day, but if they do, they'll surely have heard that racket. As will my father, if he's anywhere nearby.

I start pulling wood aside, cursing as splinters pepper my hands, and on the other side of the window, Ren does the same until the window is clear.

"Hi," he says, pulling himself up to sit on the sill. "Are you all right?"

"As well as can be expected."

He folds his legs and jumps down into the room, landing badly on the twisted one. But it doesn't stop him limping over to me and holding my arms, his face uncharacteristically serious as he looks me over.

"What's going on? Why did your da lock you in?"

I hesitate. I wanted to warn Ormscaula about the creatures before I left. And I am still leaving—of course I am, now more than ever. Staying to fight monsters—that kind of nonsense is for the dying type. The hero type. That's not me. I'm the surviving type. But Ren—who's about as trusted as I am by the villagers—wouldn't have been my first choice of messengers. Needs must, though.

"Come with me," I say, leading him back to the study. "I have to show you something."

He's slow to follow, trying to peer into every room in the house. He pauses at my bedroom, and I pull the door closed.

"Don't I get a tour?" he asks, wiggling his eyebrows.

"You'll get a smack," I joke, though my small smile falls when we enter the study. The book is waiting on the floor, still open to the page showing the creature's vast maw. I lift it onto the desk, then stand back.

"That's why my father locked me in. Because of those things. I saw one last night."

Ren looks down at it and grimaces.

"You saw *that*?" I nod. He's silent for a moment, staring at the drawing. "Where?"

"Outside this cottage. On my way back from the *feis*, I stopped to look at the loch, and when I turned to come inside, it was between me and the door."

Ren peers at me. "You're not joking, are you?"

"No. I'm not."

"Where did you find this book?"

"Hidden. Locked away. There are another six of them." I point to the window seat. "I think they might be *Naomhfhuil* logs, really old ones. From before the earthquake."

I watch him try to decide if he believes me. He looks between me and the book, chewing his lip while he weighs it up, and I hold my breath, hoping against hope. Because if I can't convince Ren, I don't stand a chance with anyone else.

When his expression hardens, I know I've lost him. "Listen," he says. "Whatever they are, whatever you think you saw last night, you've got a bigger problem right now.

The reason I'm here is to warn you that Giles Stewart is on the warpath. He's after your father."

The back of my neck prickles. "Why?"

Ren looks grim. "After we left last night, the *feis* was halted, and everyone was sent home. First thing this morning, a bunch of men went out looking for Jim Ballantyne's horses. They found them in the woods. All dead." He pauses. "They were completely drained of blood."

"Jesus." I swallow. My gaze falls on the drawing of the creature, and I put two and two together, then pray I've made five. *Let me be wrong. Please.* "I don't understand what that's got to do with my father. He was here last night; I can vouch for that."

"There's more." He pauses. "Hattie Logan and Aileen Anderson never made it home. They walked part of the way back with Cora and some others, then left to go to the Logans'. But they never arrived, and no one has seen them since."

"They got lost, maybe?" I say. "Or—or Aileen's gone into labor somewhere, and Hattie is with her?"

Ren shakes his head, expression grim. "They found Aileen's *earasaid* out near the bridge. Torn. *Shredded* is the word Gavan used. And it was bloody."

This time we both look at the book.

"Gavan and his search party came to mine an hour or so ago, wanted to know if I'd seen anything unusual," Ren continues. He doesn't meet my eyes when he speaks next. "Alva, I told him your father thought there was a lugh on the loose. And he told Giles. I passed them all in the square on my way here. Giles was riling up the crowd, telling them there was only one man to blame."

I close my eyes, thinking about the noise last night from the *feis*. The light from the fire, the music, the singing and dancing. The heat we must have given off. The life. We lit a beacon in the middle of Ormscaula, and those *things* came to it like moths to a candle.

"Alva?"

Ren is staring at me. "Did you hear me? Giles will come here. He's probably on his way right now."

Of course he is. It's the chance he's been waiting for. He couldn't get revenge on my father for my mam, but he will make him pay, somehow, for Hattie and Aileen.

And he *should* pay for this. He knew those creatures existed, and he did nothing, told no one. If Hattie and Aileen are dead, then he killed them as surely as he killed my mother.

"You look pale," Ren says. "Do you need some water?"

I nod, and Ren takes my arm, and we go through to the kitchen. I sit, and he fills a glass. When I sip from it, the water tastes faintly of smoke and peat, last night's whiskey still clinging to the sides.

I look at the clock. Two hours until Duncan leaves. And with him, my only chance. I've waited too long, worked too hard for this not to take it.

"You should go," I say, standing up. "Before Giles gets here. And I should clean up. Board that window."

"I'll board the window."

"No, best if I do it." My eyes dart again to the clock.

Ren follows my gaze. "What's wrong? Why do you keep looking at the clock?"

"I'm not," I snap. "I just think you should go."

There is a pause. Then understanding lights Ren's face. "One o'clock is when the mail cart is leaving, isn't it? I heard you asking Duncan yesterday."

"Oh, for mercy's sake." I move, but Ren's hand darts toward me, his fingers closing over my wrist.

He scours my face, his eyes narrowed. "Did Duncan offer you a ride? No . . . You're stowing away, aren't you?"

I force myself to sound calm. "Murren Ross, I'll say this for you—you have one hell of an imagination. And that's coming from the girl who saw a monster last night."

"You only ever use my full name when you're lying," he says, triumphant.

He releases me suddenly and darts out, heading toward my bedroom.

I follow in time to see him awkwardly kneel and peer under

my bed. He gives me a wicked smile as he reaches under and starts to pull the bag out.

"So if you're *not* planning to stow away, what, may I ask—"

We both freeze at the sound of boots outside my window. Our eyes lock, his expression as horrified as mine. And then a key slides into the front door.

THIRTEEN

I hiss at Ren to get under the bed, not waiting to see if he obeys as I race to the hall, my heart in my mouth. Da. He will see what I've done. His bedroom and the kitchen are ransacked; there's wood and glass all over the washroom floor. And in his study, the window seat with the forbidden *Naomhfhuil* logs lies open, one of the books on the desk, there for all the world to see.

My father enters the cottage, the long guns over his arm, his plaid splattered with mud.

He starts when he sees me standing in the hall. Then he looks beyond me to his bedroom, where the drawers are pulled open, his clothes on the floor. When he turns back to me, his eyes burn with dark fury.

He turns and walks to his study.

"Alva," he barks over his shoulder. "Get in here."

My whole body is screaming at me to run, but I force myself to follow. I hover in the doorway, watching as my father sees the logbook.

He puts the long guns down on the desk one by one, bracketing the book, a bag of ammunition beside them. Then he sighs, closing his eyes briefly, a hand rising to rub the bridge of his nose.

"Why did you have to do that?" he says softly. "Why did you have to look?"

I can't move. I can't speak. I can't do anything but watch as he takes the flintlock pistols from the holster at his waist. He puts one on the desk, and the other . . .

The other he hefts in his hand.

And I know, right there and then, that I'm going to die like my mother.

Everything happens so slowly. My father's fingers tighten around the handle of the pistol, his head lifting, his gaze meeting mine, eyes cold. My thoughts flicker briefly to Ren, hidden under my bed. I hope he has the sense to stay there until he can chance an escape.

Finally, this is how it ends.

It's almost a relief.

But the next moment, panic hits—I don't want to die, not like her, without a weapon, without hope.

I hear a rushing like wings as my death approaches, and I

bend over, making myself small, covering my head, keening the word *no* over and over. I want to live. *I want to live.*

Suddenly, I'm hauled upright, my father gripping my shoulders, lifting me until we're face-to-face. The gun he'd held is on the desk.

"What the hell, Alva?" His voice is rough, shocked. "What did you think I was going to do?"

"You shot her . . ." The words fall from my mouth like water.

He freezes. "What?"

"You shot her," I say, my voice louder.

My father lets me go and staggers backward, into the desk.

"I heard you." Seven years of fear and grief and rage and bewilderment leave me in a torrent, unstoppable as a winter thaw. "I heard you fighting, and I heard her screaming, and then you shot her. Four times. *Bang. Bang. Bang. Bang.*" I spit the words at him, my own bullets.

He stares. His face is gray. "Alva . . . I . . ."

"I knew it." We both turn toward the voice in the doorway. "All this time, I was right."

Giles Stewart stands in the hall, Jim Ballantyne and Dizzy Campbell, the baker, just behind him. Giles's face is maniacal, almost gleeful, his smile twisted as though he's caught between laughing and screaming.

I turn to my father. His eyes are wide and panicked. We both look at the guns on the table, and as he reaches out, I dart forward, pushing them aside.

"No, Da. Enough!"

Then Dizzy Campbell pulls me away as Jim Ballantyne, muscular from years of hustling giant, log-dragging horses for a living, yanks my father's arms behind his back and forces him to his knees.

Dizzy holds me firmly, though his grip is gentle as he pins my arms to my sides. But I don't struggle. My father isn't struggling, either. He's docile as a lamb.

There's something wrong with seeing my da like this: cowed and silent, his head bent meekly like a man at prayer. For years he's been my enemy, a waking nightmare that's hardened my heart and my mind. My entire world has revolved around keeping him happy to keep myself safe. This should be a triumphant moment.

But it's not. It doesn't feel right. This isn't how I thought it would end. I didn't think I'd have to witness it.

Giles enters the room, coming to me. He takes my chin in his fingers and turns my head side to side. "You lied to me, my girl," he says softly. "I asked you, after your mother disappeared, if he hurt her. You told me no. You told me she'd left."

"She was a child," my father growls.

"She's not a child now," Giles says, and something about the way he says it makes my skin crawl.

My father hears it, too, I think, because his gaze darkens. "Let her be. It's me you want."

Giles turns to Jim Ballantyne with a crooked smile. "Take him to the jail," he orders, and Jim doesn't hesitate.

As my father stands, we lock eyes.

"I'm sorry," he says.

I turn aside, wincing when I hear him stumble as Jim forces him out the door.

Giles jerks his head at Dizzy. "Go with him. I'll deal with Miss Douglas. And take the guns—they're evidence."

Dizzy does as he's bid, picking up all four of my father's guns and carrying them out of the house, leaving me alone with Giles.

He looks me over, sizing me up like a man at a livestock market, gaze lingering on my legs, my chest, my face. I half expect him to open my mouth and inspect my teeth. I'm in danger here, I can feel it.

"You could hang, too," he goes on. "The two of you could swing together. You're an accessory, Alva. You lied to me. And to a sheriff."

My mouth is dry. "I had no choice," I say. "I was scared he'd kill me, too. I've been scared for the past seven years."

Giles laughs. "Oh, aye. Do that on the stand. The big eyes, that tremble in your voice. The jury will love it."

"It's true."

He hesitates, then gives a single nod. "You're lucky. I believe you. That's why I'm not going to arrest you." He smiles. "In fact, I'm going to take you home with me. No more running wild up here. You'll be safer that way."

I grit my teeth. "With all due respect, I don't think I will be."

"Come, now, you can't think to stay up here alone on the mountain." He takes a step closer to me, and his voice drops low. "I'm a wealthy man, Alva, you know that. You've seen my house—all the luxuries a young woman could need. You'll want for nothing."

I scramble for a reason to stay. "What about the loch? Someone has to be here to keep an eye on it."

Giles's expression turns ugly, and I realize I've made a mistake. "Oh, aye. That's another thing. Why have I not been notified the loch is so low? The reed beds look half dried out. How am I supposed to run my mill if there's a water shortage?"

"It's your mill using up the water," I snap before I can stop myself.

"Be careful, girl," he sneers, his lip curling with anger. "You're on my generosity here."

"And I'm grateful," I say, trying to sound it. "But you can see that someone needs to be here to monitor it, now especially. With my father gone, I'm the only one who knows how."

Giles shrugs. "It can't be that hard. Low is bad, high is good. Have I got it?"

I gesture to the shelves of records and logs behind us. "This isn't all for show, you know. There's an art to it."

He smiles, a nasty, knowing smile. "You're a prickly wee

thing. Your mam was the same when she was your age. Proud. Too proud to admit her mistakes."

Mistakes. He means my father. Me. I tamp down the flare of anger. I won't give him a reason to take me away.

"Is that all of them?" He nods at the shelves.

It's then that I remember the old log on the desk, wide open to a picture of the creatures. Now is the time to tell him about them.

But when I look over, the book is closed.

Understanding breaks over me like a wave. My father wasn't going for the guns when Giles appeared. He was closing the book. He didn't want them to see. Why was he so desperate to keep those things secret?

Dizzy appears in the doorway. "You'd better come," he says to Giles, then lowers his voice. "Aileen's been found."

There is an unspoken question in Giles's face, and Dizzy answers it with a short shake of his head.

"What's happened to Aileen?" I ask, trying to keep the note of panic out of my voice.

Giles ignores me. "Pack your things and go straight to my house. By my reckoning, it takes an hour to walk down the mountain, so I'll expect you there in an hour and a half at the latest. Do you understand? I mean it, Alva," he says in response to the protest he reads in my expression. "Woe betide you if I have to come back up this accursed mountain and fetch you. Even my mercy has an end."

"Listen, Giles, I have to tell you—" I begin, only for him to whirl around and cut me off.

"And *I* have to deal with a grieving family. Pack. And you will address me as Mr. Stewart."

"But—"

"Get to it."

I hear the front door shut behind them. I walk out into the corridor, covering my mouth with my hand to keep my scream in. Hopelessness washes over me. *What am I going to do?*

I close my eyes. When I open them, Ren is in front of me.

He must have heard it all.

His mouth moves as though he wants to speak, but no words come out. He just looks at me, shaking his head, and I see myself as he must.

An accessory to murder. A liar.

I find I can't bear the idea of him being disappointed in me.

I try to speak, but I don't know how to begin. My mouth crumples.

He puts a hand on my arm. "Don't." His expression is as soft as I've ever seen it, and he gives me a sympathetic, close-mouthed smile. "It's all right. What could you possibly have done?"

He holds out his arms, and I step back, raising my hands. If he touches me then I'll cry, and if I start, I might never stop.

"I can't," I say.

He nods, crossing his arms. "Well, if you weren't already planning to leave, I think you should give the idea strong consideration now."

I smile weakly. "You were right. I was planning on leaving. Today's the day." There's a relief in saying it aloud, and his eyes lift to mine. "Wait here."

I turn on my heel and go into my room, fetching the letters from under my pillow. I hold them out to him, address side up, so he can see who they're for. "I wrote these. One says the loch is drying up because the mill is using too much water. The other is a confession about the night . . . the night she . . ." I force the words out. "The night he murdered her. I was always going to tell Giles, you see. I'd already written this. And I know I should have told someone before." He starts to speak, but I hold up my hand. "I should have, but I was scared. Scared he'd kill me, too. Or that he'd be taken and hanged and I'd be left behind, all alone."

"You wouldn't have been alone," Ren says. "For the record."

We both fall silent then. "What about the monster you saw?" he says finally.

"So you do believe me?" His pause is a little too long, and my heart sinks. "You don't."

"I believe you think you saw something." He says it so gently that I can't be angry.

"Will you do something for me?" I ask Ren.

"Anything."

I take him at his word. "I need to tell someone else what I saw last night. Someone who can do something, who knows they're out there, especially if they're what attacked Aileen. Giles won't listen, not to me."

He looks thoughtful. "What about Maggie? People listen to her."

Maggie Wilson. Of course—why didn't I think of that?

"Perfect. If I write to her, will you deliver it? Along with the book that has the drawings?"

Ren nods.

I return to the study with Ren in tow and pull a fresh sheet of paper from my father's desk. I start at the beginning: my father appearing with a slashed net, and then later that night, the scream outside the cottage. But when I try to explain the creature I saw, I stop, sucking the end of my pen.

How do I explain them without sounding like I'm mad?

"What is it?" Ren asks, searching my face.

I put the pen down. "I don't know what to say."

"Tell the truth," he says. "Write that you think terrifying monsters are on the loose by the loch and that it's possible they hunt and kill people."

I look up at him. "I might need a bit more than that."

"Like what?"

I pause, trying to gather my thoughts. "I don't know. Some history and context, maybe. It could help Maggie."

"Is there history and context?"

I wrinkle my nose. "Maybe? I think so? You remember at school, when we learned that before the one true god and the earthquake and all that, people believed everything had a god, and they all had to be respected or else? So say Johnny Logan got sick because he didn't make an offering to the tree gods before he chopped off a few branches for his fire. Or Mary Black broke her leg because she picked flowers without asking permission from the flower gods. Well, obviously the loch had gods, too. What if they weren't gods, though? What if they actually existed, and the logs prove it?"

I open the book, wondering again why my father closed it before Giles could see, flicking through until I find one of the pictures. Then I point at the creature, tapping the page for emphasis.

"My da said they called them gods because they needed a word to explain what they were. It's what the role of *Naomhfhuil* was created for—to deal with these so-called gods. So there might be something in the book that will help, something we used to do to keep them away." Then I shudder as I realize the stories I heard as a bairn weren't stories at all, but real events. "Maybe not. They did human sacrifice." I grimace.

Understanding lights Ren's face. "So is that their skin on the logs?"

"What?" I stare at him.

"The sacrificed. Alva, did you not know? The books your da had locked away are bound in human skin."

FOURTEEN

In silence, I walk past Ren to the kitchen, running the tap and scrubbing my hands. The water isn't enough, and I search for the lye soap I wash our clothes with, the caustic sting doing nothing to make me feel clean. I don't think my hands will ever feel clean again. *Human skin.* Jesus Christ.

Ren stands behind me.

"It's not much different from cow leather. It's all just skin."

I give him a look. "I'm not going to ask how you know what tanned human skin looks like."

"Come on," he says, reaching over and turning the tap off. "We don't have much time. You have to get out of here before Giles realizes something's up, and we still need to explain your monsters to Maggie."

Your monsters. The doubt is still there, but I can tell he's beginning to believe. At least, I hope he is.

I lead the way back to the study and sit heavily on the desk chair.

"So we know what they are, or what people thought they were," says Ren, beginning to pace. "Do we know where they came from?" He nods at the book. "Any clues in there?"

My thoughts catch again on my father and how he closed the book. He had seconds to make a decision, and instead of going for the weapons that might have meant he could escape, he chose to shut it? To hide them?

"My father doesn't want Giles to know about them," I say slowly, realization dawning.

Ren stops and turns to me, expression incredulous. "You think he's protecting them?"

I shake my head. "No," I say. "When he went out after them, he was armed to the teeth. But he definitely didn't want *Giles* to know about them. I think that's why he was so worried about people coming up here. Why he wouldn't report that the loch levels had fallen."

The loch levels.

My stomach swoops like I'm falling, and I grip the side of the desk.

"The hole," I say, surprising us both. "The hole we saw the other day, in the bank on the north shore. I thought it was too big to be made by otters—I said that to you. What if those things live inside the mountain?" My mouth falls open in a perfect O of realization as it all comes together. "The water traps them there—has done ever since the earthquake, when the underground loch merged with ours, making the water so deep it covered their entrance. It didn't kill them, it imprisoned them. That's why they vanished then and why—"

"Why they're back now," Ren says. "Because Giles Stewart is draining the loch with his mill. Their escape route is open again." He pauses, staring off into the distance, testing it. Then he nods. "That could be it. So we know what they are and where they come from. All we need to do is figure out how to stop them."

"You believe me now?"

He rubs his forehead. "I *want* to believe you. But—" He freezes suddenly, eyes locked on the clock on the mantelpiece. "Alva, it's nearly one."

I'm out of my seat, flying into my room. Duncan will be leaving Ormscaula in a few short moments. Leaving me behind.

I drag the bag out from under the bed. Then I stop, back bent, hands stilling on the ties.

If I stay, I'll lose my job. I'll have to live with Giles Stewart. I'll see my da hanged. But if I go . . .

I'll never know what happened here. Whether Maggie listens to Ren about the monsters. Whether more people are killed. Whether they stop them.

I turn and look at Ren helplessly.

"It's your only chance," Ren says softly, as though reading my mind. "Go. I'll take the book to Maggie. I'll tell her everything you've told me."

He walks over to me and gently takes my bag, placing it over my shoulder. His thumb strokes my cheek, his eyes tender.

"Go," he says again, lowering his hand and stepping back. "You can still catch the cart."

I pass him and start to run.

It must be close to two by the time I reach the river, each breath a hot blaze of pain, a stitch beneath my ribs. There's a raw patch on my left knee from where I skidded and fell in my haste.

I try to fight down my panic as I reach the village. I keep my head bent and my *earasaid* up as I dart through the back streets, following the same path I used yesterday to avoid the square and the main lanes, making for the road out of Ormscaula. I'm an hour behind Duncan, but I can make it up, if I run. I just have to—

"My house is back that way." Giles Stewart stands before me, Dizzy Campbell at his side.

I skid to a halt, panting. He steps forward.

"I'll take that for you, shall I?" he says, and without waiting for an answer, he jerks the bag from my arm. I watch in horror as he drops it to the ground and tugs the drawstring, opening it and rifling through. My stomach turns as he pulls out one of the fine dresses.

"Very smart for a girl who lives in the mountains," he says thoughtfully.

"It was my mother's," I lie.

He looks at the gown with renewed interest, and I don't think I'm imagining the care with which he folds it before gently placing it on top of the cloak. My heart stutters when his fingers brush against the *earasaid*—the gun that killed my mother is still wrapped inside. If he sees it . . .

Instead, he pushes it aside, covering the pocket with the bullets in it, and pulls out my writing case, pawing through it disinterestedly. When he finds the purses of money, he gives me a knowing look.

"You seem to have come prepared, Miss Douglas. Empty your pockets, please."

The only thing in there is the cameo of my mother. I pull it out and hand it to him.

Giles cradles it in his palms, staring at it for a long moment.

"I'll keep hold of this," he says.

"It's mine," I reply sharply. "It's all mine."

"Of course," he says soothingly. "I'll look after it for you. Keep it safe. Come on." Giles throws my bag over his shoulder and takes my arm, just above the elbow. "Let's get you home."

If I go with him, I'm done for. Forget the bag, forget my stuff. They're just things. Maybe I can still get away, and as long as I'm free, I'm fine.

"I want to see Mrs. Logan first," I say. "Offer my condolences. I heard about Aileen. Just now." I remember at the last second that he never told me what happened to her.

"They're not ready for visitors," Giles replies. "Save that for the funeral. If you're brave enough to show your face."

I suppress a growl of frustration as he continues. "You'd probably best not go at all. But we can decide that later. In the meantime, your place is with me." His grip on my arm tightens, and he begins to walk, taking me with him.

I've seen rabbits caught in snares; trying to fight makes it worse. Every time they try to escape, the wire tightens, until they're dead, strangled by their own struggle. So I don't argue or protest, just trot meekly beside him, my cheeks flaming when Maggie Wilson steps out of the store and watches us pass, bidding Giles a good day. He nods tersely, and we keep moving. I feel her gaze as she looks after us, all the way down the street.

The Stewarts' house hasn't changed at all since I was a child. The hallway where Giles drops my bag is still gloomy, paneled in dark wood. There's a long rug running the length of it, the middle faded from years of footsteps. To the left is the receiving parlor, and beyond that is the family parlor—only the Stewarts are grand enough to have two. Ahead is the door to the dining room, scene of those weekly dinners of my childhood, the kitchen behind that.

But it's up the wide stairs Giles leads me, grip still firm on my arm.

"Where's Mrs. Stewart?" I ask. "And Gavan?"

"My wife is abed. She took the news about Aileen hard," he says. We pass what I assume are the family bedrooms. "And Gavan is out with the others, searching for Hattie."

At the end of the hall is another staircase to a third level. But instead we make for a small door that looks like it might be some kind of cupboard. I'm surprised when Giles pulls a key from his pocket and opens it, pushing me inside, even more so when I see another staircase there: narrow, high steps, the wood less fine, leading up into the dark.

"Go on," he says.

Apprehensive of what awaits me at the top, I go, gripping a rope that's been attached to the wall to serve as a banister. My eyes adjust as I near the top and find another door, a key in the lock.

"Where are you taking me?" I ask, but Giles is at my back, reaching past me to unlock it, using his body to force me inside.

It's a small room, a round window set with thick greenish glass casting an eerie light through it. There's a mattress on a small brass bedstead, a chipped chamber pot visible beneath, and a wardrobe. No desk or chair, even. A bed, a wardrobe, and a pot.

I turn to Giles, who is blocking the doorway. "You can't seriously mean to keep me up here."

"It's just for the time being," he says.

I take a step toward him. "I want to go back downstairs."

"Why don't you lie down for a bit?" he says. "You must be tired."

"I don't want to lie down."

He looks at me as though I'm a child, and when he speaks, it's slowly. "Listen, Alva, you have to understand, there's a lot of bad feeling in Ormscaula right now. A lot of uncertainty and fear and anger. People are out for blood. They need someone to blame—for what happened to your mam, all those years ago, and what happened last night. And I'm afraid that with your father locked up, they'll take it out on you."

"Then I'll stay in the house," I say. "Away from the windows so they can't see me."

He shakes his head, smiling faintly. "People will be coming and going. No, it's best for now if you stay up here, safe and sound."

"I don't want to." I don't want to be locked in somewhere again. Especially not here.

His face darkens, his pupils becoming pinpricks. Then he

forces himself to smile once more. "So like your mam when she was your age. Just as headstrong." He turns to leave.

"Where are you going?" I try to keep the desperation out of my voice.

"To the mill. I'll be back later with a tray for your supper."

The mill. If Ren and I are right and the water level dropping means those creatures can get out, then every inch of water he uses is an inch more freedom they have.

The door shuts behind him, and the key turns in the lock.

I fly across the room and hit the door with my fists. "No, Giles—Mr. Stewart—listen to me, there's something I need to tell you! Something about the mill. You have to stop. Listen to me. Listen!"

There is only silence. I continue to batter the door and shout until my throat and hands are raw. Despair floods me. No one knows I'm here. No one will miss me. And no one will hear me. I'm three floors up, behind locked doors. I look around the room—neat and tidy, the bed made—and my skin crawls. How long has he been planning this?

I head to the window, searching for a latch, but there isn't one. The glass is thick and full of bubbles, making it impossible to see out of, though I'm pretty sure I'm at the back of the house. With nowhere else to sit, I cross to the bed, sinking into the ancient mattress.

Now what? I think of my bag downstairs—the clothes, the ink and pens, the money in it. My gun. If I had that, I could shoot out the locks. I could have forced Giles to let me go. Threatened him. Wildly, I remember when I pulled it on Ren, him telling me he knew I wouldn't shoot him because I never cocked the gun.

Ren.

He's going to Maggie to tell her about the creatures, and Maggie knows I'm with Giles. Surely she'll tell Ren. He'll come for me, won't he? He'll help get me out of here.

As I lift my legs onto the bed, I find my skirts are stuck to the gash on my knee from when I fell earlier. Bracing myself, I peel the fabric from the wound and pull up my skirt to inspect it. The gash is bleeding again, the edges ragged and raw. I spit on what I hope is a clean bit of skirt and dab at the cut. I tear the bottom of the inner skirt and tie it around my leg as a makeshift bandage. Then, with nothing to do but wait, I curl into a ball.

I must have fallen asleep, because I sit up suddenly, confused about where I am, just in time to hear a key in the lock. Before I can swing my legs off the bed, Giles is in the room. He locks the door as I stand, pocketing the key.

"What time is it?" I ask.

"Four. Teatime." He takes a step forward, and I see it.

The dark shape of a gun in his hand.

"Get on the floor. Facedown," he says pleasantly, as if remarking on the weather. "Please."

I stare at him in shock.

"Alva, if you want to eat, you'll do as I say. Otherwise, I'm happy to wait for you to come to your senses."

I remember the rules of staying alive. *Rules three and four*, I remind myself. Be useful, and don't make them angry. I swallow.

"All right," I say. "I'll do it. But there's something I need to tell you. About the mill."

"Floor, Alva. Now."

I swallow my words, wincing as my wounded knee meets the wooden floor. I kneel, then lower myself onto my belly, clasping my hands behind my head. I listen as Giles opens the door once more, see the golden light from a candle flood the room as he brings something inside. Then he locks the door again.

"See, that wasn't so hard, was it? You can get up now."

I rise and look at what he's brought.

There's a tray, the kind with legs that you give to the lady of the house so she can have breakfast in bed. On it is a candle in a brass holder and a plate covered in a silver dome. A small jug and a wooden cup, like those from the *feis*, sit beside it. And a pile of white fabric. The dress he examined earlier, taken from my bag.

"Put it on," Giles says softly.

"Where's my bag? Where's my money?" I ask.

"Safe. You don't need it anymore. There will be no running away now." He laughs. "Don't deny that's what you were planning; it's obvious you were hightailing it out of here when I caught you." He shrugs. "But that's over. You're here."

My heart sinks.

"You just be a good girl and put it on." He points at the dress with the barrel of the gun. That's when I realize it's one of my father's flintlocks. He took it for evidence, he said. "I'm going to close my eyes and count to ten," he continues. "You either put it on yourself, or I'll put it on you."

He means it. He wants me to dress up nicely for afternoon tea in the dress he thinks was my mother's.

He wants me to be my mother.

"Go on," he says when I stand, staring at him, frozen with shock and horror and disgust. "Take off your *earasaid* and vest, and then I'll shut my eyes. If you're fast enough, I'll see nothing I shouldn't."

He takes a step toward me, and my hands fly to the pin holding my *earasaid* in place. I unclasp it, slipping the plaid from my shoulders, unfastening it from my waist. Then I unbutton my vest, my hands shaking so much that my fingers slip twice. My cheeks burn with humiliation; my mouth and throat are as dry as the loch bed. I want to cry and scream all at once. His eyes are on me the whole time, a strange light burning in them.

Once I lay my vest and *earasaid* on the bed, Giles raises the gun and points it at me. "I'll close my eyes to preserve your modesty. But if you try anything, I'll shoot. Don't think I won't, Alva."

"All right," I say slowly, my mind racing. My hands move to the ties at my waist. "Close your eyes."

He smiles and does so. "One . . ."

I stick my first two fingers up at him, both hands.

"Two . . ."

He doesn't flinch. He has played fair in this, at any rate. I drop the dress to the floor and pick up my *earasaid*.

"Three . . ."

I open it as wide as I can, gripping the edges in both hands.

"Four . . . Tell me something, Alva. What was all that money for?"

He wants me to speak, to be sure I'm where I ought to be. "I'm a little busy right now," I say, muffling my voice behind the *earasaid* as though it were a blouse being pulled over my head. I take a step closer.

"Five . . . Surely you can talk and dress?" he says, smiling.

I make a small grunting sound, as though trying to force a dress over my head in a hurry.

"Six . . . It sounds like you're struggling, there, Alva. You are a little bigger in the hips than your mam was."

This time, my grunt is one of disgust. Pig.

"Seven . . ."

I take a deep breath, readying myself. I have one chance to get this right.

"Eight . . ."

I make a sound of panic, disgust blooming when I see him fight a smile.

"Nine . . ."

I wait.

"Te—"

Before he can finish, I launch myself at him, using the *ear-asaid* to pin his arms and my weight to drive him backward.

The gun goes off.

FIFTEEN

I wait for a burst of pain, but it's Giles who moans and writhes beneath me.

"I'm shot," I hear him gasp from under my *earasaid*. "My leg."

"Good," I hiss, keeping a tight hold on him.

"I can't breathe!"

"Good," I repeat. "You don't deserve to breathe, you pervert."

I keep the thick cloth over his face as he thrashes weakly, trying to free himself. When he finally goes limp, I loosen my grip slightly, but I wait a few more moments before I pull the *earasaid* from his face, reaching for the gun at the same time. I take his pulse to be sure he's truly unconscious, and because he bloody deserves it, I give him a sharp slap, then peel back one of his eyelids. His pupils remain unfocused. It's only then that I get off him.

Girding my stomach, I lift his kilt to check the bullet wound and sigh with relief. It looks like the bullet merely grazed his thigh, and sure enough, when I check the floor, I see it embedded in the boards. He'll live, then. It might not even scar. More's the pity.

I make short work of going through his pockets, finding two loose keys and a full set on a ring, as well as the cameo of my mother. I take it all, and my father's gun, too.

I put my vest back on and walk out, leaving Giles on the floor, tangled in my *earasaid*. I debate whether to lock him in but decide against it. I don't plan to stick around Ormscaula long enough for him to regain consciousness and come after me.

I find my bag in the receiving parlor and take the new *earasaid* from it, putting it on and pocketing the revolver. I won't be parted from that again. I put the flintlock in the bag, too. Everything else is still in there, down to the purses of money. I sling the bag over my shoulder and walk out, smack into Gavan Stewart.

"Alva? What are you doing here?" he asks, eyes wide.

"Ask your da," I say, moving past him, heading for the front door.

"What do you mean?" he says, following.

"Your father brought me here." I don't break stride, but he keeps up, walking beside me down the wide hall. "By force. He said he'd arrest me if I didn't come."

Gavan shakes his head as though to keep my words from reaching his ears, but I keep going.

"He locked me in your attic and told me it was for my own good. And just now, he came up with a tea tray and a gun." I pause at the door, Gavan stopping beside me. "He wanted me to put on some fancy white dress and sit down for tea with him, so when he closed his eyes to *preserve my modesty*," I spit, "I knocked him down, and he fired the gun. The bullet grazed his thigh—he's fine," I add quickly. "He's up there now."

Gavan blinks at me.

"Are you all right?" he says at last. "He didn't . . . hurt you?"

I shake my head, then say with some malice, "No. He didn't have a chance to."

He nods. "Good. And he's breathing? Conscious?"

"Not exactly conscious," I admit, my hand on the latch. "I kind of . . . sat on him until he fainted so I could get away."

Amusement flickers over his face, lips quirking into a swift smile that comes and goes faster than a summer storm.

"I checked the wound; he won't even need a day in bed," I say. "I'm sure he'll be fine."

Gavan nods again. "Leave him to me. You go on home. I'm sorry about this, Alva."

"Actually." I take a deep breath. There's no point in hiding my plans now. Giles has already figured them out. "My father has been arrested, so I'm not going home."

"What?" Gavan says. "Where are you going?"

"I have a job in a town. I was going to stow away with Duncan to Balinkeld and get the stagecoach, but he's long gone. I'll have to start walking now if I want to get to Balinkeld in time for the coach tomorrow." I lift the latch, and Gavan reaches out to stop me.

"But there's a lugh out there. It's already killed Aileen Anderson and the horses, and Hattie's missing, too. You can't just walk down the mountain in the dark."

"It's not a lugh, Gavan," I say. "It's something else. I've seen it. It's . . . Talk to Maggie Wilson. Talk to Ren. They can tell you."

Gavan shakes his head. "No, *you* tell me," he says, bracing a hand against the door. "Half an hour, Alva—you can spare that. After all, you shot my da." I hesitate, and he smiles suddenly. "Come on, I need a cup of tea. I'm parched. And I've even got an idea to get you down to Balinkeld and make up the lost time."

I hesitate—it'll start getting dark in a few hours, and I want to put as much distance as possible between the loch and me before then.

"I'll keep my da locked up overnight," he adds. "As an extra thank-you."

I smile. "You'll want these, then," I say, holding out the keys I took from Giles.

I end up making the tea and carrying it through to the dining room while he goes to check on his father. When he returns, we sit in the same seats at the same polished table we sat at all those years before; I do it without even thinking.

"How is he?" I ask, nursing my cup.

"He'll live," Gavan says in a measured voice. "Just a scratch, like you thought. He's not even bleeding."

"Shame," I say, then hesitate. "And how are *you*?"

He exhales slowly. "This time yesterday, we were still setting up for the *feis*. It feels like such a long time ago now. You know, I saw Hattie trip you during the dance." I am ashamed at the bolt of vindication that shoots through me when he says this. Gavan continues. "I actually said to James, 'Hattie'll get herself murdered if she carries on like that.'" He pauses. "It was a figure of speech. But now she might really be dead."

I reach over and pat his hand. "Gavan, it's not your fault."

"No. It's your da's fault, apparently," he says plainly. "Or so everyone is saying. He knew there was a wildcat about. He knew, and he didn't warn anyone." He leans forward. "Only you say that it's something else."

I pull my hand away. "It's going to sound impossible. Just try to believe me."

He listens in silence as I talk, as calmly and clearly as I'm able, about what I saw by the loch and then in the old books.

I tell him my father knows, and that Ren knows, too, and that he's taken the little proof we have to Maggie Wilson.

I explain that I think the creatures are free because his father's mill is draining the loch so that they can walk across the bed. And that if the mill keeps going, draining more and more water faster than it can be replenished, they'll be out there for a long, long time.

Gavan says nothing, doesn't interrupt. After I've stopped, he remains still as a carving for many minutes. The only sound is the ticking of the clock.

Then, though it must be cold now, he picks up his tea and drinks, tipping the cup back until it's empty. He sets it down. "This is all true?" he says. "You swear to me?"

"I swear." I put my hand on my heart. "Gavan, I *saw* one."

"Do you have any idea how many there are?"

"I only saw the one. But the way my father spoke, and the images in the logbook . . . it made me think there are more."

"Then I have to catch one."

I'm too stunned to reply for a moment. "What did you say?" I ask at last.

"No offense, Alva, but the word of a Douglas and some old book probably isn't going to get us very far." He holds up his hands. "Oh, I believe you. But I suspect I would be in the minority."

He's right.

"And I can't imagine anything other than coming face-to-face with one will convince my father to shut down his mill," Gavan continues.

"I don't know if it's possible to catch one."

Gavan's chin lifts in a gesture I recognize as pure stubbornness. "There's only one way to find out."

He asks me to wait in the dining room, telling me he'll be as fast as he can, and then he leaves. I hear the front door open and close. I contemplate making a break for it and have to force myself to finish my tea, bitter from steeping for so long. I can trust Gavan; I feel sure of it.

But as the hands on the clock over the fireplace turn, marking how long he's been gone, I take to pacing around the room, trying to stay calm.

Finally it's too much, and I hitch my bag over my shoulder, ready to go, when the front door opens and, a moment later, Gavan enters wearing his plaid, his cheeks flushed.

"Sorry," he says, breathless. "Everything's sorted. Let's go."

"What's sorted?" I ask as I follow him to the front door.

"I told you, I had an idea to get you away, so long as you don't mind traveling first thing tomorrow instead. I've arranged a loan of Jim Ballantyne's donkey for you to get down to Balinkeld. If you go at first light at a clip, you'll make it in time for the stagecoach. You can still get away, and it means you don't have to be on the road at night."

I stare at him, stunned at this overhaul of my plans and not sure whether I like it. "What about your father?" I ask. Because if there's one thing I've learned, it's that Giles Stewart doesn't forgive. He didn't forgive my mother for falling in love with another man, and he won't forgive me for besting him or exposing him to his own son. He won't forgive Gavan for helping me, either.

"He'll be fine. I left the keys with my mam." He hesitates. "She says she's sorry, by the way. I told her a bit about what happened. I don't think it surprised her."

I swallow. "Gavan . . ."

"I'll take you somewhere to spend the night, somewhere you feel safe." He holds the door open for me, and we leave his father's house, entering the empty square. "Where would that be?"

I think for a moment. "Ren's house," I say at last. I have no idea how Liz Ross will feel about it, but it's the only place in Ormscaula I think I might feel safe. If Gavan is surprised, he doesn't show it.

"Ren's it is. Should we go there now, then?"

I nod.

"You have the gun, don't you?" he asks.

For a moment, I think he means the pistol against my

thigh, and I freeze; I don't want anyone to know about that. Then I realize he means the flintlock his father was shot with.

"It's in my bag. But I don't have any more bullets for it. You can only load one at a time, and it was fired."

He chews his lip. "That's a shame. I was going to ask if I could borrow it." He pauses. "Do you think Ren would be willing to help me? You said he knows about the creatures. I'll need a second pair of hands."

I watch him for a minute, then make up my mind. "Third," I say. "You'll need a third pair of hands."

He smiles at me tentatively. "And that would be you?"

"If I can't leave until first light, I might as well help you. Where could I be safer than chasing monsters?" I smile.

Gavan grins back at me. "All right. I don't suppose you have any bright ideas about how to catch one?"

We walk along, both of us lost in thought. "We have cages," I say, breaking the silence. "My da keeps them to catch the odd sick cat or wolf that came down the mountain."

"How does he know if they're sick?" Gavan asks.

"No healthy animal would come near humans," I say. "Believe me."

"Says a lot about these creatures, then," Gavan replies.

I say nothing.

I've never been to Ren's home—he's always made sure of that. And I know very little about Liz Ross; only that she's from Albion, she takes in mending and laundry, she buys the bruised and damaged stock from the Wilsons' store, she sometimes has a man around, and she likes drink a lot more than it likes her.

We don't see a single soul on the way there, everyone staying inside; the cottages we pass are shuttered against the growing dusk. Gavan seems to know the way, leading me through the silent lanes toward the run-down part of Ormscaula. As we move past the last of the well-kept homes, we pass the Logans' neat cottage, the curtains closed, the cottage somehow forlorn, as if the stone has absorbed the family's sadness. Then we pick our way out to where the paths become untidy and muddy, the stonework in the walls haphazard and in need of repair.

Gavan leads me along a path to a tiny, ramshackle cottage. There can't be more than one room inside. Behind it, I spot an outhouse. The door leans against the opening, clearly long divorced from its hinges.

If the Logans' place felt forlorn, the Rosses' cottage feels like it's dying. Everything about it is dirty or decaying: the thatch on the roof smells sour and dank, even from a distance; black mold clusters around the tiny windows, one of which is boarded up. There's a horseshoe nailed above the door, half hanging off, the silver dulled to black. The plaster around it is crumbling away, exposing the daub and wattle inside. It must be freezing in winter.

Quite suddenly, I don't want to be here. I don't want Ren to know I was here. I didn't know he lived like this, and he clearly didn't want me to. I remember how I teased him by the loch about wanting time off from the mill, and I'm ashamed of how it hurt him. I understand now. But Gavan is already knocking on the door, the knock of a person who's used to being welcomed wherever he goes.

The door opens, and Liz Ross appears. She does not look welcoming. Her stringy hair, the same dirty blond as Ren's, falls in her face, her blouse hanging from one shoulder, her underskirt made transparent by the light behind her. An unpleasant smell drifts out from inside: spoiled milk and rot. *Oh, Ren.*

"If you're here for the rent, you can tell your father I don't have it," she says to Gavan. "So go away."

"I'm not here for the rent, Mrs. Ross," Gavan says gently. "I'm looking for Murren."

"He's not here." Her voice has taken on a little of the mountain burr, the *t* dropped.

"Do you know where he is?"

"I'm not his keeper," she replies.

Then she peers beyond him, her eyes finding me and sharpening. "Is he not with you?" she says to me. "You're the Douglas girl, aren't you?"

I nod, surprised to be recognized.

Liz Ross looks back at Gavan. "If he's not with her, then I don't know where he is."

With that, she closes the door.

Gavan turns to me. "Where else might he be?"

I'm reeling at the fact that Liz Ross not only knows who I am but expects Ren to be at my side. I think. "Mack's Tavern, maybe?"

He's not in the tavern, though. There's a sign on the door saying it's closed on account of the curfew. That explains why the streets are deserted.

"Who called for the curfew?" I ask Gavan, already knowing the answer.

"My father," he confirms. "After what happened to Hattie and Aileen. Keep people inside, where it's safe."

We peer into the pub anyway, but it's empty. Even the cat is missing from its regular perch.

"Maggie's, then," I say, and we turn toward the store, heading for the door to her private rooms at the back.

I wait outside while Gavan does the asking, returning after a few minutes with a grave expression. He shakes his head. "She's not seen him. She asked about you, though."

"She did?" I say, surprised, and he nods grimly.

"Said she saw you with my father. Told me to check on you. I said you were safe."

"But no Ren?" I say.

"No Ren. She hasn't seen him at all today." He looks at me

thoughtfully. "Ren was going straight to her to deliver the letters, wasn't he? Odd that he never arrived."

I shiver. That means he never made it down the mountain. Both of us turn to look at the black mass above us. It'll be dark before we reach the loch.

"We should check my cottage," I say at last. "We have to go up the mountain anyway to get to the cages. If you still want to catch one."

His jaw sets. "I still want to catch one. The one you saw was blind, you say?"

"I think so," I say cautiously. "It seemed like it."

"Then we move slowly and quietly. And we pray."

The moon is still almost full, waning by a hair, and the sky is clear, so the path is lit well. Above us, an uncountable number of stars litter the sky, making me dizzy when I look up for a moment. We move slowly, each step taken with the greatest of care, mindful of any loose stones that might make a sound or any twig that might snap underfoot. My right hand hovers beside the pocket with the pistol in it. I have six shots, if we need them.

I repeat that in my mind the whole way, a litany of reassurance: *I have six shots.*

We make it to the loch path, the last stretch before the cottage, and my nerves tighten again as I recall the night before. Once more, the world is cast in silver and black, but tonight there's no charm in it. Now the shadows are hiding places for unnatural things, the cold moonlight reminiscent of the creature's bloodless skin.

My head swivels like an owl's, looking to the scrub on our left, the loch on our right. Ahead of us, I can just make out the shape of the cottage; behind us, the path remains mercifully clear. We see nothing, hear nothing other than the water, but I can't help feeling that eyes are on us.

Hunting us.

As we approach the cottage, the hairs on my arms and at the back of my neck rise. I hear Gavan's breath hitch. Without saying a word, we move back-to-back, turning in a circle so we can see all around us.

Out in the loch, something screams.

I grab Gavan's hand, and we race for the cottage door, clearing the ground in a matter of strides. The door isn't locked, and I pull him inside, slamming it behind us.

I go to throw the lock, but barely a split second later, something hurls itself hard against the door, knocking it open.

Pale fingers curl around the edge. Gavan throws his weight against the door, too, and they withdraw, another screech rending the night.

I manage to throw the lock, and we both back away, horrified, as the thick wood trembles under the attack. If Gavan didn't believe me before, he does now.

Suddenly, the banging stops, leaving the hall ringing with silence. I'm grateful now that my father locked all the shutters.

Then I remember the washroom with its broken window.

I pull my bag off my shoulder and draw the pistol, not caring if Gavan sees it, racing to the back of the cottage, finger on the trigger.

When I open the door, heart pounding, I find the window has been boarded up. Ren must have done it.

"Oh, Ren," I say aloud.

And in the darkness, a voice answers. "Alva?"

SIXTEEN

I whirl on the spot to find Murren Ross, dressed only from the waist down, coming from my bedroom. His hair looks rumpled, as though he has been asleep.

I don't think. I throw myself at him, flinging my arms around his neck and pressing into him with all my strength. His chest is warm under my cheek; I can feel his heartbeat. Then his arms come around me, slipping under my *earasaid*, holding me just as firmly. He's alive. I'm giddy with relief, squeezing him until he makes an undignified squeak, then laughs into my hair.

"You're here," he says, voice muffled. "Why didn't you go?"

"Long story," I tell his rib cage. "I'm going tomorrow. You've got one more night with me yet."

His arms tighten around me, and I feel his mouth graze the top of my head. My stomach flips over.

"Hi, Ren," Gavan says. Ren and I release each other immediately, both of us taking a step back. "Glad to see you hale and hearty. We were worried."

"Gavan?" Ren looks between the two of us. "What's going on?"

Suddenly, my relief at his being alive is obliterated by fury that he didn't do what he'd promised. "I don't know," I blaze at him, causing him to take another step back. "What *is* going on? What happened to finding Maggie Wilson and telling her about the creatures?"

"I . . ." He stares at his feet. "I wanted to be sure."

Fury builds in my chest. "I see. You never believed me, did you?"

"No, that's not—"

A barrage of crashes and screams from outside my bedroom cuts him off, and I yank him behind me, raising the gun and aiming it.

"Do you believe me now?" I hiss over my shoulder, gun trained on the door.

We hear the unmistakable sound of nails tearing at wood as the creatures try to rip the shutters from the window. But my father never let anything get old or broken. When you live by water, you learn to take care of your home. Any warped or split timber was replaced the moment he saw it, the hinges and locks oiled every few months. Unlike Ren's house. If the creatures got that far, a single push of the door would probably shatter it. They could blow his house down.

I remain focused on the window, the gun steady in my hands.

Finally, the noise stops. We all wait, listening to the night, long minutes passing until we're sure it's gone. I let out a shaky breath, rubbing my eyes with my left hand.

When I turn back to Ren, his eyes are on the gun, his lips parted. I shove it into my pocket.

"Trapping one will be interesting," Gavan says quietly.

Ren looks sharply at Gavan. "You want to trap one?"

Gavan nods. "To show the village what really killed Aileen. And what we're up against. Proof."

"I thought the same thing," Ren says. "That's the reason I stayed." He turns to me. "I knew you had cages in the sheds, so I went and set one up. I didn't think the book and your word—our word—would be enough. So yes, I wanted to see for myself if they were real." He lifts his chin, defiant. "But I also wanted proof so that I could convince the others."

I relent slightly. Only slightly. "I suppose that makes sense."

"Did you bait it?" Gavan asks.

Ren nods. "I used one of your chickens," he says to me. "Hope that's all right. For the cause. And I found a few eggs, so I brought them in, too." He gives me what he clearly thinks is a winning smile.

"Put a shirt on," I say. I pick up my bag and take it into

my room, ignoring my bed, which has obviously been very recently vacated, a dent in the pillow where a head was resting, the covers thrown back.

When Ren follows to find the rest of his clothes, I leave and go to the kitchen. The fire in the stove is almost out, so I spend a few minutes feeding it, stirring the embers until the flames take hold. Then I head to my father's study and fetch the *Naomhfhuil* log. When I return to the kitchen, Gavan is sitting at the table, looking around the room with the same interest as Ren this morning. I place the book in front of him.

"There are pictures of them in here," I say. "So you can see what we're up against."

Gavan opens the book, and I begin to make tea. Ren comes and leans against the stove next to me.

"Why didn't you leave?" he asks quietly.

"Something came up," I reply, shooting a warning glance over my shoulder at Gavan.

Ren raises his brows, and I stare him down.

"But what about . . . ?" he asks.

He means my job. My new life. "It's sorted. I'm off in the morning. Gavan has arranged loan of a donkey to take me down to Balinkeld. I'll still make the coach."

"Good," he says, turning away, but not before I catch the relief on his face. It stings to know he's eager for me to be gone.

Behind us, Gavan slams the book shut, and we both turn. "So," he says, looking pale. "I guess I know what we're up against. When do we think we might catch something?"

"The attacks on the horses and Aileen happened at night. Alva saw her one after dark, too," Ren says. "And I didn't see anything up here all day. My guess would be that they're nocturnal. We'll check the trap at dawn, when it's safer."

We all look at the clock on my mantel. Dawn is hours away.

"In that case, I'm going to rest while I can," I say. I place a mug in front of each of them and carry mine out, picking up a candle on the way. It makes me feel strange to think of Ren in my bed, so I bypass my room, going instead to my mother's parlor, taking my tea and curling up on the sofa. After a few moments, the boys pad through with their mugs, Gavan sitting on the sofa opposite me, Ren on the floor between us.

"I remember your mam," Gavan says, looking around at the pretty room. "I liked her. Not as much as my father did, mind." He instantly looks horrified, clapping a hand over his mouth. "I mean . . . it's not a secret. Is it?"

For a moment, I stare at Gavan, and then I burst out laughing. He joins in, leaving Ren looking back and forth between us, utterly bewildered.

After that we fall silent, the candle burning down while we wait the night out. We doze sometimes, jerking back to wakefulness when we hear the unearthly shrieks of the creatures, though they sound mercifully far from the cottage.

Just after the clock in the kitchen has gently chimed four in the morning, a volley of shrieks from nearby sends me scrambling to my feet, the gun raised, Ren and Gavan flanking me.

The creatures are at the cottage in seconds, banging on every window, screaming, attacking the front door over and over. I hear a clang: metal hitting the stone stoop. Then the cries move, coming from outside the parlor window, followed by the frantic sound of bodies crashing into the outer shutters so hard the inner ones shake. They know exactly where we are. Wide-eyed, I turn to the boys to see their faces stark and pale. Gavan presses fingers to his ears, and I do the same, the gun dangling loosely from my thumb as I keep my gaze on the shutters, praying they'll hold.

The whole thing lasts around a minute. Then it stops, and the night is as silent as before. I take my fingers from my ears and listen. Nothing.

"What the hell was that?" Gavan sounds as shaken as I feel, and I lower myself back to the seat, my legs turned to jelly.

Ren remains standing. His eyes are gleaming. "I think that was retaliation. I think it means we got one."

"Should we look?" Gavan asks.

I shake my head. "No. Ren's right. Let's wait for the sun to come up."

There's no chance any of us will sleep now, so we take the candles back to the kitchen, and I start pulling out food, preparing to cook. While Gavan leans over the *Naomhfhuil* book once more, Ren gently jostles me aside, taking the bacon and eggs from my hands.

I stand back and watch in silence as he cooks, heating a skillet and adding butter before laying the rashers in the spitting fat. He takes a handful of chives growing on the windowsill and tears them up, sprinkling them over the bacon, then cracks the eggs in alongside, their yolks cheery and wholesome. It smells amazing: smoky from the bacon, sharp from the chives. My mouth starts to water.

"Butter some bread," he tells me, and I find the last of the loaf I made, a little stale now. I slice it, then toast it, spearing it and holding it to the flames inside the stove, working alongside Ren as he tends the eggs and bacon.

Out of nowhere, I remember his suggestion that we run away together to play at being husband and wife. I think of his arms around me, my cheek against his chest.

Hoping any blush can be put down to the heat of the stove, I sneak a glance at him. His hair is falling into his eyes again. *How does he see at all?* I think, stopping myself from reaching up to push it aside. His hands are sure as he moves the food around the pan, flipping the bacon and tilting fat up over the yolks.

"Plates?" he says, and I leave my toast resting on the lip of the door, dashing to fetch plates, returning in time to stop the bread from burning.

I balance the plates along the hob to warm them, putting a slice of toast on each and buttering it. While Ren adds bacon and eggs, I butter three more to make the toppers.

When Ren squashes his down, golden yolk oozes out from the sandwich, and he smiles: a pure, joyful smile.

He carries his and Gavan's to the table, and I take mine, nudging away the *Naomhfhuil* log so we are spared the images for a moment.

We chew in silence, the food fortifying us, taking away some of the horror of the night and giving us fuel for what's to come. I lick yolk from my fingers, coloring when I see Ren watching me, his usually pale eyes darker. We look away from each other at the same time.

When I carry our plates to the sink, I see a chink of gray light fighting its way through the gap in the shutters.

I look at the clock. Five thirty. "Dawn's coming," I say. "We need to decide how we're going to do this."

"You're the one with the gun," Ren says.

"Speaking of, do you have any others?" Gavan says.

"I have the flintlock," I say. "And now that we're here in

the cottage, I have bullets and gunpowder. Have either of you used a gun before?"

Both of them shake their heads.

"Then you're not having one."

"How do we defend ourselves?" Gavan asks.

"We stay behind Alva." Ren grins.

"Fine," I sigh. It is a fair point. "One of you can have the gun, after I show you how to use it. And there's an axe, wherever Ren left it. But also, yes—stay behind me."

In the end, Gavan takes the axe, and I give Ren the flintlock gun. I make him show me how to cock and fire, over and over, only loading it when I'm happy he knows what he's doing.

"You only get one bullet at a time," I remind him. "So don't fire too soon. And aim for the chest."

"Surely the head would be better?"

"Aye, if you knew how to shoot, it would. But we're going to have to proceed assuming you're not a crack shot. The chest is larger, so you've got a better chance of hitting it, and it'll slow it down, at least." I shiver.

"Do we even know if bullets can kill them?" Gavan asks.

"Of course they can," Ren says, but he doesn't sound sure, looking at me for an answer.

I hadn't even considered it.

"I don't know," I say slowly. What kind of creature can survive a serious gunshot? "I suppose we'll find out." I try to sound confident.

Neither boy looks convinced.

We stand at the front door, straining to hear beyond it. I wonder if the creatures are standing on the other side, doing the same thing.

"All right. Gavan, you open the door and let Ren and me deal with anything out there," I say. Gavan nods, and I turn to Ren. "Now, remember—you only get one shot, so make it count. On three," I tell Gavan, his hand ready on the latch, while Ren and I point our guns. "One. Two. Three."

Gavan opens the door, and Ren fires the gun.

The sound echoes into silence.

"Are you joking?" I speak at last through clenched teeth. "What did I tell you?"

"I panicked!"

I growl and move forward, my gun raised and ready. Beyond the door, the sky is pale lavender on the horizon, still deepest blue above. Once I reach the frame, I turn, looking around. There's no sign of the creatures, but the shadows are still too long for my liking. I want to be able to see more. Especially as Ren has just announced to them that we're here.

I step back and close the door.

"Are they out there?" Gavan asks, his knuckles white on the handle of the axe.

"I can't see anything, I think it's still too dark. Let's give it another ten minutes or so," I say, before adding, "We can reload the flintlock and give Ren another lecture about responsible gun use."

"I look forward to it," Ren says, gleeful malice in his eyes. "Who better to teach me?" And I remember pressing the mouth of that selfsame gun to his temple hard enough to leave a mark. Apparently, so does he.

My face burning, I snatch the flintlock from him, gritting my teeth when he laughs, and head to the study to reload the gun. Ren follows, laughing softly.

Ten minutes later, we leave the cottage once more. Ren grips the axe, and Gavan now holds the gun, having been thoroughly drilled in its use. Outside, those shadows have lessened, revealing nothing sinister in their wake.

As I step outside, I stub my toe on a blunt object and look down to see a silver horseshoe on the stoop. For a second, I'm confused. It's supposed to be above the door. Every house in the village has one to keep evil out—

Oh . . . I wonder then if the evil in question is the gods— monsters—whatever they are.

Well, it seems to have worked so far, so who am I to argue

with it? I pick it up and fling it inside the house, making a note to put it back up when we return, locking the door behind me.

Dawn is coming in fast, but we move faster, with Ren on my left, watching the scrub, and Gavan to my right, his eyes on the loch. There's a fine mist draped over it, like a lacy shawl, but it stays on the water, so we see the sheds clearly as we get closer.

And as the sun breaks over the mountaintop, bathing us in light the same golden yellow as the yolks we ate earlier, we see the hunched white thing caught in the cage.

"We did it," Ren breathes. "We got one."

"Keep looking around," I remind him. "For all we know, its friends are still nearby."

But I don't heed my own words. I can't take my eyes off it.

My heart soars with triumph. I realize I never thought Ren's plan would work. That these things were too clever, too *unreal* to be caught in anything so mundane as a cage. And yet there one is, caged.

As we get closer, I can see more. The explosion of chicken feathers that means the bait did its job, poor wee thing. Then there's the creature itself. It's on its knees, hunched over, arms hooked over its head as if it's shielding itself from us. If this is the same creature I saw that night, then it looks grayer in the sunlight than it did in the moonlight, its skin cracked and papery. It doesn't move, even as we walk right up to the cage.

"Is it sleeping?" Gavan asks in a whisper.

A strange feeling comes over me. My skin begins to crawl. Something's wrong. Very, very wrong.

"No," Ren says, and his voice is grim. "It's not sleeping."

Then he steps forward, poking the handle of the axe through the bars, driving it into the creature's side.

SEVENTEEN

"Ren!" Gavan cries as the axe makes contact.

And the thing disintegrates.

I watch with horrified fascination as it collapses in on itself. Within a matter of seconds, it's a pile of dust on the ground, a few particles drifting in the air before settling on the mound of gray ash that used to be the creature.

"To think we've been scared of them," Gavan says, relief in his voice. "They're weak as anything."

"No," Ren says bluntly. "Look at it, it's ash. It's like it . . . burned up." He looks up thoughtfully, shielding his eyes as he finds the sun, and I follow his gaze, then look back at what remains.

He's right. It's like when a log in the stove burns from

the inside out. It looks whole until you try to move it with a poker. Then it crumbles. Exactly like the creature did.

I look again toward the sun, squinting. So far, all the attacks or sightings have happened at night. There's been no sign of them in the day. And now this.

"They're not just nocturnal. The sun destroys them," I murmur. "It must do."

This makes everything harder. If we had one, we would have something real to show the village. But even Ren—who knows me better than anyone—didn't believe me until last night. No one else is likely to.

"Come on," Ren says. "We'd better get down to Ormscaula."

"What's the point?" I say bitterly. "Let's face it; no one is going to believe us. Not without proof."

"Never mind that. Gavan and I will get proof." He looks at the other boy, who nods in agreement. "You have a donkey to collect, don't you? This is your chance, Alva. The creatures aren't your problem."

But I think they *are* my problem, because they come from the loch my family is supposed to tend, and they're documented in my family's secret books. They're the *Naomhfhuil*'s problem. My father neglected to do anything about them. I don't want to do the same. I don't want any more deaths on my conscience.

I make a split-second decision. "The stagecoach goes every week." I shrug. "I'll go next week. My employers will understand."

"You're a fool," Ren says. There is anger in his voice.

"Why do you care?" I ask, bewildered.

"Because I'm a fool, too," he says. "That's why." Then he is walking down toward the shore, leaving Gavan and me staring after him.

"It'll be fine," I say, though it sounds more like a question. My job will wait, I tell myself. They'll give me a week to make an appearance. They have to. And if not, then I have money, enough to get by till I find something else.

I want to see this through, I realize. I want to catch one, and I want to be here when we tell the village what it is. I want to know the truth. I want them to know it.

I want them to see I'm not like my father.

"We'll try again tonight," I say, iron in my voice. "We'll lure it indoors so that it's under cover when morning comes. Then we'll bring the villagers to it."

"Where can we set the trap?" Gavan asks.

I think for a minute. "At the cottage." I square my shoulders. "I'll get the cart."

"I just want to say again that I think this is a really stupid idea."

Ren's arms are crossed as he watches Gavan and me carry the cage into the hallway of my cottage. Grayish powder still sits in the bottom. He stood and watched as we lifted it onto the cart at the sheds, avoiding the remains of the creature as they sifted through the bars to the ground. He wouldn't take a turn pulling the cart either, his expression dark and brooding as he followed us back.

"Thank you again for your thoughts," I grunt as we lower it to the floor. "Your actual help wouldn't go amiss."

Ren stays where he is as Gavan and I turn the cage so the entrance faces the cottage's front door. It leaves deep welts in the wood as we drag it around, but that doesn't matter now.

"That should do it." I straighten and rub my hands.

"I still don't see why we couldn't set it up inside one of the sheds," Ren says.

"Because they'll be wary of anything near the sheds now. Animals learn to avoid places that are dangerous to them."

"Are they animals, though?" Gavan asks.

"They're not people," I say.

"Still, it's surprising that one went into the cage at all," Gavan says. "Surely it could see what it was?"

"Not if it was the blind one," I say, thinking aloud. "Remember, the one I saw was blind. Maybe it heard and smelled the chicken but couldn't see the cage. Could be that others are blind, too," I add. We can only hope.

"What are we going to bait it with tonight?" Gavan asks while Ren glowers.

Good question.

My goat is dead. The nanny we've had for as long as I can remember is lying on the floor of her shed, her throat torn out. The chickens are dead, too, their own necks a bloody mess. The coop is a riot of blood, gore, and feathers.

"Jesus," Ren says, resting a hand on my shoulder, his annoyance at me forgotten in the face of the massacre before us. "This is savage. They didn't even eat them. Just . . . slaughtered them. Poor things."

Gavan turns and walks back to the cottage in silence.

Hattie. He's thinking about Hattie, and wondering if she's dead, and whether it was like this. I hope not. I hope if she is dead, then it was faster and cleaner. I hope she isn't dead at all.

"Let's burn them," Ren says swiftly.

We make short work of it, me building a bonfire from the pile of wood at the back of the cottage while Ren gathers up the corpses. I go into the cottage for matches and pause by the study door, now closed. Gavan must be in there. I raise my hand, poised to knock, but in the end I take the closed door at face value and return outside.

"How's Gavan?" Ren asks, lowering his voice.

"I think he wants to be left alone." I bend low and strike a match, holding it to the kindling. "I don't blame him."

We watch the fire take hold, the pops and crackles making me think of the *feis samhaid*. A lifetime ago, as Gavan said. When the blaze has reached its zenith, Ren throws the chickens on. It takes both of us to carry the goat, and we haul it on, too.

The air is filled with the smell of roasting meat, and I feel sick when my mouth waters.

"Come on," Ren says, covering his nose and mouth. "Let's go for a walk."

I nod. I could do with fresh air, and the creatures surely won't be out now, in full sunlight. Even so, I make sure the gun is in my pocket.

We leave the fire behind and head toward the loch, turning right and following the bank. Ren's limp is more pronounced than usual, as if the lack of rest is wearing on him. I don't mention it, though I do slow my pace. He matches me, a brief smile claiming his lips.

"So, you *are* still going, then?" Ren asks as we approach the path down the mountain. "Still leaving?"

"Of course. Haven't I been planning this for years? I just need to see this through first."

"Good."

"Anyone would think you wanted me gone," I say, kicking a stone.

He snaps at me. "I don't *want* you gone."

Bewildered, I stare at his profile. "Then why are you angry? Christ, Ren, I'm not a mind reader."

"Because you're not safe here."

"Tell me about it."

"No." He stops, and I stop, too, turning to face him as he continues. "Not just because of the monsters. Because you kept your father's secret all those years ago. Like Giles said, you were complicit. What if a judge decides you should be punished, too? Or what if the villagers don't want to wait for a judge to decide? What if they do it first? For your mam, and now for what's happened to Aileen and Hattie. Frightened people do stupid things, Alva. They don't listen to reason."

My blood chills at his words. I never planned to stick around to see what happened when the villagers discovered my father's guilt. I haven't thought about what would happen after, because why would it matter when I was miles away? But Ren's right—I'm not miles away. I'm right here, and in the middle of another crisis my father covered up. Perhaps I will end up in court beside my father, begging for my life, pleading that I didn't know any better as a judge pulls a black hood over his head and sentences my father to death for murder and me alongside him for lying and covering it up.

"I was so happy to see you last night," Ren says quietly. "And then so . . . angry. I thought you were safe, riding off into the sunset on the mail cart to your new life. But you're still here, and every single minute you are, you're in danger."

"Ren . . ." I don't know what else to say.

"If you end up dead because of this, I will never forgive you," he says, looking back at me. "I mean it."

For a moment, his eyes blaze bright, cold fire burning into me.

"Fine," I say in a shaky voice. "I promise not to die."

He scowls as though I've said something ridiculous, then reaches out, grabbing my hand and lacing his fingers through mine. He starts to walk back toward the cottage, tugging gently. "Come on."

I fall into step with him, mystified by the last few moments, wondering how they've culminated in Murren Ross and me holding hands.

I'm even more surprised to find that it's nice. Our hands fit.

"How did you end up keeping company with Gavan Stewart?" Ren asks, breaking the awkward silence that's fallen between us.

"I can tell you, but you're not going to like it," I warn him. "Seeing as my safety is so important to you."

He looks at me from the side of his eyes, unamused. "Go on."

I take a deep breath and begin, telling him everything that happened after I left him yesterday. The only part I omit is going to his home; something tells me it will shame him to know I was there.

And I was right—he doesn't like it *at all*. When I get to the bit where Giles Stewart told me to get changed at gunpoint, he tries to tear his hand from mine, and I know if I let go, he'll be straight down the mountain and shortly afterward in the cell next to my father on much the same charge. So I keep a firm grip on him.

"I dealt with it," I say. "It's over, and it won't happen again."

He pulls me around to meet his gaze, his other hand rising to cup my face, thumb tracing my cheekbone. I can't remember the last time someone looked at me so softly—treated me so softly. Like I'm precious. Not precious like china or glass, something cold and brittle to be wrapped up and kept away from harm, never taken out in case it gets damaged. But precious like I'm necessary. Precious like I mean something.

And I know, with the certainty of someone who has spent the last seven years relying on her instincts to keep her alive, that he's going to kiss me. And I want him to. I want Murren Ross to kiss me, and I want to kiss him back.

A breeze blows my hair across my face, and Ren brushes it behind my ear, using the motion to move closer, his face lowering to mine.

Then he stops and looks behind me before stepping away.

I turn to see Gavan coming out of the cottage.

"There you are," Gavan says, seemingly oblivious to the moment he's interrupted.

"Here we are," Ren says. "We had to get away from the fire. The smell."

"Yes," Gavan says, nodding grimly. "Anyway, I've been thinking about what else we should use for bait."

"And?" I ask.

"Me," he says. "I'll be the bait."

Ren and I stare at him.

"What are you suggesting?" Ren asks. "That we put you in a cage, and then what? When it gets in with you, we shoot it?"

"That's plan B. Come and see plan A."

I exchange a glance with Ren, and we follow Gavan back inside, to my father's study.

Where it seems that instead of grieving, he's been working.

On the table is a drawing of a huge trap, easily big enough to fit Gavan and one of the creatures inside. Before Ren or I can say anything, Gavan speaks.

"What we need to do is create a double trap using a second cage. Lashed together, it looks like one long cage. See?" He points at his diagram and pauses to check that we're keeping up.

"But then you're stuck in there with that thing." Ren frowns.

"Not so fast. We'll actually remove the back of the second cage so it'll only *look* closed," Gavan says. "The creature will think I'm caught inside, but as soon as it gets in the first cage, the trapdoor will spring and close the front end. Then *I'll* trigger the trapdoor of the cage I'm in, it will fall down and become the back wall of the first cage, and the thing is captured. All you two have to do then is untie the back of the second cage, I'll get out, and we'll have it."

"And if we don't manage to trigger the door in time?" Ren says. "Those things move fast."

"Then Alva will shoot it. Plan B."

"Why don't we just shoot it in the first place?" I ask. "We don't need it to be alive to show the village what it is."

Ren shakes his head. "Firstly, we don't know that bullets will kill it, so let's not waste them. And secondly, even if they do, it might disintegrate like the other. We don't know for sure if that happened because of the sun, or because it died of shock, or something else. We need it trapped."

I think of how the first book in the hidden chest fell apart when I touched it, too old to take even the slightest contact. We don't know how old these things are. Maybe Ren is right. Maybe they're so ancient that they fracture completely in death.

Even so, this plan is madness incarnate.

"You can't think this"—I point at Gavan's drawing—"is a good idea. I mean, it *is* a good idea," I say hurriedly when Gavan looks hurt. "But it's too risky."

"I think it could work," Ren says thoughtfully. "So long as Gavan can trigger the second door in time. We need something they can't resist. If they liked human sacrifices way back when, then this might be it. And after last night, they'll want vengeance. That might override their survival instincts."

"So when I say let's bring a cage to the cottage, it's a stupid plan, but when a boy says he'll get in the cage and be bait, it's suddenly fine?"

"You know that's not what I mean."

He's right. I do. I just don't like it.

I scowl at him as he continues. "It needs to be more secure, though. Alva has a point." His eyes turn skyward as he thinks. "We'll need to make sure none of the others can get inside the cottage. We'll cut a hole in the door and bolt the cage to it. The creature will be in the cage, any others will be locked out, and it won't be able to get to us."

Gavan nods. "And so the sun doesn't get to it, we'll cover the front trapdoor with a piece of wood. Right, who wants to come with me to get the second cage?"

The rest of the day passes swiftly, thanks to the amount of work we have to do. By the time Gavan and I get back to the cottage, Ren has almost finished making the hole in the door, ready to bolt the cage to it. I take over for him, and he helps Gavan saw the backs of the cages off.

The first problem we encounter is how to tie the two cages together. It doesn't matter if we use twine for the back of the second, because we need it to be easy to get Gavan out. But when we try using twine to lash the cages together, it soon becomes clear it won't be strong enough to hold.

I can't help the creeping doubt that this isn't going to work.

"Chains!" Gavan says, dropping the rope he's been twisting in his hands. "Jim Ballantyne has chains for dragging the logs to the mill. I'll ask him to lend me some. Ren, you'll have to come and help me. They're heavy, so we'll need the cart."

Ren gives me a questioning look, and I nod.

"Go on. I'll finish here and then think about dinner."

"How domestic." Ren grins dangerously. "I'll look forward to coming back to a home-cooked meal."

"I said I'd think about it, not that I'd make it," I say, moving aside so they can pass. "You'll be lucky if I serve you bread and butter."

"Aye, I would," Ren says. He follows Gavan out, ducking under the barricaded part of the door, still beaming to himself, as I shake my head. As soon as he's out of sight, I smile, too.

I cobble together a stew using the last of the vegetables from the pantry, leaving it low on the heat while I have a quick wash and put on clean clothes. I think about refitting the silver horseshoe above the door before I remember we *want* one of the creatures to cross the threshold. I don't know if the horseshoe thing works, but now isn't the time to find out. I leave it on my nightstand when I go to my room, intending to take a nap so I'll be fresh for the night ahead— suddenly the thought of sleeping where Ren slept isn't quite so strange. But instead, I find myself standing up and walking back to the study. I take out the last three books, laying them gently around me.

The creatures appear in all of them, drawings and sketches spaced throughout, and as I stare at the writing between them, flicking back and forth, I see that some symbols recur over and over: the moon, horseshoes, certain flowers, scratches beside them making a tally.

A list. Or dates. Maybe when they came and how many were lost to them.

I fetch a fresh sheet of paper and try to work it out, starting with the most recent entries and working back. Slowly, I begin to make sense of it. The flowers are what's in season and blossoming; a thistle must mean June or July, which makes sense because they're hot months during which water levels naturally fall. The moon symbol is the moon phase: waxing, waning, full. This is when they came before. In the earlier books, little pictures of animals are drawn. Sacrifices, I guess—they must have tried animals first. Then come the later tallies, the human sacrifices. Sometimes there are as many as five before the entry stops.

I work out that over a period of three hundred years, the creatures came back once every twenty years or so. I put the books down, staring as I try to imagine living like that. Seeing the loch level start to drop and understanding what it meant. Praying and bargaining, hoping for rain. Knowing if there wasn't a miracle, people you knew would die. They might be chosen to die.

They must have just kept going, kept asking or begging for

volunteers, hoping it would be enough until enough rain fell to trap them again. We don't have time to wait for rain. And if it wasn't for Giles Stewart's greed, we wouldn't have to.

The boys take a long time returning, so long that the turnips I threw in the stew are almost edible, so long that I start to worry they won't come back at all. I sit on the stoop once more, a mug of tea in my hands, watching, relief like shade on a sunny day when I finally catch sight of them, one of Gavan's hands raised in a cheery wave, the other dragging the cart behind them. I put the mug down and go to help.

They're both breathless and sweaty, but Gavan is glowing with purpose, and Ren is full of grim determination, refusing when I try to take the cart handle from him, even though I can see his leg is hurting. They barely pause for water before they get back to the cages. And not a moment too soon, because over the loch, the sky has turned pink. We don't have long.

We lash the two cages together, winding the thick chains between them, the three of us pulling them tight before looping them again and again. This might actually work, I realize. A flicker of hope flares in my heart.

As the sky turns purple, we padlock the chain, the two cages now one, and then Ren bolts it to the door, hammering nails into the brackets they've brought back with them. With that it's done; the trap is set. All that remains is the bait.

"How long do you think we have?" Gavan asks.

"Not long," I say, looking at the sky.

"I'll eat in the cage."

"Gavan. You don't have to do this."

"I'll be fine. You'll be nearby with the guns. Leave a knife where I can reach it. That way, if it all goes wrong, I can cut my way out."

His faith is staggering. I hope we can live up to it. I hope I can.

Gavan crawls into the cage with remarkable cheer, and I tie the false back on, putting a knife nearby, as he asked. While I do, Ren dishes up the stew. The bowl won't fit between the bars, so Gavan has to have his in a mug, topped up over and over and passed through to him, as Ren and I sit on the hall floor, eating with him. The scrape of spoons against bowls and the soft ticking of the kitchen clock are the only sounds. All our attention is on the gaping hole before us, the door we've opened to let the monsters inside.

The night is still, no birds, no otters chirruping. No breeze to make the reeds rustle. Even the loch itself seems mute, the wash of waves absent.

We wait. We leave one candle burning, partly so we can see and partly to act as a beacon, drawing the creatures to us. We don't play cards, too scared even to talk in case we miss something outside. I keep the revolver in my lap, the flintlock loaded next to me. Ren has the axe once more. We hold our breath.

The first hour passes peacefully. There's no sign of the creatures or anything else, and Ren goes to make tea, though Gavan refuses it on account of spending the next ten or so hours in a cage. He is already starting to fidget, shifting his weight, stretching out his legs, then drawing them up. There's no room to stand or move around. It's too long to stay in there, I think.

"We should take turns," I say, crossing to the back of the cage and pulling at the knot.

Gavan twists. "What are you doing?"

"You can't stay in there all night; look at you." I nod to where he's rubbing the back of his calf. "We'll take turns. I'll sit in for an hour or so, then Ren can switch with me."

"I'm fine."

"You're clearly not. Stop being a hero."

He looks as though he might protest, but I see the relief in his eyes at the idea of being allowed out.

"Fine," he says with a sigh that doesn't fool me at all. "We need to move fast. Ready?"

I release the back and wait for him to crawl out before slipping into his place. I leave the flintlock gun outside but keep mine with me, clutching it like a talisman.

"Wait." Ren comes back, tea in hand, as Gavan makes to refit the rear, then returns to the kitchen. He reappears with a cushion, tossing it to me, and I shove it gratefully beneath me as they tie the back of the cage on.

My heart climbs up my chest, lodging itself in my throat as I face the open end of the cage.

The hole before me is a yawn, stretching out into the night, and I shiver.

"Here." Ren holds out my mug of tea between the bars.

No sooner do I think of reaching for it than a white shape appears in the dark, and from behind the cottage, something screams, high and sharp. It sounds like the word *no*.

EIGHTEEN

"They're here," I whisper as my heart starts to thump painfully, my stomach clenching with fear.

Ren sucks in a sharp breath, reaching for his axe, as Gavan picks up the flintlock gun. My own fingers tighten on my gun and the spring for the inner trapdoor.

The urge to trigger the door and shut it now is overwhelming, but I grit my teeth, fighting it.

I can't take my eyes off the hand that's wrapping around the doorframe, and I brace myself to come face-to-face with one of them again, breathing in shallow pants as I try to prepare for it.

I'm still not ready when it finally looms into view, crouching just beyond the entrance to the cage.

Like the one I saw outside the cottage, it's hairless and

naked, but where the other was wasted, this one is muscular. Still hungry-thin, but its thighs are taut and strong beneath that coarse-looking skin. It squats, feet splayed like a spider, upper body bent low as it looks in at me.

This one isn't blind. It sees me.

Its eyes are black: no irises, nothing but drowning pools that fix me in place as surely as if it had nailed me down. Its head tilts as it watches me.

Whatever these things are, they've been here for so long. Eternity rolls off it in waves, endless and fathomless; I feel so small, an ant beneath its foot. I am prey. Nothing more than prey. I am the rabbit in the snare; I'm the ptarmigan in a field with a gun trained upon it. I'm weak.

It smiles at me.

No. Not a smile.

Its thin lips curve and part, and I get a firsthand view of how those long canines fit inside.

I would give anything not to know.

Its mouth keeps opening, its jaw unhinging as its fangs descend like those of a snake. They're longer than my little finger, wickedly curved. Behind them, the back row of teeth waits to tear.

My fingers tighten on the trapdoor as Ren breathes, "Alva," his voice shaking.

The thing stops moving and looks up at the top of the trap, where the door waits to fall.

Then it closes its mouth and makes a clicking sound.

And another one appears.

I know instantly that this one is either older or more important; it's something in the way the first ducks its head and almost croons at it, deferring. The creatures click softly to each other, and Ren whispers my name again.

"Get out," he spits through clenched teeth. "Something's wrong."

But this is our chance.

"I'm fine," I say in a normal voice. The volume is jarring, but I'd hoped it would be. Immediately, the creatures stop communicating with each other and look at me, their attention drawn by the sound of my voice. The younger one bares its teeth at me again, then turns to its elder.

They both watch me for a moment, then look back at the cage door, their heads moving synchronously on too-long necks as they peer at it. The older one makes a sound, and the other one responds. Then, to my surprise, the older one sits on its haunches, and the younger one copies it, both watching me passively.

"They know what it is," I say. "They know it's a trap. They won't come in."

"Fine. Then get out," Ren says, his voice tense.

Without taking my eyes from the creatures, I reach slowly behind me.

The moment I move, they leap back; it happens so fast I

don't see them do it, only their pale bodies glowing in the dark, suddenly a few feet away, chattering urgently to each other. I was right. They know what we're doing. They know what happened to their friend, and they fear it.

Which means that if we want to catch them, we have to make them forget their fear. Override their instincts.

My fingers close around the knife, and I pull it into the cage.

"Don't you dare. Alva, don't you dare."

"Gavan, stop him," I shout as Ren starts pulling at the twine on the back door, trying to get to me before I can see my idea through.

When Gavan obeys, pulling Ren back, I hitch my skirts up, right hand still ready to spring the door, press the knife to the graze on my knee, and scrape the blade over it.

Crimson beads of blood well in the wound; only a few drops, but they're enough.

The scent of salt and metal and *life* rises, catching on the air.

I don't see it move, but it does. The younger creature screams and throws itself into the cage, triggering the door, which slams down behind it.

And I spring the second door as Ren wrenches the back off the trap.

His hands come under my arms, and he pulls me out, both of us skidding over the wood, his arms around me, my gun flying out of my hand and across the hall, landing by my bedroom door.

The captured creature shrieks with rage, launching itself against the bars of the cage, and we all watch in horrified fascination as it flings itself from side to side, battering the sides of its prison, frantic and furious as it realizes it's trapped.

"We got it," Ren says in my ear, pulling me to my feet. "We did it!"

Gavan's plan has worked.

All three of us end up in a tangle of a hug, my heart still ricocheting off my ribs, my body limp now the danger has passed, adrenaline and victory making us giddy, as all the while the creature hisses and shrieks behind us, railing against the jail we've locked it in.

My ears are so full of Gavan's laughter and Ren telling me I'm a lucky, lucky fool that the first moment we notice something is wrong is when the sound of metal against metal punctures our bubble.

As one, we turn in time to see the second creature lifting up the trapdoor at the front of the cage, its long fingers wrapping around the handle at the top and turning it before pulling it up, the way no lugh or wolf ever could.

And the one trapped inside the cage reaches up and copies it, opening the back of the cage.

"Go!" Ren screams, hurling me into the kitchen, slamming the door behind us, bracing against it.

"Gavan? Ren, Gavan's still in there!" I force him aside. "We have to help him! Where's the gun?"

"I don't know. Alva, no!" I throw myself at the door and open it as Ren tries frantically to stop me, his fingers scrabbling at my skirts.

One of the creatures is bent over Gavan, fangs elongated, desperately trying to bury its face in his neck as he attempts to push it away.

There's blood beneath him. He's already bitten.

I let out a horrified sob, and his eyes find mine as he mouths my name. I dive to where the flintlock gun is lying against the wall, rolling over and firing at the creature. I miss the head, the bullet burying itself in its chest, where its heart should be.

But it doesn't die.

It rears back from Gavan, screaming. It falls to the ground, clawing at the wound, as Gavan reaches out to me.

And the second creature comes from nowhere.

The last thing I know are its teeth as it bears down on me, slamming me back into the wall, where my head cracks with a sickening thud. I drop the gun and hear Ren screaming my name.

Then everything is black, and I know nothing.

NINETEEN

When I wake, it's dark, I'm lying facedown, and someone is crying nearby.

I try to sit up, and a sharp, searing pain flares inside my skull. Tentatively, I touch the back of my head. My hand comes away sticky. Slowly, carefully, I shift onto my side, breathing heavily as another burst of agony blooms behind my eyes. I hold myself still while I take inventory of the rest of my body, relieved when, aside from the pain in my skull and the graze I reopened on my knee, I find I'm whole.

And alive. Unless this is hell, this claustrophobic, oddly warm place, where every breath tastes of metal and dust. My eyes are open, and yet I can see nothing, the darkness is so total.

No, I'm not in hell, I realize. I'm in the creatures' den. Where else could I be that smells musty and feels so gritty and dense beneath me? I must be in the caves out on the loch. I strain my ears, hoping to hear water, but it's silent, other than that muffled crying.

Why am I not dead? Why have they brought me here? And who else is here with me?

I force myself to sit up, battling another surge of sickness. "Ren?" I whisper. "Gavan?"

"Alva?" a female voice asks softly.

"Yes. Hattie? Hattie, is that you?" Hope rises.

She's silent for so long, I start to wonder if I've imagined her. Then, on a breath: "No. It's Cora. Cora Reid."

"What?" Cora Reid has not been missing, as far as I know. "What are you doing here?"

Again, she's quiet for the longest time. "I was with James earlier. We heard Gavan and Murren Ross asking to borrow his father's chains, and we got suspicious. So we followed them back up the mountain to your cottage. We hid in your henhouse, waiting to see what you were all doing. The next thing I knew . . ."

"They came," I finish for her. I remember that scream—No!—just before the creatures attacked. It must have been her. "Did they take James? Is he here, too? Is he all right?"

She starts to cry again, harder, a sad, definite answer to my question. He's dead, then.

I shuffle toward the sound, bumping against her a few seconds later. I reach out with my right hand and pat her awkwardly. "I'm sorry," I say quietly.

"What are they?" Cora's voice shakes. "Their mouths . . . their bodies . . ." She swallows. "Is that what killed Aileen? Did they get Hattie? What about us?"

I hear the climbing panic in her voice, how her breathing sharpens into gasps.

"We're going to be all right," I say firmly, rubbing her arm more vigorously. "We're going to get out. Just leave it to me, Cora. OK? We're going to be fine."

"How?" she says, sounding more like herself. "What can you possibly do against them?"

I find her scorn comforting. There might be monsters in the world, and we might be in their lair, but Cora Reid still thinks I'm worthless. The whole world hasn't turned completely upside down.

"I'm going to get us out of here," I say with more certainty than I feel. "We need to figure out exactly where we are. Were you awake when they brought you in?"

"No, I fainted. I woke up in here. Did you see anything?"

"No. I passed out, too. I hit my head."

"Where are Gavan and Murren?" she asks.

I can't think about Gavan, a hard lump forming in my throat when I remember the desperation in his eyes as he reached for me. But Ren might have made it. If he stayed in the kitchen and managed to keep them out, he'll be alive. He'll be able to alert the village and tell them what's happened.

Or he might be dead, like James.

I swallow, fighting to stay calm. "I don't know."

"What if the monsters come back?" Cora asks.

"We'll be long gone," I lie. Both of us panicking is the last thing we need. "Come on," I say brusquely. "Let's see if we can find a way out. Give me your hand so I don't lose you."

Cora slips a slim hand in my left, and I stand again, reaching out with my right, feeling blindly. What I need to do is find a wall. If we follow a wall, eventually we'll find a door or an opening. And then we can follow that, and so on, until we get out. *Easy*, I tell myself, pushing down the bubble of fear that threatens to burst and drown me. One step after another.

I move slowly, hand stretched out before me. I can't make anything out, the black so perfect and penetrating I can't imagine ever seeing again. I thought the darkest it could ever get was blowing out my candle on a moonless night, but this is true darkness.

After a few paces, my foot nudges something that gives, and I bend, groping for it. My fingers press against something cold and waxy, and I frown into the darkness, feeling around . . .

I snatch my hand back with a muffled yelp, staggering into Cora.

"What is it?" she asks, gripping my hand.

I fight to steady myself, pushing down the surge of horror

that threatens to overwhelm me. "It's nothing," I say. "I just gave myself a fright."

"Good." She says it too fast. But for once, Cora doesn't question me, and I'm grateful.

"When you woke up, was anyone else here?" I ask her, trying to keep my whisper as casual as I can.

"I don't think so. I didn't hear anyone—I called out, but there was no reply."

"Was anyone brought in after you?"

"I heard a thud, like something had been thrown in. It must have been you. Unless there's someone else here. *Is* there someone else here?"

I ignore her.

Though it's dark, I close my eyes. I have to know. I have to know if the body I just felt is Ren or Gavan.

"I'm going to let go of your hand for a minute," I say. "I need to check something."

"What if you can't find me again?" Cora says.

"I will. I promise I will. Just stay still."

I shuffle forward until my toes find the body again. Then I bend slowly and reach out. Swallowing my revulsion and gritting my teeth, I feel for the shoulder and follow it to the neck, trying not to gag at the feeling of the cold, unyielding skin beneath my hands. I force myself to breathe slowly and concentrate on that.

My fingers meet hair, long and soft, and in my mind I see

it: red, curling around a finger as its owner gazes at Gavan Stewart.

Poor Hattie.

There's no point in telling Cora I've found her missing best friend; I need her to stay calm. I reach back and take her hand again. "Come on," I say.

There's a reason they've kept us alive. I just don't want to think about what it is. I edge past the corpse, keeping Cora behind me. Then we creep on in the dark, taking tiny steps forward, ducking and straightening as the ceiling lowers or allows us more room. When my fingers finally connect with rock, I could cry.

"Cora, I've found a wall."

"Congratulations. But we need a door," she snaps.

I take a deep breath, counting to five. "So we do. And now we have a wall, we can use that to find one."

She gives a soft snort, and I bite back a curse and begin to move again, right hand in constant contact with the wall, occasionally dislodging small stones that fall to the ground and make us both freeze at how loud it sounds in the dark. We walk, and walk, and walk, and yet there is no gap.

"How big is this place?" Cora asks, giving voice to my thoughts.

Without light, it's impossible to tell. It could be huge, or it could be tiny, and we're walking in circles; the careful steps we're taking are so small that I have no idea.

"Cora, do you have anything in your pockets? Like a knife?" I ask hopefully.

"I don't have a knife," she says wistfully. I hear the soft rustling of cloth as she checks her pockets. "A bit of paper and a pencil," she adds. "That's all."

"Can I have the pencil?"

She places it against the hand I'm holding. From there I take it, and measuring the height of the wall against my shoulder, I feel around, fingers tracing the rock, until I find a crack. I wedge the pencil in it, hoping it stays.

"Let's go," I say.

This time I count our steps, leaning against the wall instead of using my hand to feel it, listening for the sound of the pencil falling, praying that it doesn't.

One hundred and fifty-two steps later, my shoulder knocks the pencil from the wall, and it clatters to the ground with a hollow wooden rattle. And I have my answer.

"There is no door," I say.

"What?" Cora's voice is sharp with fear.

"I put your pencil in the wall, and I've just hit it again. Which means we've been walking around in a circle and not found a door."

She's quiet for a moment. "Maybe it's a wee one. Only big enough to crawl through."

"No," I say slowly. That doesn't make sense. She said she heard a thump when I was brought here. I was *dropped* in.

I look up, seeing nothing. I need to find the body—Hattie—again.

"What are you doing?" Cora asks as I move past her, stepping away from the wall and moving tentatively toward what I think is the center of the cave.

"Looking for—" I stop as my toes nudge Hattie's body. Closer than I'd thought. This place is small.

Then I reach up, finding only air above me. Fresh, moving air—I feel it against my fingertips. There is no ceiling here.

"We're in some kind of hole," I say. "It can't be that deep, because neither of us has a broken neck."

"How are we going to get out of a hole?" Cora asks, her voice high with fear.

"We're going to climb. But first I have to let go of you. I need both hands to feel. I need to find the edge."

"Alva . . . I . . ."

"We don't have time. You're going to have to trust me," I say, pulling my hand from hers.

I begin to feel above me, waving my hands back and forth, jumping a little. When I find what I think is an edge, I follow it around, until I can see it in my mind. The hole is about three feet across, in roughly the middle of the chamber. Wide enough to drop a prone body through, and far enough away from the sides to stop us easily climbing out. But not impossible . . .

"I think I've got it. You have a choice. Either you kneel

down and I climb on your back to see, or you climb on my back to see."

"I'm not kneeling for you." I can hear the scowl in her voice, and it gives me courage.

"Fine," I whisper breezily. "You climb up. And if you come face-to-face with one of the creatures, punch it in the mouth."

A pause. "I'll kneel."

She kneels, and I climb onto her back, then fall straight back down again. Balancing is hard enough normally, but without my eyes it's impossible.

I try again and again, ignoring her swearing and moaning, snapping at her to hold steady.

Until finally I'm slowly straightening, raising my arms out, then up. When I find the lip of the hole, I dig my fingers into the rock and start to pull myself up.

Only for Cora to wobble, and once again I fall.

"Maybe you should get on my shoulders?" she says, eager now.

"Let's try."

She crouches down, taking my hands to guide me, grunting when I slide a leg over her back, settling myself there, fingers knotted together, arms held out to help us balance.

Cora lifts herself slowly, and I feel the breeze on my face.

"Walk forward," I whisper, more scared now that my voice will carry and bring the creatures to us. "Slowly."

Cora is struggling under my weight; I can feel her

trembling, rocking me back and forth. I have to fight not to tighten my legs around her so I'm not unseated. Slowly, carefully, I shift my weight back, let go of her hands and put my own out in front of me.

When I feel the lip of the hole again, I move my hands over it, then my elbows. I haul myself up, unhooking my legs from around her.

The moment I try, I realize with terror that I don't have the strength to pull myself up.

"Help me!" I hiss, and she does, grabbing my legs and pushing them upward as I dig my fingers into the rock and drag myself out of the hole, scraping the skin on my arms as I do.

I roll onto my back, panting, my shoulders burning from the effort, my forearms stinging.

Moving onto my belly, I inch forward, finding the hole.

"Are you all right?" I call softly down to her.

"Yes. What's it like up there?"

I look around but can still see nothing.

"Dark. I can feel a breeze, though. That must mean a way out." I shuffle forward and reach down. "Grab my hands. I'll pull you up."

"No, you won't." Cora sounds strange. "You can't. You couldn't even pull yourself up. If you try to pull me up, you'll end up back down here."

"Cora, we can try—"

"And what? You land on me and break something, and

then we're both stuck? No, thanks. You need to get out and find help," she says firmly.

"I'm not leaving you."

"Then we'll both die. And so will everyone in Ormscaula, because they won't know what's happening."

"Cora—"

"Every second you're wasting here is a second closer to me dying in this pit," Cora spits at me. "Just go and get some proper help." Her voice is firm. "Please."

It's the last bit that gives her away. I hear how brave she's trying to be. For me. She's trying to be brave so I'll go. She'd never normally say please. Not to me. She's trusting me to get help and to come back.

"All right," I say, my heart heavy. "Just hang on."

"Aye, I'll wait here," she says, the faint tremor in her whisper the only sign that she's as petrified as I am. "Nowhere else to be."

I sit up, turning my back on the hole, facing the breeze. Then I look over my shoulder. I have to tell her about Hattie. I don't want Cora to stumble across her body.

"There's something you need to know . . ."

"I really don't," she says. "I don't plan to move a muscle until help gets here. So I don't need to know anything. You can tell me everything later."

My newfound respect for Cora grows.

"I promise I'll come back," I say. Then I get on my knees.

I move sideways until I find another wall, then begin to crawl forward. I stay on my knees, partly in the hope that the smaller I am, the less attention I'll draw, and partly because if I come across any more pits in the ground, I'm less likely to topple into one if my body weight is spread out. Still, I move slowly, testing every time I put a hand down.

It's so silent here. So still. And endless. I keep going and going, and the only thing giving me hope is the cool air, stronger on my face as I move. The fact that there's no sign of light isn't encouraging, but I put that thought aside, telling myself it might still be night. Instead, I concentrate on the breeze. I just have to follow that. That's all I need to do.

One hand in front of the other. Then a knee. Repeat.

Easy.

The wall comes to an end, and I stop. Bracing my foot against it, I stretch forward and feel around the edge, relieved when I find that the tunnel continues on my left, the breeze on my cheek reassuring me.

But when I do the same on the right, I find there's a passage that way, too, and the faintest whisper of air on my face. So which way do I go? Left or right?

The choice is made for me when I hear clicking echoing from the right. Calling and answering, heading toward me.

It's enough to send me to my feet, my heart thudding as sweat prickles across my back, the heat of panic spreading.

They're close.

Dread wraps me in its fist and squeezes. I stop thinking, stop breathing, stop being quiet and careful. Instead, I run.

I have enough sense to keep my hand on the wall, knowing I have one chance. One chance to get out of here and get help. I can't think about the darkness, or that I don't know where I'm going, or what might be ahead of me. I know what's behind me, and that's enough.

My feet pound the rock, and I slip and stumble, the dark so complete it makes my ears ring, but I manage to stay upright, one hand outstretched before me, the other on the wall, following it as I run, my breath too loud.

There's a bright, beautiful moment when I realize I can no longer hear the clicking sound, and I think I've left them behind.

Then one of them screams: a cry of pure rage and hunger that echoes through the caves, making my blood run cold. The bones in my legs turn to liquid, and I know with blinding certainty that I'm not going to make it.

I'm going to die down here.

TWENTY

Somehow, I keep moving, splashing through puddles I can't see, the water soaking into my skirts and making them heavier. Behind me, I hear stones skittering and the thuds of powerful feet gaining on me, more screams farther back as others join the hunt. There's a stitch under my ribs, my head is throbbing once more, and my shoulders still ache from pulling myself out of the pit. I'm too weak for this.

When the tunnel turns, it takes me a few seconds to realize it, and I almost miss it, veering sharply around.

And I see it. The most beautiful sight in the world.

The soft, safe light of dawn.

I pelt toward it, the shrieks of the things behind me desperate now. I stop feeling the wall and use my arms to drive myself forward, pumping them hard as my feet pound the earth.

As I get closer, there's another moment of sheer terror when I realize the tunnel is narrowing, closing in, but I keep going, throwing myself to the ground when the ceiling gets too low to run, crawling through the puddles left over from when the loch was high enough to flood these tunnels.

Then I have to get down on my belly, elbows digging into the rock for purchase as I wriggle toward freedom.

I'm almost there when something grabs my foot and pulls, dragging me back, but I kick out with the other, viciously glad when it connects and my ankle is freed. I lunge forward again, pulling at the rocks.

My head breaks the entrance, my shoulders following and then the rest of me tumbling out, as if the cave has birthed me.

When I land on the boggy ground, I don't even pause for a breath, pushing myself to my feet and turning.

I see a stark white arm scrabbling for me and watch as it starts to blacken and burn before vanishing back into the dark.

The sunlight. We were right. They can't bear the sun.

It can't get me.

With that, my legs give out, my body exhausted as the last of my adrenaline vanishes, leaving me a weak, shaking mess. But alive. Gloriously, miraculously alive.

I let myself lie there in the mud, the warmth of the sun on

my face, but only until my limbs stop trembling. Carefully, I push myself into a crouch, keeping back from the hole, and peer toward it. I think I catch light from a set of black, hateful eyes before they vanish.

I want to lie down in the dirt and sleep; I'm so tired the edges of my vision are blurry, and I sway from side to side with every step. But I can't. Cora is still down there, and I need to get help. So I walk.

I let my brain empty of everything, push all the terrible things I've seen and that I know to the back of my mind, locking them away. I think of nothing but putting each foot in front of me. I stop twice to bend to the loch, cupping water in my hands and drinking it, sluicing it over my head to try to soothe the headache, the coldness of it buying me a few moments of alertness. The sun climbs in the sky, drying the mud and blood on my skirts, making them stiffer. I take off the outer ones, discarding them, walking on in my underskirt and blouse.

When I reach the road that leads down the mountain, I pause. I want to go back to my cottage, but I don't think I have the mettle to face it. I don't think I'll survive seeing Gavan, throat torn out on my hall floor. And Ren . . .

I can't. I can't think of it. Even testing the thought of it is too much.

I turn toward the path down the mountain instead.

Once again, I'm grateful it's downhill, and I offer myself

up to momentum, allowing it to work with my body as I half jog, half stumble along the track. When I round the bend and look out over Ormscaula, I see the lanes are deserted, the square empty. For a moment, I'm filled with the frightening conviction that there's no one left alive down there. They've all gone, and I'll be alone in a ghost town, waiting for nightfall, when the creatures will come and finish me off.

My ears start to ring again, heat spreading through me, black spots dancing at the edges of my vision. I crouch and force my head between my knees, sucking air through my teeth, my fists clawing the ground, trying to beat the dizziness.

Once I'm sure it's passed, I look up and see a figure below, making for Maggie Wilson's store—Mhairi Campbell, I can tell from the blaze of her red hair. The sight of her gives me hope. She's alive, at any rate.

Somehow, I start moving, traveling the last of the path, crossing the bridge into the village, dragging my feet through the streets and over the square until I reach the Wilsons' store.

I summon what remains of my strength and lean against the door, forcing it so hard it swings back, smashing into the wall with an almighty crash.

Maggie Wilson and Mhairi Campbell turn to me, mouths open in shock.

"There are monsters," I manage. "Monsters, living in the caves by the loch."

Then I pass out.

I wake on my back with a cool cloth on my forehead and Maggie Wilson glaring down at me.

"Are you going to be sick?" she asks.

I consider, testing how I feel. "No."

"Sit up, then," she demands, and though her words are short, her hands are gentle as she helps lift me, then holds a cup to my mouth.

The warm, weak tea tastes like the nectar of the gods, and I reach for the cup, scowling when she slaps my hands away.

"If you rush, you will be sick. You fainted."

I'd figured that out for myself, but I keep my mouth shut. She feeds me tiny sips of tea like I'm a wean or a baby bird until it's gone. Then she puts the cup down and crosses her arms.

"Well?" she asks. "Monsters, is it?"

The last thing I said before I passed out. *Cora.*

I nod. "They have Cora Reid. They live in the caves by the loch, and that's where they took us. The water is so low now that they can get out. It was them that killed Aileen, and Jim's horses. Hattie Logan and James Ballantyne are dead, too. I found Hattie's body in the caves, but Cora is still alive, or at least she was. She helped me escape," I say, my voice sounding as if it hasn't been used for a thousand years. "I can show you where they have her. It might not be too late." *It can't be too late,* I pray.

I don't realize I'm crying until I feel water drip onto my hands, and I look down, surprised. I'm even more so when I see I'm no longer wearing my filthy blouse or underskirt. Instead, I'm dressed in a very matronly, heavily starched nightgown, the high collar scratchy under my chin. I look around me at the neat room, the lacy covers over the arms and backs of the immaculate chairs, the dried flowers in gleaming vases on the well-polished side tables, the scent of beeswax and lavender. I'm in Maggie Wilson's private parlor, dressed, I assume, in one of her nightgowns. It's sobering. I wipe my face with my hands.

Maggie is watching me carefully.

"Did you hear me?" I ask.

I make to swing my legs off the sofa I'm lying on, but she pushes me back. When I try again, she does the same. "I heard you, lass. But you'll not get far, the state you're in. The back of your head looks like someone took a cudgel to it."

"I'm fine." I lift my hand to my head and feel the blood now matted in my hair, the skin beneath tender and sore. "I'm fine," I repeat. But I'm not. Even sitting up has exhausted me. I've barely slept since the night I first saw the creatures.

So what? Cora is counting on me. I can rest later.

222

"Listen, we have to tell everyone," I say. "We need to get a rescue party together for Cora. And I think Gavan—"

"Gavan Stewart is fine, if that's what you're worried about," Maggie says, cutting me off. "He was in a bad way when he got here, but fifteen minutes ago, he was snoring fit to bring my roof down. And Murren Ross is well, too, for that matter."

My heart threatens to burst out of my chest at the news that the boys are alive. "Can I see them?" I ask, trying again to get up.

"Will you sit back and calm down?" Maggie says, shaking her head at me. "You can see them both when they wake up. They need the rest. So do you." She clasps and unclasps her hands. "Now. These monsters. Murren gave me your letter and the logbooks. I can make neither head nor tail of what they say, but the pictures speak for themselves. That's what we're facing, I take it."

Dumbfounded, I stare at her. "Wait, you believe me?"

She raises an eyebrow. "Hard not to, seeing Gavan Stewart with a great chunk missing from his neck, young Murren Ross raving like a madman, and your father's books. Not to mention what happened to Jim's horses. I saw the state of them when they were found, and it was clear to me no lugh did *that*. And . . ." Maggie hesitates, clearly reluctant to say the next part. ". . . it would appear someone else has seen them, too," she finishes in a rush.

"Who?" I ask, astounded.

She shakes her head. "Never you mind. The main question is, what are we going to do about it?"

"We have to let everyone know," I reply instantly. "That's the first thing. And then put a rescue party together for Cora. And"—I take a deep breath—"Giles needs to stop running the mill so that we can refill the loch. That's the only way to trap them in the caves."

Maggie gives a scornful laugh. "I thought you of all people had the measure of Giles Stewart. You know what that man is. He won't be happy until Ormscaula is renamed Stewartstown and he owns everything and everyone in it. He won't stop the mill."

"But they attacked his own son!"

"Giles is telling everyone *you* attacked *him*. In his own home," Maggie says.

"Aye, I did. And I'll tell everyone why: because he was trying to make me undress in front of him at gunpoint."

"That's not what he's saying. According to him, he took you in out of the goodness of his heart, and in return, you shot him and kidnapped Gavan."

"He's lying!"

"I know he's lying," Maggie snaps. "And I expect half the village does, too. But as long as he's paying their wages, they're not going to say anything about it. They can't afford to."

"So what, then?" I ask, tears of frustration pricking my eyes. "We do nothing? Leave Cora down there with those *things*? A human sacrifice, like the good old days? Let Giles Stewart keep running the mill until the loch is empty and those monsters can stroll into town and take us all whenever they like? Keep our traps shut so King bloody Stewart doesn't get his knickers in a twist? People will *die*," I choke out. "People *have* died. We have to do something."

"Alva?"

I whip around to see Murren Ross standing in the doorway of Maggie's parlor, looking drawn and pale. I've woken him with my shouting.

"You're alive."

Ren walks over, staring all the while, as though I'll vanish if he takes his eyes off me. He sits carefully at the end of the sofa, by my feet, looking me up and down.

"I thought . . ." He doesn't say whatever he's been thinking. "Where were you?"

"In their den. We were right—it is in the mountain, in the caves there. When the loch is healthy, the entrance floods, so they can't get out until the water drops. Ren . . . it's huge. It goes right back under the mountain, as far as I can tell."

If possible, he looks even more shaken. "How did you get away?"

"Cora was in the cave, too; she helped me."

"Cora? Cora Reid?"

"Aye, she was at my cottage last night. She and James got suspicious seeing you and Gavan together, and they followed you back up the mountain to see what you were doing. They hid in the henhouse, but those things found them. They killed James and took Cora." I swallow. "I found Hattie's body, too, where they kept us."

The bell on the wall jangles, making Ren and me jump. Maggie frowns. "You two stay here," she says, rising. "Not a sound."

She leaves us, closing the door firmly behind her. Ren stands and crosses to the window, peering out.

"It's Mhairi Campbell. She looks vexed." He ducks back quickly. "I think she saw me."

"She was here when I arrived," I remember.

A thought catches on my attention like a thorn, but I lose it when Ren crosses the room and squeezes himself next to me on the sofa, pressing his leg against mine.

He looks at me with soft eyes. "Don't worry," he says. "You're all right now."

His hair looks like a haystack sticking up from his head. I fight the urge to smooth it down. Then I give in and do it anyway, only to sigh when it just springs back up.

"You really need a haircut," I say.

"I'm ready when you are." His gaze moves to my arms. "Did they hurt you?" he asks, running a gentle thumb across the gauze Maggie has bound the grazes with, then looks at me.

"No. But, Ren, Cora's still down there—"

I stop abruptly as we hear footsteps in the hall, and Ren shifts forward, shielding me.

When the door opens, we both jump, but it's only Gavan. There's a bandage around his throat, and he's even paler than Ren. He looks as though there's not a drop of blood left in his body.

"I thought I heard you, but I didn't see how . . ." Gavan says, peering at me in wonder. He moves like an old man, edging over to Maggie's chair and dropping into it. "What happened?"

I swallow. James, Hattie, Cora. Two of his best friends dead and the third in that pit.

I tell him everything as clearly and cleanly as I can, Ren watching me all the while. I get to the part about Cora telling me to leave her and go, and Gavan closes his eyes.

When I'm finished, he goes to stand by the window.

"We'll get her back," Ren says to him. Gavan gives a jerky nod, then lowers his head.

"I'm glad you're all right," I say to Ren. "Both of you."

"I tried to get to you," Ren says. "But that thing just picked you up and ran."

"What about the one I shot?" I shudder as I remember the wild way it screamed.

"It got away," Gavan says, still facing the window.

"The sun burns them for sure," I say. "I saw it happen."

"At least we have that," Ren says. "It means we're safe in the day . . ."

"Until winter," I point out. After the *feis samhain*—the autumnal sister festival to the *feis samhaid*—the nights will start to draw in. At best we have six hours of sun, less if it's cloudy. Which will give those things eighteen hours of darkness per day. Long enough to decimate the village. To find new hidey-holes closer to the village. To get down to Balinkeld . . .

"Surely the loch will be full again by then?" Ren asks. "The rains—"

"If the mill keeps running, that won't be enough."

"Then Giles has to shut the mill down," Ren says firmly. "Or we have to shut it down for him."

"That'll take time. And we don't have time. Cora needs us. We have to kill those things, the sooner the better."

"Kill them?" Gavan says, still with his back to us.

I watch him, puzzled. "They're monsters, Gavan," I say.

"Are they?" He turns now, his expression unreadable.

Ren and I exchange a look. "You saw them," I say. "Of course they're monsters. They killed Aileen and Hattie and James. They took Cora and me. Attacked you. What else would you call them?"

"They're predators, aren't they? Trying to survive." He shrugs. "Maybe we're just not used to being prey."

"We're nothing like them," I say. I glance at Ren, whose

expression is thoughtful. "I've seen what they can do. I've looked in their eyes. And I'll call them what they are. So should you. Both of you."

I swing my legs off the sofa and stand.

Ren tries to catch my arm. "Alva, wait."

"Wait for you both to discuss whether those things have feelings? No, thanks."

I'm limping and dizzy, which means my exit isn't as damning as I'd like it to be, but I keep my chin up, ignoring both of them imploring me to listen.

"Where do you think you're going?" Maggie stops me in the corridor, Mhairi with her. "You're in no state—"

"Am I the only person who gets this?" I shout. "They've got Cora, and God knows how long she'll be alive down there. And if you don't care about her, then think about this: They'll come back tonight. And every night until we're all dead. We have to be ready for them. We have to stop them. If no one else is willing to do anything, I am."

I storm through the store, still in Maggie's nightgown, my feet bare. She catches up with me at the counter, reaching for my arm.

"Alva, wait," she begs, pulling me with her toward her private quarters, and I hear something in her voice that should make me stop, but it doesn't. Cora's house—that's where I'll go. She has brothers. They'll help me.

"We don't have time for this," I hiss, wrenching free.

"Alva, get away from the door," she barks, her eyes wide and horrified.

I look around and gasp.

On the other side of the glass stands Giles Stewart.

TWENTY-ONE

He stands frozen as he stares at me in disbelief, lips pulled back in a furious snarl, and I realize too late that Maggie was trying to warn me.

Giles pulls open the door, his hand snaking out to grip my wrist before I can stop him, dragging me outside.

"Get off me." I bend my knees, shifting my weight back. "You have no right."

In response, he twists my arm behind me and presses it against my spine until I cry out, tears springing into my eyes. "I have every right after what you did to me, you wee bitch. You're under arrest. Now walk," he commands, pushing me forward. I notice he's limping and feel a flash of vicious pleasure, until he squeezes my wrists so hard the bones grind, and I cry out.

"On what charge?" Maggie says, hurrying after us.

"Assault. Kidnapping—my son has been missing all day. Accessory to murder. And that's just for starters."

"Kidnapping?" snaps Maggie. "Gavan is inside. You know damn well he wasn't kidnapped by that slip of a girl—he'll tell everyone so himself. And I shouldn't think you'd want to bandy that word around after locking her in your attic and telling her to take her clothes off in front of you. Don't think I don't know about that."

"You watch your mouth, Maggie. You don't want to cross me." He smiles nastily. "You could lose your store if you do. And then what will you have in your life?" He pauses. "Tell my son I'll be back for him."

Maggie puffs up at his threat, but she lets Giles yank me away from the shop.

"Where are you taking me?" I ask.

"Where you belong," Giles replies.

He means the jail, then. I shudder again, wondering if I'll be in the cell beside my father.

I slip, and his grip on my arm tightens. People are staring out of their windows as he hauls me through the streets, their faces pale and shocked, and my own burns in humiliation. Maggie's nightgown is too long, and I keep tripping over the hem, though I'm grateful it's at least covering me.

"You have to listen to me," I gasp through gritted teeth, forcing myself to talk. "The thing that killed Aileen, it's not a cat—"

"Shut it," he says, kicking my ankle so I stumble, then jerking me upright by the arm. I cry out, tears on my cheeks, as fire blazes through my wrist.

He means to break it, I realize. That's what all this pushing and pulling is about. He's hoping I'll go down and it'll snap under his fingers. He's furious that I escaped his house, and he wants to punish me. But I have to make him understand about the mill.

"Giles, listen—" I say as we round the inn and enter the village square.

I don't know if it's because I used his name or because he's reached the end of his tether, but he kicks me again, hard, behind the knee, and my leg collapses, me with it.

My vision whites out with pain as my shoulder is wrenched from the socket. I scream, a high, shrill release of agony.

"What the bloody hell are you playing at?" I hear a man's voice, and then the pressure on my wrist is gone, my arm falling uselessly to my side as I drop to the ground. Nausea rises, my stomach heaving from the pain, and I start to retch, curled over myself. I release a thin stream of tea and then sit back, gasping.

"Alva, pet, are you all right?" a tender voice asks, the owner rubbing my back gently, and I turn to it, blinking up at Deirdre Gray, one of the mill workers' wives. When I nod, she helps me to my feet, whimpering as every single motion jars my dislocated arm, and I face Giles. Dizzy Campbell stands at his side, though for once he doesn't look like his henchman. Instead, he's poised to stop him if he tries to reach for me; I can see it in the set of his jaw, the readiness of his hands. It calms me.

"She's under arrest," Giles says again, though he sounds less sure now.

"She's sixteen," Deirdre replies, unfastening her *earasaid* and tucking it around my shoulders, taking care not to jolt my left arm. "And she's not dressed."

I nearly smile at that. Bless her sense of modesty.

I can't miss my opportunity to tell them about the creatures. I raise my voice, loud as I can. "I need to tell you something," I say. "All of you. It's about Aileen and Hattie."

By now, others have arrived; they must have followed Giles and me through the streets, and so a crowd gathers around as I screw my courage together. I look for the Ballantynes and the Reids, but if they're here, I can't see them.

I clear my throat and begin. "The thing that killed Aileen wasn't a cat. It was something I've never seen before. There are lots of them, living in caves in the mountain. They look like us—they walk on two legs, and they have arms and hands—but they're not like us. They're monsters." I think of Gavan's protest and pause.

It's enough for Giles to find his footing again, an ugly smile distorting his mouth.

"Are you hearing this?" He steps forward, a finger pointed at me like a malediction. "Monsters, she says. Aye, we know there are monsters in Ormscaula; they go by the name of Douglas."

"She's telling the truth." Mhairi Campbell's voice booms from the back of the crowd, which parts like a wheat field in response.

Mhairi Campbell has birthed five sons, one after the other: big granite lads made of brawn. She's tall and broad and would be well able to help Jim Ballantyne shift the logs he cuts for the mill, if she wasn't a woman, at least. She's eye level with Giles Stewart when she faces him, thick arms folded before her.

Behind her come Maggie, Gavan, and Ren. The boys move immediately to me, Deirdre Gray stepping aside so they can stand at my left and right. Giles's eyes follow his son, lingering on the bandage at his neck, as the crowd begins to whisper and nudge one another. Maggie stops beside Mhairi.

"Are you all right?" Ren whispers.

I nod, trying to ignore the agony in my arm.

"What's this, now?" Giles says, though some of his surety has left him, his smug smirk replaced with wary eyes. "Mhairi, I thought you were a sensible woman."

"Don't you try that on me. I said Alva Douglas is telling the truth. There are beasts up in the mountain. I know, because I saw them with my own eyes."

That's why Mhairi was at Maggie's. *She* is the person Maggie was referring to. She's seen them.

Mhairi steps closer to Giles, challenging him with her presence, and though he refuses to move back, I see the bob of his throat as he swallows. Next to him, Dizzy smiles briefly. He is proud of his wife, I think.

Mhairi doesn't spare him a glance, though; all her attention is on Giles. "Last night, I was sitting in the window. I couldn't sleep after what happened to the Logan girls—I don't think many of us have."

The crowd nods and murmurs.

"Our back room overlooks the brook, and I sat in there so as not to disturb Dizzy. I saw what I first thought was a person. But it wasn't human."

"What do you mean?" someone in the crowd calls. Giles frowns, and Mhairi continues.

"They were too tall. Too pale—milk white. *Bone* white. They've claws instead of nails; I could see that even from a distance. And they were as naked as the day they were born." She hesitates, and I understand why, though I'm still surprised when she says it. "They had no parts to speak of. Nothing down there at all. I saw two of them skirting the bankside, looking into the village. Scouting, like animals do.

I watched them turn and run, faster than anything I've ever seen, back up the mountain." She turns to me. "I take it that's when they got you?"

I feel my skin heat again as the throng of people, who seem to have forgotten I'm here, all turn their attention back to me. I look as many as I can in the eye.

"They got you?" Giles says to me.

"They carried her off." It's Gavan who answers, stepping forward. "I saw them. So did Ren. This is what they did to me." He peels the bandage back from his neck. The people gasp as one at the cut that slashes Gavan from ear to collar-bone, livid red against his pale skin.

"James was killed by them," Gavan continues. "Cora was taken, with Alva, to their lair. She helped Alva escape to warn us. We have to rescue her. And we have to be ready. For when they come back."

"What about Hattie?" Connor Anderson steps forward, his face puffy and swollen, his eyes red. "Did you see her?"

I can't bear his desperate expression. "She's dead, Connor," I say. "I'm so sorry."

A shudder runs through the mob like a wave; people pull their loved ones closer, as if that will keep them safe. At the back of the group, someone peels off, to find the Reids and the Ballantynes, I assume.

Giles is looking thoughtfully at me. I can almost see his

mind working, trying to figure out how he can come out on top here. Never mind what he's just learned: two more children dead, one captive, the village under siege by unnatural creatures, and his own son sporting a wound that could have been fatal. No, Giles's only concern is coming out on top. How he can rise like cream.

"Well, you seem to be the expert." He meets my eye. "What do you suggest we do?"

Clever, putting it on me. This way if it goes wrong, it's my fault.

But I have nothing left to lose.

"First we need to shut down the mill."

Giles is speechless, his mouth moving noiselessly.

"Why?" Maggie asks loudly.

I frown. She knows why; I've already told her. But then I understand. She's giving me a chance to explain in front of everybody. If the villagers agree, Giles will have to do it, if only to hold on to his status.

"Their lair is under the mountain, beside the loch." I pause. "We all know that before the earthquake, there used to be two lochs." I wait for them to nod. "Well, my guess is that those things lived in the caves alongside the underground loch. When the earthquake happened and the lochs merged, their caves were blocked off. But now the mill is using up so much water that the entrances are exposed and they can get out. They can just walk across the loch bed."

"We should be focusing on killing them, not trapping them," Giles says.

"I shot one last night," I tell him. "Right where the heart should be. It ought to have put it down, but it didn't. The only thing that we know for sure hurts them is the sun. That's why they live deep in the caves, why they only come out at night. The sun burns them."

"How do you know that?" Deirdre Gray asks.

"We trapped one," I say. "Gavan, Murren, and I. We set a trap, and we got one."

The crowd gasps, looking around.

"We found it in the morning turned to ash. When we touched it, it dissolved to nothing. And this morning, when I escaped, one tried to grab me. I saw its arm start to burn in the light. They can't abide the sun, I'm certain."

"What use is that to us?" Giles asks.

"It means they *can* be killed. At least one way."

"There have to be other ways." That's Jim Ballantyne, his wife behind him. The Reids follow, and so do the Logans. They stand beside Connor, separated from the others by their loss.

"There might be," I agree.

"Then I say we trap another," he says, talking to the crowd now. "We secure the women and the bairns tonight, and we set a trap. We keep the beast out of the sun, and we find other ways to kill them. And once we know how, we go to their lair, and we slaughter them all."

"And get my Cora back." Mrs. Reid steps forward, reaching for my hands, though she stops at the last minute, folding her arms instead. "She's alive, you say?"

"She was this morning."

Mrs. Reid closes her eyes.

Giles has finally recovered himself. "You're not seriously going to listen to the word of a murderer?"

"I've killed no one," I say, and both Ren and Gavan move closer.

"You are your father's daughter, though. The future *Naomhfhuil*. And was that not the point of the *Naomhfhuil*, originally—to commune with the things that lived in the loch? For all we know, it's you who's been up there, coaxing them out, setting them on us. Look at the victims." He turns to the crowd, happy to have found his stride. "Look who they were. Hattie Logan. Aileen Anderson. No love lost between those girls and you, was there? We all saw Alva take Aileen's place at the Staff."

"That's ridiculous," I begin, but Giles talks louder.

"Cora Reid and James Ballantyne missing, too—both friends of Hattie's. Both enemies of yours," he says to me. "Why, my own son told me they didn't like you, isn't that right, Gavan?"

There's disgust in Gavan's eyes as he looks at his father. "What has that to do with anything?"

"You don't have to be afraid of her, son," Giles says. "She can't hurt you again."

"She didn't hurt me in the first place," Gavan says angrily, but no one is listening. Any ground I'd gained is gone, and the faces that look at me now wear the same old expressions of mistrust.

Maggie must think the same thing, because she steps forward.

"Well, there's one way to find out if she's lying, isn't there?" Maggie says. "We shut down the mill, then do as Jim suggests and set a trap. We catch one and see what it is we're dealing with." She shoots me an apologetic look. "And we keep Miss Douglas far away from it."

TWENTY-TWO

I watch the action in the square from the best table in Rosie Talbot's inn, a place I genuinely thought I'd never set foot inside.

From what I can see, the trap that's being built is a grander version of Gavan's design, so he's essential to the process, standing off to the side and consulting with Iain the Smith over a hastily drawn plan, occasionally calling out instructions, while every man and woman with even the slightest hint of brawn puts it together.

As I watch, they pause to take a break, wiping the backs of their arms across sweaty brows, loosening tight shoulders, while Rosie moves among them, handing out mugs of thirst-quenching ale. My hand rises to my own shoulder, testing it. The ache is still there, but it's faint and dull, the ghost of an injury haunting the joint instead of the raw, stomach-churning pain of the dislocation and the sickening way my arm just hung there, barely part of me at all.

Mhairi Campbell put the joint back in place for me after giving me a hefty dose of cheap whiskey, but even the burn from that gut-rot didn't mask the pain of having someone forcibly push a bone back into a socket. I screamed so loud I'm sure the creatures heard it in the mountain and smiled.

Giles thinks he's won. If they succeed and catch one, then it's not my success, and I can't share in it. And if they fail, they have a scapegoat. Either way, he thinks he's back on his throne, the would-be king who brought the whole of Ormscaula together to face monsters he doesn't believe in; I see it in his eyes. He either won't or can't accept what he's been told.

He is outside with the others. He turns toward the window now, mug of ale in his hand, raising it slightly as if toasting me, and I stare back at him. He thinks keeping me in here gives him an advantage, but I'd say right now we are even. He might have locked me up, but I shut his mill down.

Actually, when I put it like that, I'd say I'm ahead.

It's eerie in the village without the rumble of the mill in the background. No hum of the pulping vats smashing and shredding the wood. No creaking and groaning of the water-wheel as it sluices water into the huge tanks and carries the wastewater out and down the mountain. Every so often one of the villagers looks up, frowning, trying to place what's missing. He's working, his friends are around him, and yet something is wrong. It's partly the fact that he's outdoors in the fresh air, the sun beating down on his neck, instead of in the dark, sour-smelling mill. But it's mostly the silence.

The door to the pub kitchen opens, and I turn.

"I've made you a spot of tea." Maggie, charged with baby-sitting me to make sure I don't interfere, walks over, laden with a tray.

I look at the clock above the bar. Five. Not long until sundown. I rise and take the tray from her, ignoring her protests, and put it on the table, careful with my left arm.

"Has anyone been sent to find Cora?" I ask.

"It was decided that catching one of the creatures was the priority," Maggie says, her voice full of apology.

"So she has to spend another night up there, alone in a pitch-black hole," I reply bitterly. "I promised I'd get her out."

"No one wanted to go there without knowing what they were up against," Maggie replies. "Even her brothers agreed it was better to wait until the dawn is on our side. Cora's tough. Believe in her."

"It doesn't matter how tough she is. You don't know what they're like."

"Aye, well, if the trap works, we all will. Now, eat up. We've a long night ahead of us."

She's put together a nice spread: cold chicken and ham, bread and butter, some hard-boiled eggs, and a block of cheese, as well as a thick chunk of pork pie, the crust crumbling into the juices of fat, silvery pickled onions. And despite everything, I'm famished. I don't need any more encouragement to dig in.

I make short work of the food, eating my way steadily through it until all that's left are crumbs and my rounded tummy. I brush down the blouse and skirts I've been lent to wear instead of Maggie's nightgown. I watch the work outside the whole time.

"I wonder what they'll use as bait. Do you know?" I ask.

I've been trying to figure it out. Our trap worked because it was contained—only one of the creatures could get in, and we had control over when the trap sprang. Of course, we didn't bank on them copying us and learning how to open the trap; Gavan will have told them that.

But this trap is out in the open. I can't imagine a creature will come alone, and even if one does and goes into the trap, how will we keep the others from rescuing it or get out to it before the sun rises without being killed ourselves? What do we plan to do with the person who's the bait? Leave them out there all night as the creatures try to get in at them? I pour a cup of tea, my mind whirring.

Maybe they'll use me, I think darkly.

Movement outside catches my eye, and I see Giles

walking toward the inn, a smug expression lighting his self-satisfied face.

Does he plan to use me? I cover my alarm with irritation. "Ugh, what does he want now?"

"Alva, listen," Maggie says hurriedly. I look at her, my stomach plunging. "He's coming for you. You're to stay with Giles tonight."

I drop the teacup, and it shatters. "No." I stand, looking around for another way out of the inn.

Maggie reaches out to placate me. "He won't hurt you."

"I'd rather be the bait in that cage. You know what he tried to do to me—I told you."

"Alva, please calm down. The others . . . Well, they're not keen on the idea of you being in the same house as them. Giles holds a lot of sway, Alva—you know that. And then there's Lachlan, in jail for what he did to your mam. It's one night, and he won't try a thing, I promise. He knows I won't let him get away with it."

Before Maggie can say any more, Giles opens the door to the inn and walks over to us.

"Oh dear," he says, voice dripping with false concern. "That's a face. I take it you've told her? Let's go, Miss Douglas."

"There has to be somewhere else," I say to Maggie desperately. "Anywhere else. What about with you?"

"No one will have you," says Giles. "It's home with me. Unless you fancy a night in the cells."

"I'll take the cells," I say.

Giles smiles a wide, ugly smile. "So be it."

A new wave of horror crashes through me as I understand that I'll be spending the night with my father.

It would only take a moment to cross the square to the jail, but I make Maggie walk me around the back of the village. I won't give Giles the satisfaction; I won't have the villagers pausing to watch me heading there, don't want to see the pity in Gavan's eyes. Or Ren's. I don't have much dignity, but I will fight to preserve this scrap.

The injustice of it is burning me, leaving a black, molten hole inside my chest, but I hold my tongue, even though I want to scream. There's no point in seething at Maggie; she's on my side, and I'm short on allies. So I walk placidly beside her as though we're just out for a stroll after supper.

The sky is darkening and streaked with clouds as we turn onto the side street by the jailhouse: a tall, slim building on the edge of the square opposite Giles's house. Mercifully, the door is on the side, so no one sees as we approach.

"I want a cell overlooking the square," I say to Maggie as she opens the door for me. "I want to watch as it happens."

"I don't see why not," she says gently, ushering me inside.

Angus Mitchell, a thin, weasel-faced man with light auburn hair and skin almost as pale as the creatures, is on duty today.

There aren't often people in the jail for more than a night or two, so there's no permanent jailer. When one's needed, Giles gets one of the men from the mill to do it. It must be Angus's turn. He stands, reaching for my arm, and I pull away.

"She's not a prisoner, Angus," Maggie warns him. "I'll see her to her room."

He scoffs. I meet his watery blue eyes, and for a minute we're just two people, amused at Maggie behaving as though I'm staying at an inn. Then the shutters come down, blanking his expression, and he pats the ring of keys at his skinny waist.

"I'm to come with you to lock her in. Mr. Stewart's orders."

Maggie tuts. "She doesn't need to be locked in. She chose to come here of her own free will."

"*Mr. Stewart,*" he emphasizes, "says she's to be locked in to keep her from trying to get her father out."

"I wouldn't," I say, but I know there's no point.

Angus gestures for us to mount the stairs. "To the top, Mrs. Wilson."

I follow Maggie up to the third floor, passing the closed door on the second floor. They must be keeping my father there, and I'm glad I'll be on a different floor. This is going to be bad enough without him nearby.

At the top of the stairs, Maggie pushes open the door, which isn't locked. There are four cells. I count the doors, two facing out on to the square, two the street behind.

"She wants one over the square," says Maggie, and Angus laughs.

"Does she, now?" he replies. Maggie fixes him with a glare that turns his skin puce. "First on your left," he mutters, and I follow Maggie to it.

Good. That's one less thing to worry about. It frees me up nicely for the horror I feel when I see where I'm to spend the night. Maybe I should have chosen Giles's house . . .

The cell is small, twice as wide as my bed at home and not much longer, with a single window high on the far wall, glassless and barred. It's barely furnished at all, outfitted with a wooden bunk, a thin-looking pillow and blanket, and a metal pail.

"Am I supposed to use that?" I point at it.

"Jesus Christ, Angus. She's a child. And she's not a prisoner," Maggie says.

"I'm just following orders, Mrs. Wilson. Mr. Stewart said nothing about luxuries or special circumstances. Only that you'd bring the girl and that she was to be locked in a cell for the night."

Maggie looks conflicted, her attention moving between me and the sparse, grim cell.

"We can tell Giles you've changed your mind," she says.

I take a breath, steeling myself. I survived seven years living in the shadow of a murderer. I survived being taken by the creatures, and I survived their caves. I can make it through one poxy night in a cell. Compared to where I spent last night, it's lovely, I tell myself. It's got a pillow, a blanket, and nary a monster or corpse at all. And it's better than being under Giles's roof.

"No. It's fine," I say to Maggie, my voice higher than usual but thankfully steady. "But if I need to use the bathroom, I'd appreciate it if Mr. Mitchell would fetch me to use a proper one."

"I can't promise I'll hear you all the way up here with the doors closed."

"You will," Maggie says, her eyes blazing. "By God, you will. And I'll take the spare keys, thank you."

"Mr. Stewart said—"

"Mr. Stewart has said enough," Maggie snaps.

She holds out her hand, and we both watch as Angus pulls a ring of keys from his belt and hands it to her in sullen silence.

Maggie turns to me. "Now, do you need a candle or anything?"

I shake my head. There's a sconce on the wall, long candles already lit inside it, and the moon will still be bright enough to see by. Besides, I'm scared of having one in a place I can't escape from. What if I tip it over and end up setting the place alight? I shiver.

"Water, food? Paper and pens? Maybe a book?"

"No, thank you. I'm fine." I don't plan to eat or drink anything that might force me to use the bucket. And I'm scared anything else, even the smallest of luxuries, will make me feel as if I'm here on a more permanent basis. My heart skips as I think it, and I force myself to be calm.

"All right, then," Maggie says.

I step into the cell, walking to the back wall and jumping up onto the bed so I can peer out of the window. I can see the square, see the cage set up, apparently ready, and the people still milling around, even though night is falling fast. I'll be able to watch it all, even if I can't help.

I climb down and go back to the door. I close it myself, ignoring how my stomach drops as the barred iron door meets its opposite. It feels important to me that I shut myself in instead of letting someone else do it. I meet Maggie's brown eyes and try to smile bravely. Neither of us is fooled.

"I'll be back at dawn," Maggie promises. "Just a few hours, really, if you think about it."

I nod, not trusting myself to speak.

"Are you *sure* you don't need anything?"

Another nod.

"All right." With that, Maggie slips the key in the lock and turns it.

It's a well-oiled lock, the bolt slipping easily home with a decisive ring.

Maggie stares at me through the bars, this woman with her iron-streaked hair and her ironclad heart, and I decide that if nothing else comes of this horror, at least she's on my side. The support of a woman like Maggie Wilson is good for the spine. I stand up taller and give her another, better smile.

It's returned full force, and she pats my hand, still gripping the bars, before she leaves. She doesn't look back.

When I hear the lock on the outer door find its home, my stomach swoops.

The first lock I could handle; I closed the door, and I expected it. But this second lock breaks me; it feels so final. The carefully collected calm I'd gathered skitters away, and terror takes its place.

Suddenly, my chest hurts; my lungs won't expand to let any air in. I bend at the waist, scrabbling at the buttons of the borrowed blouse, too tight at my neck. My heart is beating so hard I'm sure it's bruising me inside, my vision narrowed so all I can see is the lock, the lock, the lock.

"Breathe, Alva," a calm voice commands me gently, piercing my panic enough to let a lungful of air in. I do it again, and again, dropping to my knees and pressing my forehead to the cold floor, sucking in breath after breath, my muscles slowly relaxing as oxygen gets to them. The pain in my shoulder returns, tight from where I clenched it, but it's something to focus on, so I do.

Slowly, I come back to myself.

"Are you all right?" The voice is familiar; the words aren't.

No. No, no, no, no.

"Alva?" my father says from the cell beside mine.

TWENTY-THREE

I don't answer, sitting back and leaning my head against the bunk.

"Alva?" my father says again, the ghost of that same old annoyed snap in his voice, the sound of a man not getting the answer he wants from his teenage daughter. It would be comforting, if we weren't locked in neighboring cells at the behest of a man who hates us both.

"I heard you. I'm fine."

"What are you doing here? Why did Maggie Wilson bring you here?"

"I'm not talking to you."

He's silent. I close my eyes.

Though I can't admit it—not even to myself—I feel better

knowing he's there. Not because he's my father, but because I'm not alone. Next door, he's in the same boat I am. A rock-solid bed, a threadbare blanket. A pillow that smells of someone else's sweat. A bucket, no doubt dirtier than mine. But I'll walk free tomorrow.

Comforted by that, I clamber back onto the bed and peer out between the bars, fingers wrapping around them instinctively. The moon hasn't quite risen yet; everything is shadowy and dark, though I can see that some people are still outside, dimly lit by the windows that look onto the square. It seems like every lamp in Giles's house is blazing, and I watch those inside taking it in turns to do as I am, peering out at the cage.

"You told them. About the ò*lanfhuil*?"

His voice sounds different; he has moved, standing at his own window.

"That's what they are?" I ask. "*Òlanfhuil?*" Similar in sound to *Naomhfhuil*, I realize.

"It means 'blood-drinker' in the old tongue." He answers my unspoken question.

"I thought *Naomhfhuil* meant 'holy saint,'" I say. "*Fhuil* is in both words—what does it mean?"

"Blood. Not holy. The words are similar and got confused over time."

Blood saint. Jesus, that's creepy.

"Why didn't you tell anyone about them?" I whisper. "Why didn't you tell *me* about them?"

The silence stretches long and thin like twine between us. "Alva, I had my reasons," he says at last.

"What?" The words leave me before I can bite them back. "What possible reason could you have for protecting those *things*? Do you actually think they're gods?"

"I know they're not," he says softly.

"Well, then, why?" When he doesn't reply, I continue. "They killed Aileen Anderson and her baby, you know. And Hattie Logan, and James Ballantyne. By keeping your mouth shut, you killed them as sure as you killed my mam. You almost killed me."

"What do you mean?" he asks, and I hear fear in his voice.

"They took Cora Reid and me," I say. "Out to the mountain, to their den. Put us in a hole for later, saving us for their supper. Like we store the dried sausages and bacon. That's what I was to them, Da. Meat. And Cora is still there."

"Alva—"

"Spare me, Da, would you?"

"I was trying to." His tone is dark.

I don't have a clue what I'm supposed to say to that.

Below, I hear the sound of men arguing, their voices raised, though I can only make out a few words—one of which is my name. A door closes—the front door to the jail, I think—and then I hear a voice I know, cursing. I doubt he'd be using that kind of language if he knew my father could hear him.

"Ren?" I call down to him.

"Alva? Is that you? Are you all right?"

Even if I stand on tiptoe, I can't see him; the angle's wrong. "I'm all right," I call down.

"I can't believe they've locked you up; who the hell does Giles Stewart think he is?"

Best not to scream my honest answer to that across the square. I'll tell Ren it was my decision in the morning. "Is the trap ready?"

"It's ready."

"Who's going to bait it?"

"Giles has got a bunch of men drawing straws now. One of them will sit in it while the others wait in the windows with guns."

"Where will you be?"

"Maggie's. She's got my mam and a bunch of others there, too. Everyone whose house isn't secure has been brought into the heart of the village. Giles sent Mhairi around to do a census so everyone is accounted for."

I hadn't even thought about Liz Ross or any of the others who live outside the main village. That was smart of Giles, I think grudgingly, though I bet he hasn't got any of the poorer folk in his own house.

"Wait a minute . . ." Ren says.

I can't see anything, but the sound of scuffling, a thud, and a soft grunt tell me he has tried and failed to climb the wall. I smile to myself.

He steps back, and I can finally see him, his hair silver in the moonlight, rubbing his hands on the tops of his thighs as he looks up.

"You all right?" I ask.

But his attention has moved to my right, his eyes wide. Ah. He's spotted my neighbor.

"As you can see, I'm not alone," I say.

"Mr. Douglas," Ren says, nodding his head respectfully.

"Murren," my father mumbles from the cell beside mine.

"Do you mind?" I say to my father, before asking Ren, "Has he gone?"

Ren shakes his head. Someone calls out to him, and he turns to them, then back to me. "Look, I've got to go, but I'll be back in the morning with Maggie."

My heart sinks, but I nod. "All right. Stay safe."

"You too," he says, eyes darting to my father once more.

Then he turns and starts to jog toward the Wilsons' store.

I climb down, my neck and shins hurting from straining. It's starting to get cold, and I have no *earasaid*, so I throw the blanket around my shoulders, coughing at the dust that puffs up as I do. Then I settle in to wait.

I fall into a doze and wake myself up shivering, my teeth chattering violently. Without glass in the window or any kind of shutters, there's nothing to stop the cold night air from seeping into the room.

"Alva?" my father calls, his voice a whisper.

I let out a sigh. "What?"

"Here. Come to the door. Put your hand out."

Too cold and tired to protest, I do, and reach through the bars to feel something soft. A blanket. His blanket.

I hesitate. "I don't need it."

"I know you're a better liar than that," he says, and I feel a smile tug at the corners of my mouth in response to his tone. It's resigned and annoyed. But there's something else there, too. Respect, maybe.

I take the other blanket. I put them both around my shoulders, pulling one up over my head like an *earasaid*. Then I climb back up to the window and peer out.

The moon is high, but clouds have drawn in, making the light patchy. Most of the windows are dark now; only a few have faint glows inside them, though I can't guess at the time. Late enough that the world feels asleep. I see someone sitting in the cage, but I can't make out who until he stands and I see his broad back. Jim Ballantyne. I watch as he works out a kink in his leg and sits back down, pulling a blanket around his shoulders.

Then he stands again, staring ahead, his blanket falling soundlessly to the ground, and I follow his gaze.

Three of them are there in the middle of the street, watching him in the cage. It's as if they just appeared; one second the square was empty, and the next they're there, as if that's always been.

Clouds obscure the moon, and I lose them.

When the light returns, they're closer to the cage, and I can see them more clearly. The ones in the center and on the left, on the jail side, are tall, hairless, and pale like the others I've seen. But the thing on the right is smaller, closer to human-sized, with noticeably darker skin, like there's a light fuzz over its chest, back, and legs to the ankle. One of their young, I realize, brought hunting. Animals do that—take their young out to teach them to kill.

They want to teach it what they learned last night. How to open the cages.

As I watch, they push the younger one forward, and it moves, with less grace than the adults, toward where Jim is transfixed. He reaches out toward the creature, and to my horror, I see that he is beckoning it into the cage. What is he doing?

I'm distracted by movement in the side streets. Then the bottom falls out of the world, and I feel like I'm falling through the wall.

Stalking toward the square are more of them, more than I'd thought possible. From what I've seen, I'd guessed there were maybe five or six of them, a small family. But there are at least twice that many moving silently toward where Jim is trapped, some passing through the streets and some on the roofs, moving like large white spiders.

"Are you seeing this?" my father whispers. I don't have the breath in me to reply.

I freeze as the two adults that brought the young one turn to us, their heads tilting at the same time as their eyes seek us out.

"They can hear us," I whisper back.

At my faint whisper, their lips pull back from their teeth into a synchronized, silent snarl, and I break out into a cold sweat, my pulse quickening with some age-old instinct.

One of the creatures makes that hateful clicking sound, and it echoes through the square. The others freeze in place, all of them turning to the window I'm watching from.

The clouds return, and I swear, pressing my cheeks into the bars, desperate to see what they do next, if they're still looking at me.

"Alva, get back," my father barks, and the habit of half a lifetime means I do it instantly.

It saves my life.

There is a monster at my window.

It must have climbed or leaped two stories, holding on to the ledge of my window to keep itself there. It stares at me, pallid face striped by the bars between us, and then its long fingers fold around the metal where mine were just moments before.

Black eyes fix on me as it takes me in.

"Alva, are you all right?" my father calls, his voice tight with panic.

"I'm OK," I say.

The creature smiles, as if it's understood me. Slowly, it shakes its head.

No, you're not, it seems to say.

From outside, I hear shouts, screams, and the sound of gunfire as the villagers realize the siege has begun. The creature flinches, turning to look behind it, and that's when I notice a mark on its chest, a dark, circular patch. This is why it climbed up here.

I shot this one. Last night, in the hallway of my cottage. I put a bullet where its heart should be.

I tell myself I'm wrong, that it can't be the same creature. The scar looks old; it's just a coincidence that it's sporting a wound exactly where I hit one. But I know in my bones it's the same one. In addition to being faster than us and stronger than us, they can heal quickly.

And it remembers me.

Dawn, and real safety, feel a long time away.

"Tell me what it's doing now," my father calls.

"Nothing. Just looking. I . . . I shot it. Last night. I think it remembers me."

At the sound of my voice, it clicks softly. I raise my hand to my own chest and touch the spot that mirrors its wound.

When it opens its mouth and I see its savage canines elongate, I know I'm right. It is the same one, and it recognizes me. It's here for revenge.

It tugs on the bars gently; then, holding them with both hands, it forces itself backward, trying to rip the bars from the wall. I don't know whether it's strong enough to do it, but I don't plan to find out. I pick up the pail and throw it. The sound it makes as it bounces against the bars is clear as a bell, a high, metallic gong.

The creature screams in fury and slams a hand against the bars, sending a shower of mortar to the floor.

Beyond it, the others scream in answer, their shrieks mixing with the frantic human cries of the villagers.

"Jesus, Alva, what the hell's going on?" my father shouts.

I drop to the floor and reach for the pail as the thing hurls itself against the window above me, a long arm reaching through the bars and scrabbling for me, the claws dangerously close to my face when I look up.

Pail in hand, I wiggle backward and stand. It withdraws its arm and stares at me, holding the bars, the hatred in its eyes unmistakable.

I raise the pail, intending to beat its fingers until it lets go, but I don't get the chance. As I take a step forward, it turns, head rotating almost all the way around, like an owl's. Then it's gone, dropping silently out of sight.

Scared it's a trick, I edge toward the window, pail held out before me.

"What's happening now?" my father calls.

"I don't know. I think it's gone. Or it's trying to make me believe it has."

The square beyond is silent, too—no more gunfire, no more shouting.

"Stay where you are, let me see."

I wait, head cocked, listening. I hear him suck in a sharp breath.

"Don't look, Alva. For God's sake, don't look."

I look, and the pail falls from my hand, hitting the floor with a metallic thud and rolling under the bed.

Jim Ballantyne is dead inside the cage. His body is slumped forward, his neck a mess of red and pink.

His head is beside him.

I turn away and retch, pressing my hand to my mouth, the other across my belly.

"I warned you," my father says.

I wipe my mouth and look again, trying not to look at Jim this time.

Instead, I see the others. Three men lie sprawled, torn from where they leaned out of windows to shoot, holes in their throats like leering mouths, their heads almost sev-ered. Their wounds have been blackened by the moonlight, their faces unrecognizable.

In the house beside Giles's, the lower windows have been smashed. I spot two different *earasaids* caught on the glass where they've been ripped away from their owners' bodies. The houses themselves seem still, silent, and I try to piece together what happened.

While one was trying to get at me, the others must have attacked the shooters, pulling them down and breaking the lower windows to get inside. They must have taken some of the people. *Stock for the larder*, I think grimly. The survivors must have fled deeper into the house. I hope.

Please let Ren and Gavan and Maggie be all right.

"They got one," my father says, breaking into my thoughts.

I look out again, this time at the cage, and find to my surprise that he's right. Cowering in the corner, one of the creatures is caught, doing its best to make itself as small as it can. It's the young one, I realize. Short and slim, hunched over so its pelt looks like clothes . . .

"Alva, get away from the window," my father says again. "Don't look."

But his voice is different this time. The command isn't a command; it's not made out of annoyance or fear for me. It takes me a second or two to place the tone.

It's a plea.

I see it then—another young one, slinking into the square, skirting around the edges of the buildings, trying to remain in the shadows. Smaller, with that same strange covering over its head and back. Except this one's arms are bare, fair in the moonlight.

"Alva," my father says. "Please."

The creature looks up at me, and I see my mother.

TWENTY-FOUR

"Alva," my father says.

It isn't possible. He killed her. I heard the gun go off four times. I heard him taking her body outside to the loch.

My mother is dead.

My mother is looking at me.

She's changed and unchanged all at once. What I took for a pelt is clothes and hair, plastered to her body with water or grease. Now that I know what I'm looking at, I can see her moon-pale skin between rents in the blouse.

The creature in the cage looks up, and a new wave of horror breaks over me when I see that it's wearing James Ballantyne's face. I understand now why Jim Ballantyne didn't scream, why he reached out to it. He thought it was his son.

Shots are fired somewhere opposite, and both my father and I scream for them to stop. I'm at the bars again, face pressed against them, body mashed against the wall to get as close as I can. The creature that is my mother continues to look at me, black eyes vacant, then turns and runs. Faster than a normal person, but not as fast as the others. The original ones.

"How?" I say. There is silence from next door. But now I understand why my father didn't want to tell anyone about the loch level dropping. Why he went out alone to hunt. Why he wanted me to stay inside.

Why he closed the book to keep Giles from seeing that the *òlanfhuil* existed.

He knew she was one of them. That somehow, she'd stopped being like us and started being a monster.

I listen as the bed in the room next to mine creaks as weight is removed from it: my father stepping down from the window. I do the same and walk to the door, sitting against the wall between us. I have a feeling that on the other side, my father is mirroring my position.

"How?" I say again.

He clears his throat. "I'll have to go back to the beginning," he says. "It's a long story."

"We're not going anywhere," I say, and he gives a small laugh.

"You remember that she wasn't right, after we lost the bairn . . ." He pauses. "Jim Ballantyne told me it was to be expected after such a loss—his Ada had lost a baby between two of their sons. Jim said the best thing to do was be normal, give her space and keep up the routine, and she'd rally. That had worked on his Ada. So I did. I was sad, too—don't get me wrong. Desperately so. But I didn't have time to grieve."

"Why?"

"Well, there was you to think of, and your mam couldn't care for you. And it was the year Giles opened the mill," he says. "It was a success. A huge one. But it took a toll on the loch—the sheer amount of water the wheel sucked in for steaming and pulping—and it was a hot summer. Giles and I fought daily about it; I'd finish my rounds and go down with the report, begging him to slow down, and he'd tell me to deal with it, as if I could just magic more water from the sky." He hesitates. "He relished it. Having the power and the control. Making it impossible for me to do my job, knowing the responsibility was mine. And then we lost the baby."

Giles must have been jubilant—everything was falling apart for us. Maybe he thought if he could break my father, ruin him, then my mother would finally crawl to him.

"You remember she went for walks around the loch?" he says.

"I remember."

"I thought it was good for her. The air and the water. Space for her to grieve. I thought it was a good sign she wanted to get out. And it was—she was coming back to herself, I could see it.

"Then that last night, she came home and she was different. Angry. At first, I thought that was good, too; anything was better than the silence and the nothingness. I was wrong. She was changing. One of them must have bitten her."

"Wait," I interrupt him as something terrible occurs to me. "Did you know about them? Did you know they were there?"

"Yes—"

"And you didn't tell her? You didn't tell me?" I'm sickened, shaking my head as if that might keep the knowledge away. "The loch level was falling, and you didn't warn us what might happen? You let her go out?"

"It's not what you think," he says hurriedly. "I knew they *used* to be real, because I saw the same logs you found when I wasn't much older than you. But I didn't really believe they were still out there. I thought surely they must have died inside the mountain. Centuries had passed, Alva. Nothing is supposed to live that long. It was only after I saw *her* change before my eyes that I realized what must have happened. So, aye, I suppose it was my fault. But not like you think. Maybe if I'd paid more heed to the books and realized what it meant that the loch was drying out . . . Maybe . . ."

He falls silent. And I find I believe him, because if he'd told me they existed before I saw them, I wouldn't have believed it either, even if I had seen the logs. I would have chalked it up to folklore or ignorance. Ancient people using monsters to explain what they couldn't understand. Yet all the while, the creatures were waiting. Biding their time.

They would have been weaker, surely, after so many years trapped. Still stronger than a grieving human woman, but she'd managed to get away. She hadn't told us. Had kept it to herself. Returned home and begun to change, over the course of minutes or hours. That's why they have two sets of teeth, I realize. One is for eating, and one is for making us like them. I was right; they are just like snakes, poison in their fangs.

Last night, Cora saw one of them bite James—and tonight he's down in the square, trapped. It's in the bite.

"They can turn us?" I ask. "Make us like them?"

"If they don't kill us outright."

I think of Cora. Maybe I was wrong; maybe she isn't supposed to be food. Maybe they want something else from her.

"Is that why you shot her, then? That night?"

"I didn't shoot her. She came at me, teeth bared. I tried— if she'd gotten past me, she could have gotten to you, but I couldn't do it, even seeing what was happening to her. I fired four times, but I shot wild—there are holes in the wall from the bullets. I put the window out, too."

I try to remember the room, try to recall any marks on the walls, but they're covered in floral paper. I expect you'd have to look closely to see them.

There was no blood. There should have been if he'd shot her, an obscene amount, but there wasn't. Not even a drop.

I stare into the distance, astounded that I've never realized this before. I remember glass on the floor, and the gun, still warm when I picked it up, but no blood.

"She went out through the window. I went outside to look for her, but she was gone—to them, I suppose. Some instinct calling her home to them after she changed, or back to where she was attacked. And the next day, the rain came and kept coming, so the loch refilled. Stayed full. They were trapped again."

"Until now."

"Until now," he agrees.

All these years, he's known. And kept it to himself. Let everyone believe what they wanted and watched the loch, wondering if they'd come back. If she'd come back.

He told me she had left in the night, and she had. I asked if she'd come back, and he said he didn't know.

It was the truth. All this time, it was the truth.

"You should have told me." I mean that he should have told me about Mam, but he misunderstands, thinking I mean the creatures.

"I would have when you came into your majority. I would have told you everything, even about her. I would have made sure you understood. There's a tradition, passed down from *Naomhfhuil* to *Naomhfhuil*. We spend three nights out by the loch, near the mountain. It's a rite of passage to tell the old stories and pass the knowledge on. I would have shown you the logs you found. After that, part of your job would have been to study the books. Learn the symbols." He pauses. "That is, if you'd wanted to be the *Naomhfhuil*."

I never realized I had a choice. "I think I figured out some of the symbols," I say. "The moon represented the moon phase, didn't it? And the flowers were what was in season at the time?"

"That's right." His voice is warm. Proud. "That's exactly right."

"What else is in there?"

"All kinds of things. I'll show you—" He stops. He can't show me. Not if Giles has him hanged.

"But she's not dead. We saw her. All we have to do is show Giles, and he'll have to let you go. She's the proof that you're innocent."

In his silence, a voice whispers in the back of my mind that it doesn't matter. Giles won't ever let him go, not now that he has him.

"Is there some kind of cure?" I say. "What if we can bring her back? Then she can tell him herself. There must be something in the logs . . ."

He's quiet for a long, long time. "I looked. Of course I looked."

"And?"

"We'll look again. Together. When this is all over."

There's something in his voice—the tenderness of a father trying to convince his daughter that everything will be all right. It's too bad that he's lying.

"I wish you wouldn't lie to me," I say softly. "I'm not a kid anymore."

"Oh, Alva." My father tries to comfort me. But he can't. There is no comfort to be found here.

The ones they don't kill become like them, swelling their ranks. My mother. James. I think of Gavan; he was bitten. How long before he becomes one?

I was frightened before, imagining the creatures reaching Balinkeld and beyond under cover of darkness. But now it's worse. Because every time they reach a new place, their numbers will grow. They'll just keep moving and increasing, like a disease sweeping through the land. Winter will come, and there will be no stopping them. No lucky horseshoes, no bullets or—

My thoughts freeze.

Silver horseshoes on the houses.

Silver bullets in the gun.

Silver.

"The gun," I say aloud. "The gun you fired that night, with the revolving barrel. Are the bullets silver?"

"How do you—you have it?" my father says, surprised. "I thought she must have taken it somehow. Yes, they're silver. Silver is the only thing that works against them, according to legend. I bought her the gun when we got married—it's traditional for the *Naomhfhuil* to give their spouse something silver when they wed."

"And you chose a gun that fired silver bullets?"

"It's what she asked for. She wanted a gun of her own. Do you still have it?"

"It's at the cottage." I think. I hope.

"We'll need it."

"We need to get out of here first," I reply.

Then I catch myself and fall silent. *We*. He's been my enemy for so long, I can't imagine him as my ally. But now he is. He always has been. We've wasted so much time.

"You didn't kill her," I say aloud. It feels important to say it.

"No, I didn't."

"I'm sorry." That feels important, too. "I thought . . . for so long . . . I thought you did. I was scared."

"Because you thought I'd kill you, too?" He sounds so sad.

"I'm sorry," I say again.

"You did what you had to do. I understand," he says. "Come here."

I press my face to the bars of the door and see he's pushed his arm through, his hand extended toward me. I do the same, taking it. His hands are bigger than mine, the skin rough from years of work. His fingers feel cold, and I remember guiltily that I still have both blankets. The last time I held my father's hand, I was nine.

It doesn't last long—I assume he's in the same position as I am, pressed flat against the wall, shoulder contorted to be able to reach—but it's good while it does. There's so much more I want to say: that I was planning to run away; that now I don't think I need to. That he wasn't far off when he thought Ren was courting me, and that I'm not against it. That Maggie Wilson is actually not a harridan.

But I don't say any of it. I'm too superstitious. It feels like tempting fate. Like I'd be saying goodbye when it's hello that's needed. We're strangers to each other, for all that he's my father. But there will be time to fix it. We will have a chance to mend this and heal. We just have to get through the next bit first.

We don't speak for the rest of the night, but it's all right. For the first time in a long time, it's a good, healthy silence, the fever between us broken. Maybe he sleeps, but I don't. Instead, I put a plan together in my mind.

Once Maggie lets me out, I'll take her aside and tell her everything. My father is safe enough in jail, but I'll make sure someone brings him good food and better blankets. I need to get back to the cottage and get my gun and my bag.

I have eight silver bullets. That's not enough, but if we round up every bit of silver in Ormscaula, every spoon and ring, every belt buckle and heirloom, and melt them down, I bet Iain the Smith can make more. Enough for every single one of those things. Enough for every gun in Ormscaula. I'll sit outside the creatures' den for however long it takes to put one in each of them as they come out. And while they try to stop me—because I'm sure they will—a rescue party can go in and get Cora and any other survivors.

I hear shouting outside and rise stiffly, calling, "Da."

The sky is beginning to lighten, and I can see people hurrying around the cage, carrying rolls of paulin, or oilcloth. As I watch, they unroll them, throwing them over the cage and covering it to keep the creature that used to be James from burning. He—or *it*, I suppose—is still cowering, and for a moment, I feel sorry for it. I wonder how much of James Ballantyne is left in there. I wonder what it remembers—did it know who Jim was when it killed him? I wonder if it can still speak.

I wonder if she can.

Once the cage is covered, the men approach it, clearly nervous. They lift it, and Iain and three others, including beanpole Dizzy Campbell, carry the cage toward the jail. Of course they're bringing it here. Where else could they take it? Where else is built to keep things in?

As they move it, I catch sight of Giles Stewart, standing back out of harm's way, watching. Anger blossoms inside me, a bloodred flower of fury and vengeance, my heart screaming for it. Like he senses it, he turns toward the jail and looks up. I know he sees my father and me by the way he smiles. It slithers over his face like a snake, there and gone in a flash. Smiling in triumph though his best friend and likely others are dead. He can't hide his happiness that we are trapped here.

He keeps his eyes on me as he walks toward the jail, and then he's gone from sight, inside the building, following the men and the cage.

I return to the cell door and wait.

TWENTY-FIVE

I'm still locked in when they start to torture the thing that used to be James Ballantyne.

The sounds it—he—whatever he is now—makes are hideous. My skin crawls, chills riding my spine with every piercing shriek. It sounds as if it's in agony, as if they're peeling its skin away, holding flaming brands against its flesh.

He was one of us until two nights ago, I think. It hasn't taken the people of Ormscaula long to forget that.

I remember Gavan questioning whether the *òlanfhuil* were monsters and how angry I felt at the idea they might not be.

The creature gives a piteous, mewling whine, and something inside me snaps.

"Let me out!" I bellow, swinging the bucket against the bars with all the strength I have in my right arm.

There's a lull in the noise from below, as if they've heard me, but the screams begin again, and no one comes.

"They're going to leave me here," I say.

"Maggie won't let that happen," my father insists.

But as the cells fill with light, the sun rising over the mountain, still no one comes. They must have covered the windows below, because the *òlanfhuil* is still making sounds, though now it's a constant, anguished keening that's somehow worse. There's an emptiness to it, as if whatever was alive in it has fled and all that's left is pain and noise. It becomes too much, and I have to cover my ears and hum, bent over myself, to keep from going mad.

It's while I'm bent that someone comes, and it's only when I feel a hand on my shoulder that I jerk upright, almost smashing Murren Ross's nose.

Ren.

I throw myself into his arms, squeezing him tightly.

"We have to go," he says, though not before he's pressed a fierce kiss to the crown of my head. "They don't know I'm here."

"Where's Maggie?"

"Barred. All the women are. Men only. I volunteered so I could get to you. They think I've gone for more kindling for the fire." He looks over his shoulder. "You have to go; they'll realize soon enough that there's something wrong."

"My father," I say. "We need to get him out, too."

To his credit, Ren doesn't question it, just holds up a bunch of keys.

I take them from him and dart to the cell next door, eyes on the lock as I fumble with the keys, inserting one after another, not daring to look at my father until the key turns in my hand and the door springs free.

When I do look up at him, he's smiling.

I'm hugging him before I realize I've moved. His arms fold around me, and I'm grateful to find he still smells like my childhood: a bit like our cottage, a bit like the loch.

"I hate to interrupt, but you have to go," Ren says.

My father and I release each other and head for the door. My father pushes us behind him, listening carefully, before pressing a finger to his lips and beckoning for us to follow. We sneak downstairs, past the closed door to the second-floor cells. Behind it, the *òlanfhuil* is still moaning, and I feel it inside me, a kind of sharp ache.

"What are they doing to it?" I say.

"You don't want to know."

Ren, behind me, gently nudges me to keep going, and I follow my father all the way down. The front room is empty, no sign of Angus Mitchell or anyone else guarding the place. My father whispers that we should wait in the stairwell, then skirts around the walls to the door, peering out of the tiny window.

"There's a crowd," he says quietly.

I cross to the door and look out.

Maggie Wilson, Mhairi Campbell, and almost every other woman in the village is standing outside, though their attention is fixed on the window above us, where the sounds are echoing from. We're not going to be able to get out without being seen.

"Go back upstairs and tell them you can't find any wood," my father tells Ren. "You don't want to be caught up in this. Go on."

I nod to tell Ren I agree, and he turns.

"Oh, here," he says, reaching into his pocket and pulling out my revolver and the two spare bullets. Then he pulls out the cameo of my mother, his skin flushing when he hands it over.

My father and I look at the gifts he's given us.

"Be safe," Ren says, heading back up the stairs, as I murmur, "You too."

When he opens the door to the first-floor cells, the screams get louder.

I can't bear it.

The gun sitting comfortably in my hand, I make a decision. I open the barrel and count. Then I lock it in place and pull the hammer back, resting my index finger on the trigger. I put the last two bullets in the pocket of my borrowed skirt and hold out the cameo to my father.

"Da . . ." I hesitate.

He takes the cameo and looks at it, rubbing a thumb gently over the painted face of my mother. Then he smiles at me again. "I know. I understand."

His blessing warms me. "Where can I find you after I'm done?"

"I'll go to the Wilsons' store. No one will think to look for me there, and I expect Maggie will give me a fair hearing."

I nod. She will, I'm sure of it.

"I'll come to you there."

"Be careful, daughter." He reaches out and clasps my shoulder—the right one, thankfully—and squeezes it gently. "You've grown into a fine young woman," he begins, but I shake my head.

"No. Don't. Save it for when we're home and this is done."

As he turns to leave, I call out.

"You're sure," I say, "about the cure? You're sure there isn't one?"

He shakes his head. "I'm truly sorry, but no." He nods at the gun. "I can do this, if you want."

"No. You need to go while you can. This is for me to do."

He looks at me for too long, disobeying my silent plea to be normal, to pretend like everything is, and will be, fine. Then he goes.

I listen for long enough to be sure he's gotten away, peeping out to watch the women scatter like chickens as he fox-darts through them, sending them clucking into one another's arms in outraged fright.

As the floor above me creaks, I begin to run, taking the stairs two at a time. The door to the second floor opens as I reach the top step, someone on their way to check what's happening outside. Smoke billows out, obscuring whoever is there and masking me, too, for the brief moment it takes to pass them and enter the room.

The gun is steady in my right hand.

They've covered all the windows, so the air in the room is thick and close, reeking of meat and men. The only light comes from the candles in sconces on the wall and the make-shift brazier they've rigged from one of the mess pails, the wood glowing red, the metal poles waiting inside bright white.

I pause for long enough to see which cell the *òlanfhuil* is in, long enough to see the shock and disgust on Ren's face— he's standing as far back as he can—and to see the growing fury on Giles's face as he realizes who I am and what I'm about to do.

Long enough to meet the eyes of the *òlanfhuil*—James-that-was. Its skin is peeling from its body, a mess of wounds that have barely bled, the flesh hanging in strips or blackened where they've held hot metal to it.

Aye, I see now who the monsters are. Gavan was right.

Afterward, I'll think it sentiment, but right now it seems to me that it's asking for mercy, silently pleading with its eyes. They still look human. It's the teeth, and the fact that it's still standing, somehow, even after what they've done, that gives it away.

It takes a shambling step forward, silent for the first time since it was brought here, and as Giles Stewart screams at me to stop, I squeeze the trigger and unload a silver bullet into the *òlanfhuil*'s chest.

It dies in silence, crumpling to the ground like a marionette with cut strings.

Then I turn, pulling back the hammer again, another bullet sliding audibly into the chamber, and level the gun at Giles.

"I wouldn't," I say as he makes to reach for me.

The other men in the room all watch, and I notice with relief that none of them have guns. Probably should have thought of that earlier.

I look at them all in turn, fixing on Iain the Smith. "I assume the reason you brought"—*it*—*him*—*James*—"the creature up here was to figure out how to kill it?" I say. "Well, now you know. Normal bullets won't do the job, but silver ones will." I pull one of the bullets from my pocket and hold it up to the smith. "Gather every bit of silver in the village—every candlestick, plate, spoon, and trinket. Every horseshoe over a door. Melt them all, and make as many bullets as you can to fit the guns you have. We'll need them all to protect the village tonight, so you'll have to work fast. Go. Now."

He doesn't blink or question it; he leaves, his head bowed, moving so fast it's clear he's relieved.

As I look around the room, I see the rest of them—Dizzy Campbell, Angus Mitchell, Wallace Talbot from the inn—looking guilty, chins low, shoulders rounded, not quite able to meet each other's or my eyes. With the door open, the smoke dissipating and the creature dead on the floor, looking like the seventeen-year-old boy it used to be, the fire has gone from them. Whatever mob madness was fueling their cruelty has passed.

I hope they feel as sick of themselves as I do.

"You two," I say to Dizzy and Angus. "Go and help Iain gather up the silver. And you." I turn to Wallace Talbot. "You get a party of people together who are willing to go into the mountain with me to get Cora. You do remember Cora Reid, don't you? Or were you so intent on torturing that thing that you forgot one of our own is trapped with them?"

"The girl won't be alive," Giles spits.

"We owe it to her to try," I seethe. "Why are you still here?" I bellow at Dizzy and the others, who are still staring between Giles and me.

"Let's go," Ren says, and they follow him, glad to have a leader. "I'll be at Maggie's," he calls back to me, and I nod.

Then I'm alone with Giles.

"That was your son's best friend." I nod to the corpse in the cell, the gun still aimed squarely at Giles's chest. "And your best friend's son."

"*Was*. Until he turned. Whatever that thing was, it wasn't James. You saw what it did to Jim; I know you were watching. James never would have done that to his father."

"You know Gavan was bitten, don't you?" I say. "That's how they turn. From bites. Will you do the same to him?"

Giles laughs. "Gavan was scratched, not bitten. Oh, it was deep, I'll grant you. An inch or two to the left, and he'd be dead. But there was no bite. He'll not become one of them."

My relief is a pure, clean feeling, and it scrubs a little of the horror from the room. Not much, though. Because there's still the body of a boy in the cell beyond us. And Giles hasn't finished.

"But if he had," he goes on, "I'd have done the same— maybe not myself, because I do love the boy, but I would have understood the need for it to be done. They can't be allowed to live and hunt us. We were trying to find a way to put them down."

"Well, now you know. Sunlight or a silver bullet."

"You seem to know a lot about it."

"I'm the daughter of the *Naomhfhuil*, as you pointed out earlier. It's my job to know about it." I let pride leak into my tone. I am proud to be my father's daughter. "And it's my job to tell you that your mill is the reason they got out."

"Aye. But I didn't know, did I? If I'd known the stakes, of course I would have slowed the mill down. But I didn't. Your father kept that secret. So now your father is a killer multiple times over. These children. Your own mother."

"That's where you're wrong." I speak without thinking, so eager am I to absolve my father. "He didn't kill my mother. She's one of them."

His face slackens.

I go on. "She was bitten when you first opened the mill. Remember my father telling you then that you were using too much water? One made it across the loch and got her. She turned that night, tried to attack my father. He fired wild, and she ran away. And do you know how I know? Because last night, I saw her. Here in the square."

"You're lying," Giles says, his voice low.

"No, I'm not. If anyone killed her, it was you. You and your greed and your obsession. So what's your answer this time, Giles? Would you do *that*"—I point at the body—"to her? Would you let Dizzy, or Iain?"

His fists are clenching and unclenching at his sides, his face blank. His chest is falling and rising deeply again, but this time he's controlling it, taking deep, measured breaths.

Then he walks past me. I stand, stunned, listening to his

heavy tread on the stairs, the sound of the outer door opening, then closing.

I look at James's body and see that he looks like the creature we first caught, an ash sculpture of a fallen boy. I walk to the window, tearing down the covering to let the breeze in. Then I wait with him while he turns to dust, watching the fragments of him swirl in the morning sun.

TWENTY-SIX

When I finally leave, the square is empty. The bodies of the fallen men are gone. I don't know if that means they became ash under the sun or were taken away; I can only hope that any who were bitten have been dispatched. The *earasaids* have been taken from the windows, too, though the glass remains on the cobbles, glittering in the spring sunshine, ruby speckles glinting at me as I pass. It looks pretty, and I hate it.

It's our savior, but I find the sunshine blasphemous. It's like the earth is spitting in my eyes. By rights, it should surely be raining or thundering. The weather should be as gray and bleak and relentless as I feel. Not like this. Not birds singing, not bees lazily bobbing between gardens, not flowers opening and nodding at the sky. Not this *life*, as though nothing has changed, when everything has changed.

I walk to the Wilsons' store, feet dragging in the dust, my gun heavy in my pocket. Iain the Smith will be in his forge right now, making bullets.

I exhale, a deep, shuddering sigh. At least if I do it, it will be quick. That's something. I'll be clean and fast. I won't let them linger in pain. I won't make them suffer for what they are.

The thought of killing them makes me feel ill. Killing James—what James had become—was an act of mercy, and I don't regret it. But now I know they can feel pain and suffer. Now I know they're alive enough to want to die rather than be tortured. It's changed everything, and the idea of sitting outside their home and gunning them down in cold blood as they try to leave makes my stomach turn. I think I see what Gavan was saying about them just trying to survive. The problem is that for them to survive, we all have to die or turn. So they can't be allowed to live. I might have to murder every single one, and I hate that, too.

I wish the loch would refill so I didn't have to do this. If only there were another earthquake.

I stop, furious at my own stupidity. Of course I don't need to sit outside and pick them off one by one. I need to stop them from getting out. We need to cave in their lair, blocking the exits. We need to trap them again. We'll keep them from getting out and write clearly about it in the *Naomhfhuil* log, warning people what to expect if it ever happens again.

It's a long shot, but it sparks a little hope inside me.

Maggie's store is closed, the shutters pulled down. I hammer on them until she appears, a rolling pin in her hand. Her expression softens when she sees me, and she pulls me through the door and then, to my surprise, into her arms.

"Thank heavens you're all right," she says. "When Murren told me he'd left you behind, I could have flayed him alive."

I wince at her choice of words, and she falters. Ren must have told her what Giles and the others were doing. Bustling to cover the moment, she urges me through the shop, behind the counter, and toward her private rooms.

"Anyway, you're safe here now," she says. "Gavan's in the parlor, and Ren's just cleaning himself up."

"Good. A bunch of people will be here in an hour to help me rescue Cora. Where's my father?" I ask. I want to run my plan past him.

"He's already gone to the caves."

For a moment, I think that an earthquake is actually happening, that the earth is willing to save me the bother of caving in the tunnels. The house seems to tilt, and me with it, but it's only when Maggie catches me that I understand my knees have buckled, that dizziness has knocked me sideways.

"What?" I say, my ears ringing with the sound of my own rushing blood. "What are you talking about?"

Maggie helps me upright, watching me with concern. "He said that was the plan you'd come up with. He'd go ahead to the caves, scope them out."

"No . . . No, that wasn't the plan," I whisper.

Why would he do this?

But I know why. For the same reason he told me to stay away from the windows in the cottage and forbade me to go outside. The same reason he was out of the cottage, wandering around at night. The same reason he wouldn't tell anyone the creatures were back. For my mother. Because despite it all, he loves her still. Even though it's hopeless. He doesn't want me to shoot her.

I pull the gun from my pocket along with one of the spare bullets, loading it into the empty chamber. Seven bullets. It doesn't seem like much at all.

I'm going after him. I can't wait for the others.

"Do you have any rope?" I ask Maggie.

She heads back into the store, and I follow, taking the reel of thick cord she passes to me and looping it over my shoulder.

"And some candles. Thick ones that'll burn long."

"You're not doing what I think you're doing?" Maggie says, even as she walks away, returning instead with a hurricane lamp, a good-sized tub of paraffin in the bottom, and a box of matches.

"It depends what you think I'm doing," I reply, offering a

grateful smile as I tuck the matches into my pocket and hook the handle of the lamp over my wrist.

"Alva, you're just a girl."

"No such thing as 'just a girl,' Maggie," I say. "You should know that better than anyone."

She sighs but doesn't argue.

"Tell Ren . . ." I begin, then falter as he appears in the doorway between the shop and Maggie's quarters. His hair is wet, fresh from bathing and darker because of it, but it still hangs in his eyes, and the sight of it makes me smile. His feet are bare as he walks toward us, his mouth curving into a grin in response to mine.

His smile dies when he sees the rope and the lamp. "Tell Ren what?"

"You remember I told you the lochs merged after an earthquake?" I say.

A crease forms between his eyes as his brows draw together, but he nods.

"Well, we need another earthquake. Or something like it. Today, before sundown. You need to figure out a way to collapse the entrance so they can't get out. That's how we'll stop them. We'll block the caves and trap them again. Hopefully for good."

"Alva—"

"Ren, I don't trust anyone else to do this. I need you. Do you understand?"

His expression is a heartbreak. "I think so."

I swallow. "Good. Do it. No matter what happens, do it. Before sundown, Ren. I've got to go. I'm sorry."

I turn and run.

The climb up the mountain is made no easier by the fear that batters me like a summer storm. You hear of terror helping people enact impossible feats—overturning carriages to rescue trapped babies, or lifting timber from collapsed buildings to get to their loved ones—but there's no truth in it for me as I try to get to my father. I don't benefit from a burst of miraculous energy or strength. Instead, my sides pinch with stitches, and my calves and thighs burn as I push myself onward. My lungs are dry and heaving, and I sound like an old woman, but I don't slow or stop. I don't look back at Ormscaula; I can't. All I can do is keep going, because I can't lose my father now. I can't let him do anything stupid.

Not without me, this time.

At the loch, I pause for breath, leaning against a tree, hand pressed to my ribs, trying to rub the pain away. The water is a mirror, flat and gray, and I look up at the sky, surprised to see clouds thickening above me. Rain is coming. Much too late, and probably not enough. Better than nothing, though. I take it as an omen and move onward, traveling the miles to the north shore, where the loch meets the mountains.

I sit at the lochside and unfurl the rope, tying knots every foot or so: handholds and footholds to help Cora out of the pit. I'll get her out first, then find my father. I roll the rope up and sling it over my shoulder.

Across the dry loch bed, the opening of the cave looks like a mouth ready to swallow me down into the earth. There's no sign of my father, even when I get close—no prints in the hard earth, no telltale scrap of fabric caught on a sharp bit of rock. But I know he's here. Where else would he go?

Taking a deep breath, I drop to my stomach and, my heart in my mouth, crawl backward into the cave, the lamp cradled against my chest like a baby.

I don't take my eyes off the exit, keeping that block of light at the front of my mind as I slowly wriggle my way down into their lair.

Once the tunnel widens, I turn, crawling on my hands and knees until I can stand. Then I light the lamp. The glow is a friend in the dark, and though I know it's likely to give me away sooner, I'm grateful for it. It soothes the bird in my chest, beating against the bone cage.

I put my left hand on the wall and remember the path I took to escape. This time, I can see where the path splits, and I pause at the junction, listening. It's silent, save for my heart. Steeling myself against my screaming nerves, I turn right, edging toward the pit and kneeling beside it.

When I peer into it, the wide, shocked eyes of Cora Reid

stare back at me, her fists raised as though she plans to fight. It makes me like her even more.

I press my finger to my lips and wait until she nods before setting the lantern down and pulling the rope over my head. Hattie's body is still in the pit, facedown, her hair a matted cloud. There's no sign she's moved, or begun to rise, or whatever they do. Maybe she wasn't bitten but died some other way, and she won't come back. I'm tempted to ask Cora to check, but Cora is resolutely not looking at her, and the last thing either of us needs is her breaking down because she's been pushed too far.

Instead, I toss one end of the rope down to Cora, holding a finger up again, telling her to wait. There's nothing to attach the rope to, so I tie it around my waist, looping the knots just like my father taught me. I mime at her slowly, using my hands and my eyes to tell her I'm going to move away and that when she feels the rope flick, she should climb. I do it twice, so she remembers. Then I walk back a little.

Once I judge that I'm far enough away to be safe, I get on my hands and knees, digging them into the ground, trying to find purchase, working to anchor myself so she can climb up. I figure if I stay low and spread my weight, I'll be a better foundation for her. I tug the rope.

The moment she begins to climb, my body slides backward, knees, shins, and palms scraping the dirt. Then there's nothing under my feet, and the rope slackens. Cora bites off a yelp, and I twist, my stomach dropping as I see how close I was to falling back down.

This isn't going to work.

I untie the rope and look at Cora. Her eyes are wide, glittering, her throat bobbing, and I see the defeat written on her face as she tries to accept that I can't get her out.

Yes, I can. And I will.

I take six steps back and wrap the rope around my arms to try to keep it from burning my hands, then shift my weight low into my hips, bending my knees. Then I flick it. When I don't feel her weight, I do it again, harder, so she gets the message.

The second she starts to climb, I stumble two of the six steps forward, and I have to bite down on my lip to keep from screaming in pain as the rope scores over my wrists and palms. I lean back as far as I can, until my shoulders are parallel with the ground, keeping my knees bent, using my weight to counter hers.

I don't try to pull her; instead, I imagine roots growing out of my feet, burrowing down into the earth, holding me fast. My shoulder threatens to pop back out of its socket, every muscle in my body screaming, but I don't give up.

She held me up so I could get out. I can do the same for her.

I hold, and I hold, even as my vision turns red and my knees start to shake.

Then I'm falling backward, crashing to the ground, the rope slack.

When I look up, Cora is gripping the lip of the hole, one leg kicking wildly as she tries to swing it up. I rush forward to take her hands and pull her over the edge. Afterward, we both sit, panting. My limbs have turned to jelly, and I expect Cora is in a similar state.

What I don't expect is for her to hug me.

My eyes, closed while I recover, fly open, terrified at first that we've been found, that the viselike hold around me is one of the *òlanfhuil*. But it's Cora Reid, shaking gently, her head buried in my shoulder, the skin there wet from her tears. I shift so I can put an arm around her, patting awkwardly, before I push her away.

I stand, beckoning for her to follow. We don't have time to be sentimental.

Rolling the rope up, I haul it over my arm and pick up the lamp. Cora is moving stiffly, but I hurry her on, taking her to the tunnel out. I walk with her until we can see the entrance, and I point at it, silently telling her to go.

She shakes her head and grabs my arm, insistent.

In response, I pull out the gun and tilt my head in the direction of the tunnel.

Her expression becomes grim, her mouth a line, her eyes hard when they meet mine. She gives a single nod, as though sanctioning my actions, followed by another brief hug, and then she leaves. I watch until she's gone, waiting until I'm sure she's made it out to sunlight and safety.

Once I'm alone again, I turn to the darkness. I pull the hammer back on the gun, cocking it.

This time, I walk straight on, heading deeper under the mountain, trying to keep my focus on my surroundings, on what might be ahead of me. Even so, a worm of worry twists in my mind, because there was no one else in the pit save poor Hattie. And that means either they weren't brought here or that they've already turned. More *òlanfhuil* I might have to kill.

The stillness and the silence are eerie; though Cora and I were as quiet as we could be, we still made sounds. The scrapes of feet against stone, heavy breathing, barely bitten back grunts. I'm surprised nothing heard us, surprised nothing has come to investigate. I'm also surprised they don't have some kind of patrol or lookout—they know I know where they are, and surely they assume I've told others. They should be on guard, watching for me.

Unless this is a trap.

I gently press the trigger, feeling how ready the gun is to fire.

The passage begins to widen, and I slow down. Then, suddenly, the walls are gone, vanishing from either side of me as if they've been whipped away, leaving me in an open space, the floor glittering strangely in the dim lamplight.

I've stepped into the bed of the old loch. When I bend, I can see the fossilized skeletons of fish, their bones preserved in what used to be the bottom of the underground loch. Helical stones that were once snails, now calcified and permanent. The imprints of leaves and grasses pressed into rocks like feathers.

I walk farther in, fear replaced by wonder. My boot nudges something that shifts, and I look down to find a shell, conical and pale, its occupant long, long, long dead. I pick it up and marvel as I see the mother-of-pearl sheen still coating it. I put it in my pocket like a talisman, then continue looking around.

Then I see her.

My mother, standing before me, an air of waiting about her, as if she's poised for this moment.

At her feet, crumpled and still, is my father.

My stomach turns over as cold, bright fear lances straight through my heart. This is why I wouldn't let him say good-bye. It was supposed to ward off disaster. It was supposed to make sure something like this didn't happen.

My mother takes a step toward me, and I raise the gun without looking away from my father. This isn't fair. I notice my hand is shaking; it's never shaken before. The second I notice, I become aware of my whole self shuddering softly, fear and exhaustion and desolation and rage all wrecking me.

As though she senses it—smells it—my mother's mouth

curves into a smile, her lips parting to reveal a single pair of long canines, bracketing her upper front teeth.

She raises a finger to her lips and gestures for me to follow her.

I shake my head.

She does it again, raising her hand and urging me to go with her.

And through my grief and anger, I realize something.

She hasn't attacked me yet. She could have done it while I wasn't looking, but she didn't. She waited for me to see her, waited for a chance to communicate with me. She hasn't raised an alarm; she hasn't made a move to threaten me. Is it possible she doesn't want to hurt me? Could it be that she just wants to talk to me, or even help me?

Is it possible my father is not dead?

There's only one way to find out.

I point the muzzle of the gun at my father, my eyes asking the question.

Again she smiles, this time with her mouth closed, as though hiding her teeth will reassure me that everything is all right.

It's enough.

Gun trained back on her chest, I begin to walk slowly toward her. She watches every step, head tilted like a bird or lizard, her face impassively curious.

Up close, she's monstrous: her pale skin underscored by dark veins, her eyes not fully dark like the others, but the irises shot through with brown blood. She looks papery and fragile, desiccated, dry as the loch bed outside. Her hair is thinning, and I can see patches of scalp between it. And I know a thousand years from now, if she lives, she won't look like my mother at all. She'll look like one of them—smaller, but still bald and black-eyed, all the humanity stripped from her.

Maybe they were once something else, too. Before we decided they were gods. Picts, the race of giants that walked the land long before we were here. Or maybe she'll grow, nourished by the flesh and blood of the people she used to love, stretching and honing until she's designed to frighten and kill and nothing more.

I bend slowly, keeping my eyes on her, to feel my father's neck for a pulse. My fingers come away wet, and there's no drumming beneath them. I know what she's done.

When I stand, my finger is tight on the trigger again.

She steps back, wary now, and gestures once more for me to follow. Pointing at me, then her ear, before pressing her palms together.

Listen. Please.

I ought to turn and run, wait outside in the sunshine for Ren to come and blow the entrance shut.

I ought to put a bullet in her and one in my father so he can't come back and so I don't have to see either of them like this ever again, don't have to spend my life knowing they're under here. Don't ever have to worry that one day I might look outside at night and see them side by side, waiting for me.

But another small, stupid part of me wants to hear what she has to say. Has spent seven years wanting her back, and now here she is, begging me for a moment of my time.

So even though my father is lying at her feet, I look my mother in the eye, and I nod.

Her gaze drifts to the gun in my hand. Understanding, I pull the revolver's hammer back and press the trigger, uncocking the gun. At the sound of the faint click, my mother repeats that uncanny tilt of her head and gives a small smile, as if she's proud of me for being a good girl. I hate the way I feel good for pleasing her.

The gun disarmed, I put it in my pocket, hooking the handle over the edge. Just in case.

She leads me across the loch bed to my right, her footfalls silent, moving with a grace I don't remember her having before. A passage appears, a dark smear in the cave wall, and a wave of panic surges through me as I look behind us and find I can no longer see the one I arrived through, hidden by the dark. For all I know, there are dozens of tunnels, spidering out from banks of the old lochside, making paths deeper and deeper under the mountain. Of course there must be; where do I think the others are now? I curse myself for not using a stick or stone or something to mark the right way out.

Heart fluttering, I follow my mother along the passageway until we arrive in a small cavern. The walls glitter with quartz, acting as prisms and casting rainbows over us. Her skin absorbs them; they dance over mine. There's a pile of rags in the corner, and the walls are marked.

I crouch to look at them, stomach turning when I see the shapes traced in something dark and brown. A woman, a man, and a child. Our family. Daubed in blood.

I realize this place is hers. That must be why there are no others in the main grotto; they must have their own spaces like this, little hidey-holes secreted away. She's brought me to her nest.

When I look back at her, she's blocking the exit, and I shiver, a full-body shudder of foreboding. I have made a terrible mistake. I have allowed her to trap me.

We're of a height now, I realize as she steps toward me. Whenever I remembered her, she is taller, but now we're a matched set. In seven years, I've grown up and filled out into a woman. And she's become a monster.

"Why am I here?" I ask, though I know. "What do you want?"

She opens and closes her mouth, as if trying to remember how to use it. I expect before tonight she hasn't spoken in seven years. Hasn't needed to. So when she does, it's the sound of graves and earth. Her voice is an abyss.

"My daughter." Both answer and endearment.

Against my will, longing fills me. "Did it hurt?" I ask her.

I watch in horror as a clump of hair works free, scalp still attached, falling onto her arm. She brushes it aside like an insect, not caring. I get a sudden burst of memory: her at her dressing table, brushing her hair, telling me she had to do it a hundred times in the morning and a hundred times at night.

"Oh, yes." She smiles, her teeth gleaming.

I put my right hand in my pocket, finding the gun, curling my fingers around the handle until it fits just so. My index finger seeks the trigger, my thumb on the hammer. Even if I get it out in time, even if I manage to shoot her, I still have to find my way out of here, past the others that will surely pour out of their own dens to hunt me down.

It's too late, I understand. Now I die. For a while, at least.

"Close your eyes," she says. Her breath smells of meat and marrow.

Her teeth are all I see.

TWENTY-SEVEN

"Alice?"

She's gone. I blink, and then I see Giles Stewart pinned against the cavern wall, his feet dangling uselessly, my mother's spidery white fingers around his throat.

He doesn't fight her, though. Instead, he smiles, a fat, soft smile, as though she's the best thing he's ever seen.

She bares her teeth at him, leaning close to smell him.

It is only when her tongue snakes over his pulse that he looks frightened.

"Alice," he says again, a tremor in his voice. "It's me. It's Giles."

In response, she growls, a guttural sound that rumbles from deep in her abdomen.

"Alice?" Giles shoots a look of desperation at me.

I hate the man. I hate him so much I can hardly breathe for it; there's not enough room in my chest for air and my loathing of him. But I don't want to see my mother tear his throat out.

"Mam," I say.

She turns, her teeth bared, and now she doesn't know me at all.

But I have to try. "Don't." I step forward, pulling the gun out.

Giles whimpers as her grip on him tightens, and her lips peel back, her mouth opening wide, impossibly wide.

"I love you," he pleads.

She doesn't care about love. She doesn't know what love is anymore, but he's never going to understand that. All he sees is the thing he wanted most in the world, the thing he thought he could never have, restored to him and there for the taking.

"We can be together," he chokes out. The front of his trousers are stained dark; despite his words, he's wet himself.

And though I hate him, I pull back the hammer on the gun and raise it, pointing it at her.

She lets Giles go, turning toward me.

He slumps to the ground, his eyes wide, as she flies at me, hitting me so hard I see stars. I lose the gun, hearing it clatter against the rocks as I crash down, too, landing in her rags. They smell foul, and I gag, trying to fight my way out. Then her weight is on me, crushing my chest, one cold hand pressing over my face, covering my mouth as she twists my head to the side. The other scrabbles to pin my arm while I flip like a fish beneath her, trying to keep her from gaining a final hold.

I will not die like this. I will not die in a pile of rags, beneath the ground, killed by a thing wearing my mother's face.

A burst of strength has me shoving her away with my knees. She snarls like an animal, slamming me back against the ground, saliva dripping from her fangs as she tries to bite me.

Then her eyes go blank, and she slumps onto me, a dead weight.

Over her shoulder, I see a glint of silver.

And the frozen expression of Giles Stewart, his fingers still curled as though he's holding the knife that's now lodged in my mother's back, right to the hilt.

I allow myself three seconds—three rapid heartbeats—to recover, then shove her off me. Already she's beginning to crumble, her flimsy skin flaking as she turns to dust. I take the knife from her back as her skin disintegrates around it. Within seconds, she's gone, nothing more than a thin coating of ash on the floor.

When I look at Giles, his hands are shaking.

"I didn't mean . . ." he says, trailing off. "It was just for protection. You said silver . . . It wasn't meant for her. I loved her."

And then he howls.

It's a pure animal cry of grief and loss.

It's an alarm letting the *òlanfhuil* know we're here.

I shove the knife in my pocket, find my gun in the rags, and grab the lamp.

The last I see of Giles Stewart is him on his knees, gathering up the powder that was my mother and bringing it to his chest, her ash slipping through his fingers as he tries to capture her, hold her. I leave him in the dark, and I run.

In their own small dens, the *òlanfhuil* are waking, outraged, furiously clicking as they check in with each other, and I am a beacon, the light bobbing in my hand as I try to remember the way to the tunnel out, too scared to stop moving, my feet beating the ground as I run full pelt back the way I came.

When I reach my father, I stumble, a bolt of pure grief stalling me. I don't want to leave him buried down here. *We were just about to fix things. Everything was going to be fine.*

But one of the *òlanfhuil* appears in front of me—an old one, two sets of teeth eager for my flesh—and I fire, hitting it squarely in the chest.

I continue shooting as I run, unloading the next three bullets into swift white targets that try to reach me.

Then there's a light ahead of me, somehow, and the sound of a voice shouting, muffled to my shell-shocked ears.

Murren Ross reaches out and swings me in front of him, flinging me headlong into the passage. As he follows behind me, I turn and throw the lamp over his shoulder, into the entrance of the tunnel. The glass smashes, starting a small fire as the oil spills. Beyond the flames, the *òlanfhuil* scream.

We stumble along the passage, then drop to our knees to crawl, the glow of the fire behind us. There are bottles dotted along the passage, and Ren tells me to be careful. Then there's the sweet, sweet light of the outside world ahead, a bright white shape calling us home. Hope swells in my heart—we're going to make it.

I knock over one of the bottles and smell alcohol as its contents spill. I turn reflexively to watch it roll.

And see two of the *òlanfhuil* crawling behind us, reaching for Ren.

"Go!" I scream at him, pulling out the gun and flattening myself so he can pass me, rolling onto my back as the *òlanfhuil* claws for my ankle.

As its fingers wrap around it and begin to pull me back, I aim, close my eyes against the flash, and fire. Not at the *òlanfhuil*, but at the bottle beside it. The first bullet misses, and I swear, squeezing the trigger and firing again.

I scream when a sharp, searing agony ravages my ankle, so hot it feels cold, as the bottle explodes. I smell the hairs on my leg burning, but I channel my pain into motion and roll, then crawl to where Ren is reaching back for me.

I take his hand, and he pulls me into the light.

I collapse to the ground and stare at the sight before me.

Maggie Wilson and Mhairi, Dizzy and Wee Campbell, Mack from the tavern, the Talbots from the inn, Iain the Smith, Mrs. Stewart, to my great surprise, looking thin and pale, along with Cora and the Reids and Mrs. Ballantyne. Almost the whole village is there, all standing in a production line, stuffing rags into bottles and passing them along to where Gavan is poised with a torch.

As soon as Ren and I are clear, he lights the first one and tosses it into the hole.

"His father—" I say to Ren.

"He knows. Cora told him Giles went down there."

When I look at Gavan, I see the sad resignation on his face as he lights more bottles and throws them down the tunnel mercilessly, working as mechanically as the vats at his father's mill.

The hole begins to glow, orange and red, and then Connor Anderson runs forward, a large jar in his hand. Gunpowder.

"Get back," Gavan cries, taking the jar, and the crowd does.

Ren pulls me to my feet, and a searing pain shoots along my calf. I limp away, Ren's arm around my waist, joining the throng of villagers. Maggie Wilson comes over and puts her arm around my shoulders, and Ren releases me to her embrace. She smells of flour and lavender and good things.

Gavan tosses the jar into the hole and runs toward us, then past, and like sheep, we follow him, backing away from the hole, standing in the loch bed that just months before was deep underwater.

For the longest time, nothing happens.

Then the ground shakes.

It lasts only a few seconds, and from the outside, there's little to see. Just the tiniest of landslides, a few rocks and stones falling. It's anticlimactic.

At least until a profound, savage rumbling emanates from inside the mountain and a dust cloud pours out of the entrance to the caves. We have to move back yet again as it rolls toward us, shielding our eyes and faces, heads bent into our clothes. When it finally clears, leaving us all coated in a thin layer of mud, a coughing Gavan steps forward. Dizzy and Wee Campbell flank him while the rest of us hold our breath, both literally and figuratively, trying to peer through the settling grime to the caves.

When Gavan turns back and gives a single nod, the villagers cheer.

I have to see for myself, though.

I untangle myself from Maggie's hold and move forward, each step like I'm treading on knives. Gavan waits for me as Dizzy and Wee Campbell pass me, both clapping me on the shoulders before turning to each other and embracing. Dizzy Campbell lifts Mhairi into the air and whirls her around like she's a slip of a girl; Cora Reid is at the center of a scrum of her brothers, all of whom are crying openly.

All around me, people reach for one another, smiling and cheering. Ormscaula is united in a way it hasn't been for so long, all of us together, working and hoping together. A real village.

But I can't take my eyes off the sealed entrance to the caves. I step closer, heart thudding, terrified a charred, thin hand is going to plunge out of the rock and grab me, dragging me back under.

"It's possible they'll be able to dig their way out," Gavan says, joining me. "It depends whether the whole passage caved in or not. We might have bought only a few days' respite. But that's long enough to make bullets and fortify the village, come up with some other way to trap them. We can keep an eye on things here."

"Gavan, your da . . ."

"I knew if he went in, he wouldn't come back out. What about your father?" I shake my head. "I'm sorry," he says.

"Me too."

He looks up at the livid sky above us, swollen with clouds. "What happens now?" he asks. "If they are gone? What do we do next?"

"I don't know. Carry on, I suppose."

"You're the *Naomhfhuil.*"

"And you're the master of the mill. The master of Ormscaula."

Gavan's jaw tightens. "Enough of that. We need to rebuild.

People will need jobs. But there will be no more production at the mill until the loch is full again, and we will never again let it go dry."

As if in answer, the heavens open.

And the people of Ormscaula begin to dance in the rain.

I'm in no shape to dance, every bone and muscle and inch of me aching, aflame or bitterly cold, so I begin the long walk back to my cottage, grateful for the rain on my skin. After a few yards, I realize someone is beside me, and I know without turning that it's Ren. We walk in silence for a while, both of us limping heavily.

"You're very quiet," Ren says.

"Tired," I reply.

We don't speak again until we get back to my cottage.

I'd forgotten about the door being boarded up, and I have to crawl inside, my leg throbbing when I kneel on it. Ren follows me.

He stands in my hall, looking uncharacteristically awkward. "Shall I go?" he asks.

I shake my head. I don't want to be alone.

"No. Stay. Just let me wash up."

He frowns but shrugs, heading into the kitchen. "I'll make a brew."

I limp into my bedroom, seeking fresh clothes. Then I

stop, rummaging in my running-away bag, still sitting on my unmade bed, for one of my fancy city dresses. Not the one Giles wanted me to wear—the other one. I take it through to the washroom, where I use water from the faucet to clean my hair and my face and my body.

When it comes to the wounds on my legs, I'm gentle, sitting down on a stool and carefully wiping the blood away from the burned skin and the cuts.

And the neat set of puncture wounds just above my left ankle.

TWENTY-EIGHT

I knew I'd been bitten. I knew the piercing I felt in my ankle wasn't shards of glass from the bottles. It was like icicles being pushed into my body. Two sets of teeth. One to feast, and one to change.

My mother wasn't lying when she said it hurt.

I wanted very much to be wrong. I pushed the thought away the whole walk home, even though I could feel the coldness spreading through me. It's at my knees now; they feel stiff and frozen.

I don't know what happens when it gets to my heart. I guess my human heart stops and the monster one starts.

I dab at the wounds and pull the smart new dress over my head, braiding my hair into a thick plait down my back.

Then I reach into the pocket of my filthy borrowed skirt and pull out my mother's gun and the final silver bullet. I load it into the barrel, clicking through the empty chambers until it's in place.

It's not that I want to die—I want the opposite. I want to leave this place and try my luck elsewhere. I want to kiss Murren Ross until neither of us can breathe. I want to do more with him than just kiss. I want to see the sea and eat chocolate. I want to grow up. I want to be a girl with a pen and paper who can write her own world. A better one than the one I've known.

This isn't fair.

I leave the bathroom and walk through to the kitchen, every single step agony. But I paste a smile on when I see Ren at the table, two steaming mugs of tea before him.

"We can do better than that, Murren Ross," I say. "This is a celebration, after all."

"So I see." He nods at my dress, his eyes bright and fevered.

"Am I pretty?" I ask. Death makes me bold, it seems.

Ren's mouth falls open, and I laugh.

I fetch my father's good whiskey and two glasses, filling them to the brim, pushing one in front of him and lifting my own.

The first sip is fire in my throat, and I take another, wondering if it'll burn the cold out of me.

He isn't fooled for a second.

"What's going on?" he asks, leaning forward, ignoring his drink.

I place my mother's gun on the table between us.

"If I don't have the guts, you'll have to do it," I say.

He shoves away from the table so fast that he almost topples his chair.

I keep talking. "Ideally, I'd like it to be the sun. One last sunrise and then turn to dust. But I'm worried—what if some kind of instinct kicks in, if I try to run or hurt you . . ." I trail off. "With my mam, it happened fast. Within hours. The same with James, must have been. I don't . . . I don't know how much of me will be left."

Nothing good, I think.

"What are you saying?"

"Oh, Ren. You know what I'm saying."

I lift the hem of my dress and show him the wound.

He stares at it, the neat round marks, two inches apart. They look like nothing.

"I can't shoot you," Ren says.

I believe him. "Then I'll have to do it." I reach for the gun.

He grabs it, holding it like it's a snake.

"Ren, there's no coming back from this. I won't heal. There isn't a cure."

"You don't know that."

"I do. You either turn or die. Aileen and Hattie died. James and my mam turned."

"So turn. I'll take care of you. I'll get you what you need. Make sure you can't hurt anyone. It doesn't have to be the end."

"Ren—"

"No, Alva. No." He shakes his head, staring at the gun.

I'm gentle when I speak. "Ren, listen, it's going to end badly for me, one way or the other. But I can make sure it doesn't end badly for anyone else. I need you to help me with that. If you can't, then I know what I have to do."

He barks a terrible laugh. "So that's it? Either you shoot yourself now, or I shoot you later?"

I nod. Because that is it. That is the very awful truth of it.

Ren turns his back on me, and I watch his shoulders shake.

My heart is breaking.

I take my glass and walk to the front door, bending low and crawling back outside through the hole we made. I sit on the porch, watching the rain. The sky is iron; it's not going to let up for a while. It smells lovely. Clean.

Ren comes to sit beside me, his eyes red, whiskey in his hand.

He puts an arm around me, pulling me to him.

"Here's how I thought it would go," he begins in a soft, ravaged voice.

He tells me that he planned to follow me when I left. He explains how we'd have gotten jobs in Inverness. I don't say I was never going there; this is his dream now. I burrow into his chest and listen to the sound of his heart beating as he tells me how he'd have wooed me. How after many misunderstandings and a few false starts, we would've gotten our act together and fallen in love. He tells me he's pretty much there already, just waiting for me to catch up.

"For a bright girl, you're very slow on the uptake sometimes," he says, and I laugh. "But I would have waited," he says softly. "I would wait."

Ren tells me how he would have kissed me, how he'd have taken me to wed, how he would have trembled in my arms. He spins our lives out over decades, so many successes, a few failures to make the joys sweeter. How we would have grown and lived and loved. He tells me about our children and their children. Over the course of the afternoon and evening, he weaves a lifetime for us, and I let him, using his words to push away the coldness that rises through my belly, creeping up my chest with every hour that passes.

As if he feels it, too, he pulls me closer.

"Pretend I left," I say. "To Maggie, to Gavan and the others. Don't let them know what really happened."

He kisses my hair over and over, then my face, my cheeks and my eyelids, lifting my palms to his mouth and kissing them, too, before folding me against him once more. "I won't."

His heartbeat is becoming unbearable to me. I wriggle out of his arms and pull myself up, pretending I need to stretch.

It's the darkest part of the night now. No moon, hidden behind the relentless rain clouds. If this carries on, the loch will be full again before anyone knows it.

From inside the house, the clock chimes five.

For the last hour of my life, I sit beside him, no longer touching. He's too warm; I'm too aware of the heat of him, the life of him. We don't talk, because there's nothing else to say; he's told the story of us, and I want that to be the truth.

Above us, the sky begins to lighten, and my skin starts to feel too tight.

Ren presses his lips to my temple and mouths four words against my skin, old words, words that don't belong in the mouth of a Sassenach boy.

I reach across him, into his pocket, and pull out the gun, laying it gently on his lap. Just in case.

My heart drums a million miles an hour inside my ribs, cramming a lifetime of beats into the next few moments.

I close my eyes and turn my face to the sun.

ACKNOWLEDGMENTS

Biggest of the thanks are for Claire Wilson, my brilliant agent. You are the roots of the tree of me, keeping me tethered. We grow together. And Miriam Tobin at RCW, thanks for all the backstage stuff I know you do but never see.

Thanks to Team Scholastic US: my editor, Mallory Kass, and publisher, David Levithan, Chris Stengel for design, and Melissa Schirmer for production.

And Team Scholastic UK: editor Gen Herr and editorial superstars Jenny Glencross, Pete Matthews, and Jess White. Hannah Love, Harriet Dunlea, and Kate Graham in UK marketing and publicity, and all the people behind the scenes whose names I don't know but who work very hard to get my words out there.

Thanks to Catherine Johnson and Anna McKerrow for being ears and wine and hearts and hopes. A finer coven I couldn't ask for. And to Vic James, who told me this was the book that would make me. None of us could have predicted a pandemic thwarting your prediction. Next time . . .

If you've ever read my acknowledgments before, then you'll already know these names; they're the same old stalwart supporters, lifesavers, future alibis, and advisors, and I hope they never stop being the people I'm most grateful for. I owe them so much more than just thanks; I'm privileged and honored that after so many years they're still my best ones. So as always, thanks to my inner circle: Emilie Lyons, Franzi Schmidt, Katja Rammer, Lizzy Evans, Hannah Dare, Neil Bird, Asma Zbidi, Sophie and Liam Reynolds, Laura Hughes, and Rainbow Rowell; you're all the greatest, and I love you.

And as always thanks to the Lyonses, Papa and Mutti Schmidt, and the Salisburys (the good ones).

And finally, to you, if you read this, and if you've read me before, or you plan to read me in future. Mòran taing gu dearbh.

ABOUT THE AUTHOR

Melinda Salisbury lives by the sea, somewhere in the south of England. As a child, she genuinely thought Roald Dahl's *Matilda* was her biography, in part helped by her grand-father often mistakenly calling her Matilda and the local library having a pretty cavalier attitude toward the books she borrowed. Sadly, she never manifested telekinetic powers. She likes to travel and have adventures. She also likes medieval castles, non-medieval aquariums, Richard III, and all things Scandinavian.

She can be found on Twitter at @MESalisbury, though be warned, she tweets often.